For those of us who dare to dream
remaining optimistic, against all odds
moving forward, against all obstacles
because we believe.

Always believe!

Also by Kiki Hamilton

YA Historical Fantasy

THE FAERIE RING
Book One of The Faerie Ring Series

THE TORN WING
Book Two of The Faerie Ring Series

YA Contemporary

THE LAST DANCE

Key to Pronunciation and Meaning of Irish Words
(With thanks to irishgaelictranslator.com and Irish Language Forum)

An fáinne sí (un FAWN-yeh shee)
The faerie ring

Na síochána, aontaímid
(nuh SHEE-uh-khaw-nuh, EEN-tee-mij)
For the sake of peace, we agree

Grá do dhuine básmhar
(Graw duh GGWIN-yeh BAWSS-wur)
Love for a mortal person

Óinseach (OWN-shukh)
Fool/idiot (for a female)

Nimh Álainn (niv AW-lin)
Beautiful Poison

Tánaiste (Tawn-ISH-tah)
Second in command

Cloch na Teamhrach (klukh nuh TYARR-uh)
Stone of Tara

Corn na bhFuíoll (KOR-un nuh WEE-ull)
Cup of Plenty

Samhain (Sow WEEN)
Festival marking the beginning of Winter, usually
celebrated on October 31st

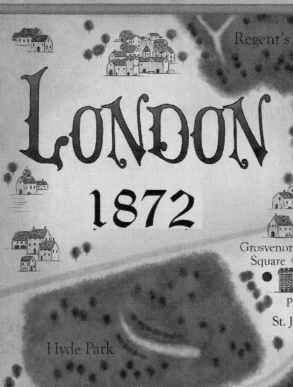

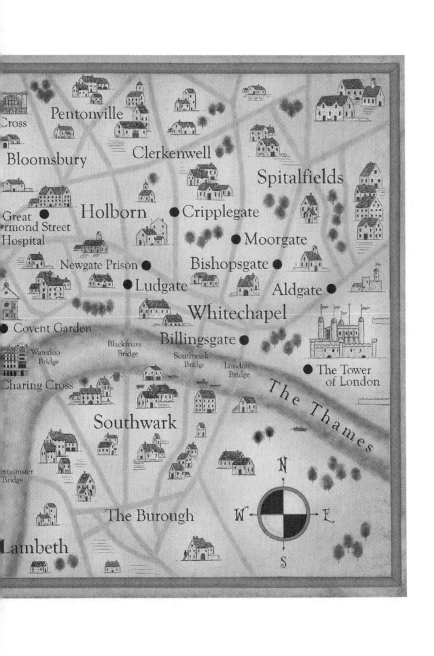

The SEVEN YEAR KING

Dear Reader,

The story told within **THE FAERIE RING series** is a combination of fact and fiction. Known as 'historical fantasy', I like to think of the books as a *'what if….'* kind of story.

Much of book one, THE FAERIE RING, is grounded in reality: Queen Victoria and Princes Leopold and Arthur were real historical figures. In fact, the story was set in the year 1871 because that was the year Prince Leopold was eighteen years old.

Many of the places referenced in the series: Charing Cross Station, King's Cross Station, The World's End Pub, St. James Park, the Birdkeeper's Cottage, Buckingham Palace, Hyde Park, and the Great Ormond Street Hospital, are real and can be visited today—should you be lucky enough to find yourself in London.

Both book two, THE TORN WING, and book three, THE SEVEN YEAR KING, take you to other parts of England, including Glastonbury Tor and The Wychwood Forest, which are both real and have legends that associate them with faeries, and in the case of the Wychwood, tales of hobgoblins, witches and other creatures abound.

The British Isles are rich with faerie lore and there are many artifacts that exist today that are said to be associated with the fey. Introduced in THE TORN WING, the Hill of Tara exists in Ireland, the London Stone is displayed on Cannon Street in London and in THE SEVEN YEAR KING you'll learn of the Luck of Edenhall – real and on display in the Victoria and Albert Museum in Kensington.

The Author's Note at the end of the book contains additional information you might find interesting, regarding some of the people, places and things mentioned in THE SEVEN YEAR KING, though to avoid any spoilers, perhaps best read **after** you finish the book.

Now—on with Tiki's story…

Chapter One

The Palace of Mirrors, the Otherworld

Firelight flickered from wall-mounted torches in the small chamber off the Great Hall as the Winter King and his court of UnSeelie advisors—Bearach, Sullivan, Cruinn and Scáthach—gathered in a circle. Dark shadows filled the corners of the room, a reflection of the perpetual night outside the palace while the UnSeelie fey reigned in the Otherworld.

Within the center of the circle lay the prisoner—the Seelie spy. He'd been beaten and tied, his wrists and ankles roped together behind his back. The glamour of the black-haired and scarred Sean ó'Broin was gone and the young man's natural features were revealed, but his eyes and cheekbones were so swollen and bruised that his face was almost unrecognizable. Dried blood dribbled from the corner of his mouth and dirt caked his hair, making the strands appear to be dark brown, rather than his natural blond color.

"You told her we had him?" Donegal's voice was low.

Bearach nodded his great head, the copper locks shifting with the movement. "The cry of the Tara Stone still echoed in the room. The new queen seemed most distressed at my news." One side of his mouth curled up with derision. "She wanted to trade."

Muffled snorts of laughter could be heard among the others.

"And Larkin?"

"Arrogant as always. Denied knowing him." Bearach's voice tightened. "Asked if he was an UnSeelie who wanted to defect." Behind him, as if sensing his animosity, one of his black hellhounds let out a low rumbling growl.

Donegal straightened. "I would expect nothing less from her." He nudged the crumpled body on the floor with his boot, eliciting a low groan. "Yet, I have no doubt that she is the one who sent him here to his death—not this newfound *queen*." He sneered the word. "We shall mark him as our Seven Year King and sacrifice him on Samhain as payment of the tithe due the Seelie Court—the very throne to which he vows his allegiance."

Bearach spoke again, his beady eyes glowing with anticipation. "Larkin may think she's clever, but she doesn't realize she has sent us the very bait we need to lure this new Seelie queen to her own death."

Donegal let out a low demonic laugh. "Or perhaps, that was precisely Larkin's plan."

Chapter Two

London, England

May 1ˢᵗ, 1872

Dusk settled over London like a sooty overcoat as a carriage left Westminster Abbey and made its way toward the wealthy district of Mayfair. The cry of *TARR~UH!* still echoed in Tiki's ears with the rhythm of the horse's hooves against the cobblestones. She clutched Rieker's hand, grateful for the sense of security his touch always provided.

The teeming streets of the City, crowded with all states of humanity, gave way to genteel landscape as the pair of black, matched horses snorted to a stop inside the coach house of Number Six Grosvenor Square.

"All right?" Rieker asked softly as he leaned close. The shadows in the carriage emphasized the aristocratic features of his face: cliff-like cheekbones and dark, sultry eyes which too often in the past had been shadowed with secrets.

Tiki gave a shaky nod. "Shocked, still, I think."

He raised his eyebrows. "Indeed. It has been a day of discovery."

Tiki forced a smile, but her lips wavered. "Almost too much to take in at once." She gripped his fingers tighter. "I'm so worried about Dain—"

The muscles in Rieker's jaw tightened as he ran the backs of his fingers along her cheek. "I know. We've got to—"

The door to the carriage swung open on well-greased hinges to reveal their driver standing at attention, his back ramrod straight. "May I assist you from the carriage, Miss?"

Rieker let out a low sigh of frustration before he answered. "No need, Geoffrey. I'll assist Miss Tara. Thank you." In a low voice he said to Tiki, "Let's go directly to my study. We've much to talk about yet." In a graceful movement he stepped from the carriage. His frame held the height and strength of his eighteen years, emphasized by the contrast to the wiry build of the small, middle-aged man next to him.

Tiki clutched the fabric of her crimson gown to step down, happy to hold on to something real in a world that was shifting and changing like a restless sea. There were still moments when she had to remind herself that the young man before her, Sir William Richmond, a noble who had grown up with Princes Leopold and Arthur of the royal family, was also Rieker, the infamous pickpocket she'd met scavenging on the streets of London. He was like a chameleon, changing his skin to fit his environment.

As they walked into the house, the patter of bare feet echoed down the hallway in their direction.

"Tiki!" Clara's high voice was tinged with excitement as the four year-old raced toward them. "Where've you been? You left without tellin' us..."

"And you missed supper!" Ten year-old Toots interrupted. He hurried behind Clara, his red hair bright even in the shadows of the hallway. Perhaps it was the constant struggle to fill his belly after his mother had kicked him out of the house at age nine because she'd had too many other children to feed, or maybe it was the endless pangs of hunger that had wracked his young body for so long, but Toots never missed a meal if he could help it.

Clara threw her arms around Tiki's waist, hugging her tight. "Don't go away again," she said, her voice muffled against Tiki's skirt. "Fiona needs you and I want you to read that book Ol' Potts gave me—the one about the lep'reecons."

Tiki hoisted Clara up and propped the little girl on one slim hip. "I'm sorry. I won't leave again, it's just that—" she hesitated.

"We were called to Buckingham Palace on short notice," Rieker finished for her. "But we're home safely now. Not to worry." He started down the hall in the direction of his study, beckoning Tiki with the tilt of his head.

"What were you doing at Buckingham?" Toots asked, his green eyes bright with curiosity.

"Did you see the Queen?" Clara chimed in, her small hand smoothing a lock of Tiki's long, dark hair, a stark contrast to the little girl's own blond curls. "Fiona told me Queen Vic has a doggie just like my Doggie an'…"

"How is Fiona?" Tiki asked, her forehead creasing with concern.

"She's in 'er room." Clara's smile faded as her voice dropped to a whisper. "I think she's still cryin'."

Tiki sighed. Fiona had developed more than a friendship with Johnny O'Keefe, a charming pickpocket they'd met at Charing Cross a few months ago. In an unexpected twist of events, Johnny had come to live with them at Grosvenor Square, but had recently gone missing when he, Fiona and the others had journeyed to Hyde Park in an unsuccessful attempt to contact Larkin.

Tiki tweaked the tip of Clara's petite nose. "Well, I've got some good news for Fi."

"You do?" The little girl's blue eyes lit up. "Did you find Johnny?"

"Sir—" The butler appeared from the foyer. Tall and robust, he was immaculately groomed as always, in black trousers with a white shirt and grey vest, a black cravat neatly tied beneath his chin. His moustache was greased to fine points beneath a hearty nose.

Rieker turned. "Yes, Charles?"

"You've a caller. A young lady. Wouldn't give her last name. Says she must see you—" his gaze moved to Tiki and his thick eyebrows rose, shifting his usually imperturbable expression— "and Miss Tara immediately. Shall I show her in?"

Rieker frowned. "Did she give you a first name, at the least?"

"Yes. Said it was Larkin—like the bird."

"Larkin?" Toots squeaked and scooted closer to Tiki. Last December, Larkin had stolen a deathly-ill Clara, intending to trade the child in exchange for the Queen's ring. Even more recently, the mercurial faerie had arranged for Toots to be taken to the Otherworld as a means to convince Tiki to do her bidding. Though Toots had been returned unharmed, his travels had left a significant impression and he now had a healthy fear of Larkin and her manipulations.

Behind the butler, a young woman swept into the hallway without waiting to be escorted.

"Ah, William—there you are."

Long, blond hair cascaded over Larkin's shoulders to frame an exquisite face. She was dressed in a fashionable gown, the color of ripe plums, and held a small matching purse. Her gaze paused for a long moment on Clara, held in Tiki's arms, before she spoke to the butler in a haughty tone.

"Thank you—" her delicate nose crinkled— "*Charles*, is it?" She flicked her wrist as she sauntered past, as if dismissing the man. "We'll carry on from here." She came to a stop in front of Rieker. "William, I have an urgent matter to discuss with you and Tara. Let's use the study."

Tiki's lips twitched as the butler's jaw sagged at the impudence of their visitor.

Clara tightened her grip around Tiki's neck and leaned close, her breath warming the skin of Tiki's ear. "You're not going to leave again, are you, Teek?" There was a hint of desperation in the little girl's voice.

Rieker didn't seem surprised by Larkin's arrival or her arrogance. He lifted an arm toward the other end of the hallway, and raised his eyebrows at their visitor. "You know the way."

Tiki's heart quickened. Though her relationship with the faerie had been fraught with distrust and deceit, for once in her life she was glad to see Larkin. Recent events had raised many questions and the faerie was her best hope of getting answers.

"Don't you worry," Tiki said softly in Clara's ear. "I'll be here." She let the child slide down to the floor. "Why don't you and Toots go play upstairs while Rieker and I talk to Larkin? I'll be up shortly."

Clara clung to Tiki's skirts as she stared up with large blue eyes. "You promise?"

Tiki cupped the child's face and kissed her forehead as she breathed in the fresh scent of Clara's skin. "I promise."

"Yes, do send the children along." Tiki started at Larkin's proximity. She hadn't heard the faerie approach. "We want to keep them safe, don't we, Tara?" The beautiful young woman leaned down and smiled. "Though it's nice to see you again, Clara."

The little girl leaned against Tiki's legs and stared at Larkin with no fear in her face. "Yes'm. Where's Dain? I haven't seen 'im about lately."

Rieker jerked around. "What do you know of Dain?"

Tiki frowned at Rieker as she placed her hands on Clara's shoulders. "Shush, never mind about Dain right now." She turned the little girl to face down the hallway and gave her a gentle shove. "Run along with Toots."

Against her will, Tiki pictured Dain's face. He was as handsome as Larkin was lovely—with a similar wild streak. Tiki suspected that like Larkin, Dain gave little consideration to rules before he broke them. In fact, not really so unlike Rieker.

Though often mocking and arrogant, Dain could also be charming. But there was something else about the young man— something Tiki couldn't quite put her finger on—that pulled at her heart when she was around him. Perhaps it was the air of loneliness that permeated his smile at times or the longing that Tiki sensed just below the surface. She imagined the look on his face as he'd traced his fingers so gently over the palm of her hand and whispered *'Have you kept my secret?* Even now, her heart wrenched at the memory.

"C'mon, Clara." Toots grabbed Clara's small hand in his own. He cast a wary glance at Larkin, as if he expected the faerie to spring at him. "Bet you can't beat me upstairs."

"Yes I can!" Clara yanked her hand free to sprint for the stairs. "I'm going to tell Fi about Johnny." Toots followed and they both dashed around the corner, their footfalls echoing on the wooden stairs. A pang of love filled Tiki's chest as their giggles and shouts receded into the upper depths of the townhome. As she followed Larkin and Rieker into his study she vowed silently that she would never be separated from them.

Rieker had barely shut the door when Larkin whirled to face them. She pointed a long finger at Tiki.

"We can't waste another moment. Tara—you are needed in the Otherworld immediately. *Cloch na Teamhrach* has spoken. You have no choice—you must claim the Seelie throne *today.*"

Chapter Three

Emotions Tiki had tried to keep at bay since leaving Westminster Abbey an hour ago, churned in her chest at Larkin's words. It was true—*Cloch na Teamhrach*—the Stone of Tara—had roared at her touch, proving she was the heir of Finn MacLochlan and the true high queen of the Seelie Court. Yet, she knew little of the mysterious Otherworld or the strange and often frightening creatures who inhabited Faerie. She'd spent her entire life living in London, believing herself to be an orphan after her parents had died of the fever several years ago—believing herself to be mortal. How could she possible go claim a *throne* in a world so alien and unfamiliar?

"Today is still May first—Beltane," Larkin said, "the day control of Faerie shifts from the Winter court of the UnSeelies to the Summer Court of the Seelies. You *must* return to the Otherworld and claim the throne from Donegal before the day ends."

Rieker stepped toward Larkin, lines of concern etched around his eyes. Dark strands of hair swept across his forehead given him a windblown and slightly dangerous look. "Did Bearach speak the truth? Have you confirmed that Dain has been captured by the UnSeelies?"

"In case you've forgotten, William—" Larkin's voice was dry— "faeries don't lie. We may twist the truth to amuse ourselves, but an outright lie results in, shall we say, 'undesirable' consequences."

She braced a hand against the back of a chair, her long, delicate fingers splayed over the brown leather. "There is no question that Dain was found out as a spy in the UnSeelie Court, but there are more important matters to which we must tend before we worry about Dain."

"Maybe more important for you, perhaps," Rieker snapped, "but not for me." He towered over the faerie's slight frame, his expression as angry as a thunderstorm. "In case *you've* forgotten, Donegal is not only holding my *brother*—the only living relative I've left—but he's also sentenced him to *death*." Rieker's eyes narrowed to dark slits. "It doesn't get more important than that."

Larkin's mood changed in an instant. Her lips curled in a snarl and she snapped her teeth as if she might bite. "William, insolence does not become you." She pointed a finger at him. "I warn you— do not test me today or I'll turn your hair into the feathers of a raven and your handsome nose into a beak to match." She swept her hand through the air and black feathers floated to the floor. "Then we'll see if saving Dain is your highest priority."

"Your threats don't scare me, Larkin," Rieker growled. "I don't think you want Dain held by Donegal any more than I do—" he took a step closer—"you just can't admit that you might care about someone other than yourself."

Larkin barked out a short laugh. "Sentiments are for mortals and fools." Her nose curled in a sneer. "We don't yet know where Donegal is holding Dain."

"How do we find out?"

"Focus on your intellect, William, rather than your emotions. Only the cleverest survive in the world of Faerie. You're going to need every inch of your wits to save your brother," she paused for a heartbeat, "and perhaps, yourself."

Rieker's expression darkened. "What is that supposed to mean?"

"Larkin." Tiki interrupted them. "What is it we need to do?" Her stomach gave a nervous twist at the thought of returning to the Otherworld. Against her will she imagined the shadowy, smoky grandeur of the Palace of Mirrors—the place where the ruler of Faerie lived. The Palace was filled with enchanted mirrors that reflected one's true form—to stop anyone from entering court in a glamour with the intent of harming the king or queen.

A place of dark opulence, the macabre ceiling of the Great Hall depicted various members of the UnSeelie court in scenes of unspeakable horror, images that were etched forever in Tiki's mind. Donegal, the Winter King, prided himself on the chaos he'd created and the lives he'd claimed. He even went as far as to hang the wings of his conquered opponents on his walls as trophies of his kills.

"The *Cloch na Teamhrach* has spoken for all in Faerie to hear. Now is the time to claim the Seelie throne and restore the rightful order of things in our world." Larkin's tone was emphatic. "We've been waiting a very long time for this day—we cannot delay."

Behind her back, Tiki tightened her fingers into fists until the pressure of her nails bit into the soft flesh of her hands. The prospect of facing Donegal again was daunting, but she knew she didn't have a choice. The killing had to stop. Donegal not only threatened the political stability of the Otherworld, but also that of England.

"Fine. Tell me what I need to do." As Tiki spoke, her promise to Clara resonated uncomfortably in her ears. She was needed in both London and the Otherworld—how could she be two places at once?

A loud sniff sounded from the doorway. "You've found Johnny?" The hope in Fiona's voice was unmistakable.

Tiki bit her lip to hold back her cry of dismay at the sight of the fifteen year-old girl. Fiona's eyes were red-rimmed and almost swollen shut, her face blotchy from crying. Her dark hair, normally full of waves, was unwashed and flat against her head. For a second,

Tiki was reminded of an old woman, worn and aged as hope had left her. She hurried to the girl's side.

"He's alive, Fi." She slid an arm around Fiona's slender shoulders. "Larkin helped save him."

Fiona clutched at Tiki's arm, her eyes lighting up. "You've seen him?"

"Well, no..." Tiki hesitated, "not exactly... but..."

"He's alive," Larkin said, "though it's not clear for how long." The faerie surveyed Fiona through heavy lids. "The *liche* left his mark and your friend is a mortal after all...." She raised her eyebrows. "What else would you expect?"

Fiona stepped toward the faerie, fearless in her concern for the injured young pickpocket. She threaded her fingers together so tightly her knuckles turned white. "Where is he? Can I go help care for him?"

A ghost of a smile crossed Larkin's face. "I don't think you want to go where your young man is now."

Fiona jerked toward Tiki for an explanation. "Where—?"

"He's in the Otherworld, Fi," Tiki said gently. "When the *liche* ran from Hyde Park he took Johnny to the Otherworld. Larkin and others were able to save Johnny, but he's still there—" Tiki's voice got softer— "too ill to return to London."

The color drained from Fiona's face and panic flickered in her eyes. "What are you saying?" she whispered.

"He's dying," Larkin said flatly. "There's only one thing that might save an injured mortal in Faerie and it's nothing you could ever get your hands on."

Fiona and Tiki spoke at the same time. "What is it?"

"It's not worth my breath to explain it to you." A look of impatience tightened Larkin's jaw. "Tara, we are wasting our time here. We need to go *now*."

"Larkin." Rieker's voice held a warning.

"Tell me what can save Johnny and I'll go," Tiki said.

Larkin propped her hands on her slim hips, a look of disgust on her face. "Fine. There is a magical vessel known as the Cup of Plenty—one of the legendary Four Treasures of Faerie. The Cup is said to hold the four essences of life, one of which is healing. Legend says that drinking from the cup will heal any ills." Her nose curled in a sneer. "Perhaps it will even cure those of a mortal."

Fiona put her hands to her mouth and turned toward Tiki with wide eyes. "We can save him, Teek."

"No, you can't." Larkin flicked a long strand of hair over her shoulder and raised her chin in an imperious gesture. "Don't waste your time trying."

"Why not?" Tiki asked. "Tell us where the cup is located and we'll go get it ourselves and bring it back to Johnny."

Rieker's arms were crossed over his chest and his jaw was set. "Remember, you want something from Tiki, Larkin. It's only fair you give her something in return."

Larkin glared at Rieker before she turned back to Tiki. "You won't be able to find the cup to help your thief friend because the cup is inaccessible." Her voice grew stern. "Leave it alone."

"What do you mean 'inaccessible'?" Tiki's brows pulled down in a frown.

"The goblins have it." Larkin snapped. She raked Tiki up and down with a scathing look. "And they won't give it up—not even to the Queen of the Seelie Court."

"The goblins..." Tiki repeated faintly, giving Rieker a distressed look. She'd heard how vicious the goblins could be.

"I must insist that we go *now*." Larkin strode toward Tiki. "It's time for you to learn to travel through the gates on your own. Ridiculous," she muttered under her breath, "a *queen* who doesn't know how to transport."

"Queen?" Fiona repeated, looking at Tiki with a confused expression. "What is she talking about, Teek?"

"Nothing," Tiki said. "I have to help Larkin with a small matter right now, Fi and—"

"But what about Johnny?" Fiona wrung her hands together. "He's hurt. He needs us!"

"As soon as I get back, we'll talk more about how to help Johnny." Tiki rubbed Fiona's arm. "Can you look after Toots and Clara while I'm gone?"

Fiona jerked her arm away. "I always do, don't I?" The bitterness in her tone was unmistakable. "How long will you be gone *this* time?"

Guilt churned in Tiki's stomach. There was an accusation in Fiona's words that Tiki didn't want to acknowledge. "Not long," she said, "I promise."

Fiona's eyes filled with tears again. "It's not only Johnny." Her voice broke. "Clara needs you, too."

"I know." Tiki bit her lip. "It's just—"

"Clara will be fine," Larkin interjected, putting her hand under Tiki's elbow and drawing her away from Fiona. "The child is adaptable."

Fiona jerked toward the door, a loud sob ripping from her chest. Tiki started to follow but Rieker put an arm out and stopped her. "Let her go, Teek." He pulled Tiki close. "Words aren't going to help Fi right now. Best to get on with what needs to be done." He pressed his lips to Tiki's temple. "After that, we can focus on how to help Johnny and Dain," he said softly.

Tiki sagged against Rieker's hard chest. He was right, of course. The Seelie Court had been at war with the UnSeelies for centuries. Losses had been great on both sides, but the last few years, Donegal, the Winter King, had turned the tide in a very deadly manner—against the Seelies. Finding the *Cloch na Teamhrach* was the first step in returning the Summer Court to power and reducing the threat to the British royals, as well as to the safety of England.

Tiki's heart tripped in her chest as a sense of responsibility settled on her shoulders like a weighty mantle. An image of the little man who had spoken at Westminster Abbey when the stone had roared filled Tiki's head. *'Donegal's killed our loved ones, our families. He's taken our homes and possessions. Enslaved some of us. We don't want peace,'* he had said. *'We want revenge. This is war.'*

Tiki took a deep breath and squared her shoulders. The Stone of Tara had roared—she was the rightful Queen of the Seelie Court. Now she needed to claim her throne.

Chapter Four

D ain stood among the shadows of the Great Hall, his hands shackled with iron, a rope cinched so tightly around his neck it was an effort to swallow. Pain radiated from his face and so many parts of his body from the beatings he'd received it was as though he'd been lit on fire. A guard stood nearby, his razor-sharp spear aimed at Dain's back, waiting to pierce his heart if he made a threatening move.

Before him, Donegal, the Winter King, sat on the golden Dragon Throne. The king watched the raucous celebration being played out among the UnSeelie Court with a furrowed brow and clenched jaw. Today was Beltane, the day the UnSeelies were obligated to return control of Faerie to the Seelies for the next six months. Donegal had murdered the previous Seelie king, O'Riagáin, and had planned to claim the Seelie throne as his own, in an attempt to rule all of Faerie—but the unexpected arrival of a new Seelie queen, confirmed by the cry of the *Cloch na Teamhrach*, had thwarted his plan. Now he was forced to concede the throne to the new queen today.

Dain closed his swollen eyes and an image of the Seelie queen filled his head. Tara MacLochlan. An emotion he was afraid to name warmed his chest.

His life had been a lonely one.

Believing he was an only child, Dain had been told his mother, Breanna, had died in childbirth, leaving him with a weighty guilt he'd tried to escape by pretending he didn't care—about anything or anyone. No one had spoken of his father, leading him to conclude the man had done something shameful that was best left buried and forgotten.

He'd been a beautiful child and had grown into a handsome young man—his looks and sharp wit giving him confidence and charm. Many sought his favor, but there were none who he'd allowed himself to care about.

Kieran, the old faerie who had raised him, had been kind and had tried to show Dain the love he craved, yet Kieran was a man of few words and had little experience in raising a child, especially one as smart and willful as Dain had been. Larkin had been a surprising ally in his younger years, but then she'd disappeared. It was only later that he'd learned she was risking her life as a spy in the UnSeelie Court.

As Dain grew older he sensed Kieran had secrets, which slowly created an ever-widening gap between them. When he'd gathered the courage to ask, the old man had said the time wasn't right yet to share what he knew.

Then one day, without a word, Kieran had disappeared. Even now, the loss was like a sharp pain in Dain's side, making his breath catch. The guilt that perhaps he hadn't shown the old man how much he'd loved him, was ever-present, even now.

He'd searched everywhere—had Kieran become ill? Been attacked? Taken prisoner by the UnSeelies? It was that quest that had given him the courage to become a spy—to risk his own life hiding among the UnSeelies, pretending to be one of them—in the hope of finding and saving the old man.

But he'd been unsuccessful.

He'd never known if Kieran had been taken against his will or if he'd simply become tired of caring for an unruly child and had decided to leave. The one fear Dain had never voiced out loud was that it had been something he had done—something that had made Kieran stop loving him—that had caused the old man to abandon him without a word.

It was only in the last few months, upon Larkin's dramatic escape from Donegal, that she'd revealed part of the truth—that Breanna had died giving birth to twins—that he had a brother who lived in London and that Dain himself was half mortal. She'd told him that his brother was equally unaware of their relationship, but had learned he had some connection to the world of Faerie.

Dain's curiosity had won out over common sense and he'd learned to cross over to the mortal world—a potentially deadly game that he began to crave as much as the danger of being a spy.

In the beginning, he'd only watched from afar. His brother, Lord William Richmond, was easy to recognize—their physical build was similar, as were their features. But soon, watching wasn't enough. He needed to know more—for the first time in his life he had a family—he *had* to know his brother.

He'd approached William while glamoured as Sean ó'Broin—tall, thin, with raven black hair and deep scars on his face—so there would be no way the young man could draw a connection between them. William's reaction had been wary until Dain had mentioned Larkin and had told him of her escape. In return, William had revealed a sordid tale of Larkin's manipulations in an attempt to wrest an unnamed prize from him and his friend, Tiki. From that point on, Sean and William had begun a semblance of a friendship.

When he'd first become aware of Tiki's existence, he'd had no idea she was part of his world, let alone a true-born queen. He'd simply known her as an acquaintance of the brother he'd only just discovered.

Dain let out a slow breath, savoring the memory of seeing her for the first time—playing in the park with a little girl, a young boy and another girl about her own age. She was beautiful, without a doubt, long dark hair swept behind her head and brilliant green eyes, but it was her kindness and the obvious love she had for the others, that had touched him most.

He'd watched as she'd laid out a picnic lunch and read to them from a book as they sat around her, enraptured. Though he hadn't thought he'd been visible to the mortal eye, the youngest girl had shot a curious glance his direction more than once. That day he'd heard that the boy, whose name was Thomas but they called Toots for some reason, wanted to learn to ride. It was then the crazy idea had taken root and he'd begun to visit the children as Dain, unbeknownst to Tiki or William.

For the first time in his life, he'd allowed himself to care about someone other than Kieran. He'd allowed himself to be vulnerable, knowing he could lose them, just as he'd lost the old faerie. Yet, the desire to be part of their lives was greater than his fear. Through Clara and Toots he'd learned more of Tiki and his curiosity grew. When he'd saved Tiki from Donegal's wrath in the Palace of Mirrors recently and they'd traveled through the Wychwood Forest together, he'd experienced emotions he'd never felt before—that he was afraid to admit to himself—respect, desire and something that felt like...

A shout echoed through the hall forcing Dain back to the present. The Court Jester, dressed in a gaudy array of colorful clothes, stood before the throne and juggled three balls of black flame. One by one, he threw the balls into the air, where they transformed into black birds with flame-colored beaks and eyes. The birds swooped in ever-widening circles above the crowd, growing in size with each sweep of their dark wings. Cries of delight and alarm rose from the crowd, who craned their necks to watch.

When the birds turned and headed toward the throne in a menacing dive, the guards let loose three arrows, which sizzled through the air to land in each black breast. As the birds plummeted toward the floor, they dissolved into balls of black flame and disappeared, leaving only the charred wooden arrows to clatter on the marble floor.

Dain watched the Jester as he pranced to the king's side, clearly pleased with himself. It was quite a feat of magic to produce birds from fire and he wondered again at the Jester's abilities, as well as his intent.

Donegal stood and clapped enthusiastically along with the crowd.

"Well done!" he cried. "Perhaps, Fool, you will create the fire-birds for the Seelie queen and her guards will not be smart enough to shoot them down." His evil laughter filled the hall until it echoed from wall to wall.

Chapter Five

Tiki's arrival with Larkin and Rieker in the Night Garden, the area surrounding the Palace of Mirrors, was similar to the first time she had visited. Darkness stretched like spider webs from twisted barren trees. Shadows shifted and lingered, nebulous beasts measuring their prey. A luminescence glowed from a number of magnificent flowers, their colorful petals the only bright spot within the garden, beckoning. Music wafted on the night air, beguiling and seductive, creating a longing in Tiki's chest, despite the dark and unsettling atmosphere.

In the distance stood the palace, perched on the rocky pinnacle of Wydryn Tor. To the right, sunlight radiated from the horizon— the Plain of Sunlight where the Seelies lived when they weren't ruling Faerie. Tiki couldn't stop herself from glancing left, where darkness, as thick and impenetrable as an inkwell, colored the sky of the Plain of Starlight. It was there that the UnSeelies lived in their madness and depravity during the summer months from May through October.

"Remember, these plants are predators who sing to call their prey." Larkin pointed to the saw-toothed edges of a nearby bloom. "That's someone's blood. Don't walk close enough to become their next victim." A corner of her mouth quirked. "They don't differentiate in their taste between royal flesh or peasant—mortal or fey."

Tiki shuddered and stepped closer to Rieker.

Larkin led the way down an uneven path, littered with broken stones. As they walked, Tiki could see glowing eyes watching their passage through the barbed underbrush. The bushes shook and rattled as creatures scuttled away.

Up ahead, Tiki recognized the statue of Danu, the original goddess of Faerie. As before, the stone woman reached towards the heavens as if in supplication, her face frozen in permanent agony. One great wing arched from her back, while the other lay broken on the ground next to her. Larkin had told Tiki a human had torn Danu's wing off to keep the faerie in the mortal world. Tiki shivered as she passed through the winged statue's shadow, as if chilled by her eternal sadness.

"It's important when we enter the Great Hall that you *command* Donegal to relinquish the throne," Larkin said softly over her shoulder. "He cannot deny the cry of the *Cloch na Teamhrach* identifying a true high queen of the Seelie Court. He is obligated to turn the power of the Courts over to you—for now. But you can leave no doubt that you are the true high Queen—just as you can never let your guard down, for he has murdered O'Riagáin already in his quest for total control and I've no doubt he will murder again."

Tiki concentrated on the path before her, as if by keeping the writhing vines snaking along the side of the walkway from wrapping around her ankles she could also keep the Winter King at a safe distance.

Larkin jerked around. "Did you hear me?"

"Yes," Tiki snapped in a low voice, the tension getting the best of her. "I heard you."

"Keep going, Larkin," Rieker said in a soothing tone. "We know what to do." He reached back for Tiki's hand.

She slid her cold, shaking fingers into his warm grip, unconvinced she knew what to do. She hadn't been the one who grew up around royals. She'd only known a middle-class upbringing before becoming a pickpocket. What did she know about *anything?*

Her heart began to pound erratically in her chest as they approached the steps. The Palace of Mirrors in the Otherworld was the equivalent of Buckingham Palace in London—the only difference was that control shifted in the Otherworld. The Seelies ruled during the summer months from May first—Beltane—to October thirty-first, known as Samhain. As summer gave way to winter, the UnSeelies took over and ruled during the dark months of the year until May first again.

Great columns lined the entry to the palace and Larkin stopped on the top step. "Remove your glamour."

Tiki whispered the words and the smell of clover hung rich in the air as her features melted into a different shape. Next to her, Rieker sucked in his breath with a low hiss and his fingers tightened on hers.

"My god, you're beautiful," he whispered.

Tiki was surprised by the ravage of emotions she saw in his usually unreadable eyes. Her breath caught in her throat at the intensity of his gaze.

"Focus, William," Larkin said, a hint of annoyance coloring her tone. "Tara needs to remain undistracted until we get Donegal off the throne." She leaned close, her words becoming more urgent. "The stone has roared for you and you alone. You are the rightful heir to the Seelie Throne. Demand what is yours."

Tiki stared at Larkin. The faerie was always so sure of herself—so powerful. If only she could borrow that confidence long enough to confront the Winter King.

"Are you ready?"

Tiki gave a hesitant nod, looking uncertainly at Rieker.

Rieker squeezed her hand. "She's ready."

"Then follow me." Larkin whirled and marched toward the lofty entry doors with her shoulders back and her head held high.

Tiki mimicked her posture. "I am the true queen," she whispered to herself. "The stone roared for me. The Seelie throne is mine." But deep inside, she remained unconvinced. Who would possibly believe she was a queen?

Larkin swept past the guards and down the main hallway into the Great Hall, her gown flowing behind her. It was as Tiki remembered. Vast black and gold fluted columns soared above their heads to support a ceiling filled with macabre paintings. This time Tiki didn't look at the disturbing contents of the ceiling. Instead, she focused on the black-haired man sitting on a great golden throne in the shape of a dragon at the end of the room. The Winter King. Donegal.

Black smoke belched from torches that lined the walls, filling the room with the acrid smell of fire and decay. Tiki's nose curled at the odor. The hall was full of well-dressed people, dancing and cavorting, drinking and celebrating, the sound of bagpipes and reedy flutes filling the air.

Larkin took a winding path toward the throne, blending with the party-goers. She paused among the last group gathered before the open space that fronted the throne. Guards stood on the four corners around Donegal, their bladed spears held at their sides, razor-sharp daggers hanging from their belts, black eyes scanning the crowd.

The gaudily dressed Court Jester sat in a relaxed pose next to the throne. The colorful stripes and patterns of his clothing were comical next to the morbid black that Donegal wore. Tiki imagined she could hear the bells jingle on the Jester's floppy three-point hat as he whispered to the Winter King, who leaned forward with an elbow on his knee. In response to the Jester's comment, Donegal sat back and laughed out loud.

When Donegal moved out of the way, Tiki's gaze riveted on someone in the shadows behind the throne. Dain stood with his wrists shackled, a rope around his neck that doubled as both noose and leash. His handsome face had clearly been beaten. Anger like she'd never known boiled through Tiki's veins until pure outrage fueled her voice.

"DONEGAL!" Tiki shouted. Out of the corners of her eyes she saw both Larkin and Rieker jerk around to look at her. The room went quiet in an instant. Even the music screeched to a stop.

"What are you—" Rieker started.

Tiki didn't wait to hear what he was going to say. She seethed with anger as she stomped forward. The crowd fell away to open a pathway straight to Donegal. Tiki lifted her chin, her face set and focused. She *was* the queen and she was not going to let him harm one more person she loved.

"I am Tara MacLochlan—" her voice was loud and confident— "QUEEN of the Seelie Court." As Donegal pushed himself to his feet Tiki pointed at him and roared, "GET OFF MY THRONE."

Chapter Six

"It is Beltane, Donegal." Larkin's silky voice sounded from close behind Tiki. "The roar of the *true* Stone of Tara was heard throughout Faerie. It's time for you to take your darkness and return to the Plain of Starlight." She waved her hand through the air is if to erase him. "Be gone from here."

Donegal walked slowly down the steps toward Tiki, his eyes narrowed in concentration. "So the rumour is true. A new Seelie Queen." There was something deadly in his words. "Where have you been all these years, my pretty?"

Tiki returned his stare. "I'm here now."

Bearach, Donegal's *tánaiste*, came to stand behind him, arms crossed over his great chest, his red hair as bright as the flames that lit the torches. "It's the same girl," he said in a low voice.

Tiki pointed at Dain. "I want that prisoner released."

Donegal swiveled to see where she pointed, then slowly turned back to Tiki, a calculating look on his face. "He's a spy. Deceitful." He raised his black eyebrows. "Untrustworthy."

"I'll negotiate."

A smile played at the corners of Donegal's lips, revealing teeth yellowed and blackened with decay. He shook his head. "Just like Larkin. You haven't even sat on the throne and already you want something of mine." Rings glittered on his fingers as he drew his black cape closed and stepped toward Tiki. "Surely you know there are no trades for spies. Only death."

He stopped so close Tiki she could see the pock marks on his face, the jewels embedded on the gold crown he wore, the malice that glittered in the utter blackness of his eyes. "Your friend has been declared our Seven Year King." His voice grew deceitfully mild. "On Samhain, I'm going to feed his heart to the *liche.*"

A laugh erupted from deep within Donegal's chest. With a smooth sweep of his cape, the Winter King disappeared, leaving only a handful of black feathers that drifted lazily to the floor. Along with Donegal, most of the occupants of the room also disappeared, including Dain.

A STUNNED SILENCE filled the air after Donegal's departure, soon replaced by the cheering of those who remained.

"Sit on the throne," Larkin said, urging Tiki up the steps.

"She's right, Teek," Rieker added, sliding his hand under Tiki's arm. "Claim what is yours."

Tiki turned to Rieker. "But, what about Dain? Did you see—"

"I saw him." Rieker's expression was grim. "There's nothing we could have done, while Donegal had him surrounded by his guards. At least we know he'll keep Dain alive until Samhain. That gives us some time to form a plan." He urged her forward. "Take the throne."

Still surging with anger, Tiki marched up the steps and sat on the seat protruding from the belly of the golden dragon. She turned and her jaw sagged in amazement at the change in the Great Hall.

The shadows and darkness were gone, replaced by light and warmth. The black and gold fluted columns were now white and gold, sparkling in the shafts of sunlight that poured in through diamond-paned windows. Verdant vines, loaded with luscious looking blooms, grew in wild abandon along the columns, the succulent scent of honeysuckle thick in the air.

Tiki lifted her head. Instead of the macabre and disturbing scenes of death and mutilation that had covered the ceiling before, now there were paintings of pastoral scenes and friendship. Her eyes riveted on one picture in particular—a well-dressed young man, clearly a mortal, held his hand out to a beautiful blond girl with an almost ethereal appearance, a pair of wings shimmering from her back.

She recognized the picture immediately. It was a depiction of *Sir Thomas' Folly*, a painting that hung in Buckingham Palace. The same painting where she'd first hidden the ring of the truce. Rieker had told her the scene was named after a play where a prince fell in love with a faerie only to lose his kingdom to her deceptions. Like the paintings on the ceiling of the UnSeelie Court, were these images snapshots of the truth, as well?

"Rieker, look—" she nudged him where he stood next to the throne and started to point to the ceiling when her attention was diverted. Those who had remained in the Great Hall after Donegal's departure had gathered in front of the throne and were bowing down to her. Even as she watched, faeries began arriving at the Palace of Mirrors.

The Macanna had been the first to arrive, great hulks of men and women who took positions around the throne and throughout the Great Hall, clearly guarding her. These were the men and women who had followed her father, Finn MacLochlan, when he'd left the Seelie Court of his father, Finvarra, and made his way to London. They held spiked mauls and curved daggers, their arms crossed over their immense red-coated chests, but smiles lit their faces as they celebrated the changing of the guard.

The trill of a panpipe started playing a jaunty tune at the back of the hall, soon joined by reedy flutes and the lofty tones of a harp. The little man who'd spoken to her at Westminster Abbey when the Stone of Tara had first roared approached the throne and swept his tri-corn hat from his head.

"Welcome to the Seelie Court, Majesty." The light flashed off the golden buckles of his long shoes as he danced a small jig. "It is at last the time for celebration." He locked arms with another little man next to him and they danced into the crowd, waving their hats above their heads.

The party grew louder and the room crowded as more and more faeries of the Seelie Court arrived. Tiki watched in amazement as they took turns coming to greet her and offer their welcome. A vast array of creatures filled the room. Many were gorgeous and almost human-looking in their appearance, while others were distinctly other-worldly and unfamiliar.

"You are very beautiful, Majesty," croaked one small man whose bulging eyes reminded Tiki of a frog. He spread his short arms in a deep bow. "Welcome."

Others came and paid their respects, nodding and bowing before her.

"At long last, a queen for the Seelie court. Welcome Majesty." The familiar scratchy tone caught Tiki's attention. She spied the speaker some distance from the throne. Wraith-thin and wrapped in rags, Tiki was sure it was the beggar who had been on the path of the Night Garden on her very first visit to the Palace of Mirrors. The creature's skin was paper-thin and did little to hide the jutting bones of its skull.

"Thank you," she said gently. Unsure if she was speaking to a male or female, Tiki's heart went out to the wretched state they were in. "Are you ill?"

The creature shook its head, greasy strands of hair shifting with the movement. Its chin was propped on its hand, as if the weight was too great to bear. "Just hungry."

Jarred, Tiki peered closer. Was this creature in this state from lack of food? Tiki would never forget the months of being so hungry that a constant ache had filled her entire being. Larkin had told Tiki and Rieker that the illusions of the faerie court hid a world that was falling apart—were faeries starving here?

Tiki leaned toward Larkin, who stood on one side of the throne surveying the crowd, a victorious smile creasing her lips. "Where do we get food?"

"The kitchens, of course. Why do you ask?" Larkin's eyes flicked to the small creature at the bottom of the steps. A frown tightened her brow.

"Because we're having a celebration and we need food." Tiki's voice grew stronger. "For everyone."

IN LESS THAN an hour, tables lined one wall of the Great Hall, laden with an astonishing array of tasty treats. Tiki whispered in Rieker's ear and within minutes one of the Macanna approached with a full plate. Steam rose from the colorful selection of food and Tiki's stomach rumbled as she inhaled the scent of the tantalizing dishes.

Balancing the plate in one hand she stood up and marched down the steps toward the creature, who had hobbled toward the wall and now sagged weakly against one of the great columns. Rieker followed Tiki, staying next to her side.

"What are you doing?" Larkin called after them.

Tiki slowed as she approached so as not to frighten the little thing. She put the plate on the ground and slid it close. "Eat what you can. There's always more."

The creature raised its head toward Tiki, great tears filling its eyes. "For me?"

Tiki knelt down. "Yes."

It stared at the plate for a long moment, as if expecting the food to disappear. Finally, it reached out a shaking finger and touched one of the rolls, the pressure leaving an indent in the soft dough. "Thank you, Majesty," it whispered in its scratchy voice.

"What is your name?" Tiki asked gently.

The creature hung its head. "Ailléna."

So, she was a girl. An image of Clara, buried in a pile of garbage on Craven Street outside Charing Cross, filled Tiki's mind. The little girl had been half-dead when Tiki had stumbled across her.

"Eat up, Ailléna. I don't want you ever to be hungry again."

Tiki stood and put her hand on Rieker's arm. "I need to go home."

Chapter Seven

"**Y**ou want to leave *now?*" Larkin scowled at Tiki. "But you've just arrived. You've just claimed the throne—there is much yet to be done."

Tiki put her hands on her hips and waited. She was sure Larkin could handle whatever needed to be done here without her. In fact, Larkin most likely preferred to handle it herself. Hadn't that been the whole point of convincing Tiki to find the Stone of Tara?

"There are decisions to be made—" the faerie swung her arm wide— "the palace is in a shambles after those disgusting dark creatures have filled these halls for the last six months. You have a court of advisors who needs to meet with you." Larkin barely paused for breath. "Do you think Donegal is going to just acquiesce to your power as the Seelie Queen?" A bitter laugh erupted from her throat. "No doubt at this moment he is plotting how to best end your reign before it even starts. And have you forgotten about the *liche?*"

Tiki had not forgotten the *liche.* An undead creature who Donegal had found staked in the Wychwood and raised through dark magic, he had murdered the previous Seelie King before setting out for London to murder Victoria, the Queen of England. Unable to reach the Queen, he had attacked her son, Prince Leopold, who was still recovering from the devastating injuries the *liche* had inflicted. Now Donegal was threatening to feed Dain's heart to the creature.

Tiki shuddered at the mental image as she held her hands up. "Stop. Don't say another word. I'll never be able to leave if I have to tend to every matter that affects this court."

Larkin raised her eyebrows, her silence more eloquent than any words.

"Oh no—" Tiki's eyes darted to Rieker, whose face was impassive, and back to Larkin. Tiki shook her head— "I never said I was coming here to stay."

"It's just for six months—until Samhain, then you have to give up the throne again, anyway—unless, of course—" her nostrils flared— "we've found a way to eliminate the UnSeelie court by then."

Tiki barked out a short laugh. "I am NOT staying here for six months. Are you out of your mind? I have a family to take care of... responsibilities..."

Lightning-fast, Larkin's mood shifted. "You have responsibilities here, as well." Her blue-green eyes flashed with anger. "There are people who depend on you—" her voice began to rise.

"Don't talk to me in that tone of voice," Tiki snapped. "You have no right—"

"Teek." Rieker's voice held a warning but Tiki ignored him.

"I've had enough of your manipulations, Larkin." There was an odd thrumming inside that Tiki had never felt before—as if the blood was boiling in her veins. "You're forever twisting people to do your bidding yet you're free to come and go as you bloody well please—" Tiki was shouting now. "Well, I've had enough—"

Rieker stepped in front of Tiki, blocking her view of the faerie. "Teek, take a deep breath." His dark hair swept across his forehead and waves curled at the sides of his chiseled cheekbones where he'd brushed his hair back. He put his hands on her shoulders and focused on her eyes as his voice lowered. "Everyone's listening."

With a start, Tiki realized the noise in the Great Hall had quieted to a low murmur. She glanced around and was met with the curious gazes of a hundred different faeries. Several members of the Macanna now stood on each side of her, their arms loose by their sides, but their eyes wary as their gaze shifted between her and Larkin.

Tiki stepped back. "It's fine," she said, tilting her chin up. "Everything is fine." She fixed a cold gaze on Larkin. "We'll be returning to London now. Larkin will be my escort." Without waiting for a reply, Tiki marched down the hallway that led behind the Dragon Throne—the same hallway in which Dain had helped her escape from the Palace of Mirrors previously.

She walked until she was out of sight of the crowd in the Great Hall, aware that Rieker, Larkin and several of the Macanna followed her. When they reached an intersection of hallways, Tiki stopped and jerked around.

"You need to teach me how to transport between here and London." She spoke to Larkin in an imperious tone, still angry at the relentless demands the faerie continued to place on her. "I haven't got time to walk through the gates when I want to come and go. Surely, as queen, I must have the ability to transport at will."

Tiki didn't know the first thing about the Otherworld, but she was loathe to admit it in front of these Macanna, who seemed to be watching her every move. Instead, she simply repeated the terms she'd heard Dain use when they'd talked about traveling to London.

Larkin's eyes were slits in her exquisite face, though her voice remained neutral. She motioned at the three men who had followed them. "Your services are no longer needed."

A tall young man, his shoulders as wide as Rieker's and half again more, took a step closer to Tiki. His brown hair reached his shoulders and was laced with braids and beads, but muscles bulged from his arms and there was no question he could do serious harm to a body should he choose.

"We stay with her Majesty." His words were simple and non-negotiable.

"Callan—" the corners of Larkin's mouth pinched— "while I appreciate your dedication, it's not necessary. I can keep—"

Callan held up a huge hand. "We stay with her Majesty." He crossed his arms over his great chest and turned away from Larkin to survey the hall, first one way and then the other.

Larkin's nostrils flared as her lips pressed in a thin line. "Fine." She shifted her attention back to Tiki. "Visualize where you want to go and will yourself to be there. It shouldn't be difficult for you." She raised her chin. "When will you return?"

"I don't—"

"When do you suggest Tiki return, Larkin?" Rieker asked in a smooth voice. "She's been concerned about Clara and Fiona. I think she feels the need to check on their welfare. Once she knows they're all right, then I think she can commit to staying here for a longer period of time." He shot Tiki a sideways glance. "Is that right, Teek?"

A surge of irritation shot through Tiki. Why was he always defending that faerie? "Yes, I'm sure I can spend some time on these... matters...when I return." She slipped her hand under Rieker's elbow and pictured the square in front of Number Six. To her amazement, the room before her began to shimmer, then disappeared from sight.

THOUGH NIGHT HAD settled on London, a warm breeze ruffled the leaves of the trees that filled Grosvenor Square. For the first time in months, stars sparkled from a clear night sky. Tiki stared in amazement at the row of townhomes across the street from where they stood, lights casting a cheery glow through shuttered windows.

"We did it!" she exclaimed as she turned a slow circle. "We're back."

Rieker's grin was broad and he held his arms out wide. "Well done, Teek." Tiki threw herself into his arms and he whispered in her ear, "or perhaps I should say, your Majesty."

Tiki laughed, resting her cheek against his hard chest, her arms wrapped tight around his slim waist. Beneath her ear she could hear the slow rhythmic beating of his heart, like a metronome to which her own heart kept time.

"If you call me that, I'll be forced to call you Sir William and somehow that makes you sound like a stuffy aristocrat." She leaned back to smile at him. "And we both know that's not the case."

Rieker smiled as he rested his hand beneath her chin. "Lord knows I have no intention of ever being stuffy. Certainly not while you're around." His mouth lowered to hers and Tiki rose on tiptoes to meet his lips. She slid her arms around his neck, savoring the moment. A different kind of hunger burned in the pit of her stomach and she pressed closer, wanting to feel his body against her own.

A small cough sounded and Tiki pulled back with a start. Callan and two other members of the Macanna stood nearby, each scanning the area in different directions.

"What are you doing here?" Tiki asked in a loud whisper, glad the dark night hid the color she was sure stained her cheeks.

"Majesty," Callan gave a half-bow as if Tiki had just walked into the room instead of being caught snogging with Rieker. "We are your bodyguards. Where you go—we go." He pointed in the darkness. "There are several other members of the Macanna watching in the distance."

"Bodyguards..." Tiki repeated faintly. She couldn't have bodyguards following her all over London. Especially men who looked like Callan. Even Rieker looked a bit startled at this new development.

"You'll remain unseen to the mortal eye?" he asked.

Callan quirked a brow at Rieker. "If that's what Majesty wants, of course."

"Yes, I want that," Tiki said quickly, realizing she had yet to don the glamour she'd grown up with in London. "Otherwise, it might be difficult to explain your presence." She smothered a wild laugh as she murmured the words to change her appearance and the smell of clover permeated the air. Bodyguards—for her? It was ludicrous. "D..do you need anything before I go in?" she asked, hesitantly looking from one to the other. Only Callan met her eyes.

"No. We're here to serve and protect you. You need not worry about us."

"All right, thank you." Tiki hurried across the cobblestone street, Rieker close at her heels. As they clattered up the front steps she clutched at Rieker's arm.

His brow furrowed in a frown. "What is it?"

She looked at him with a horror-stricken gaze. "I just realized—I forgot to ask about Johnny."

Chapter Eight

The *liche* stood outside the UnSeelie rath, hidden among the shadows between the gnarled and stunted trees within the Plain of Starlight, and contemplated the visit he'd just concluded with the Winter King. A few months ago, Donegal had freed him from an agonizing death staked within the Wychwood Forest—for a price. As payment, the *liche* had been tasked with killing the Seelie King and Victoria, the mortal queen of England. The murder of the Seelie King had been relatively easy, but Victoria had protected herself well, making it impossible to get close enough to accomplish the task.

Now, Donegal had given him another assignment: to kill the new queen of the Seelie Court.

The *liche's* fingers trembled as he threaded his long black hair behind one ear. He was still dressed in the elegant black cape, jacket and trousers that he'd been wearing when he'd run from London. His freedom and very life were at the mercy of the Winter King.

An image of the girl the *liche* had tried to take from Hyde Park floated in his memory. He drew in a deep breath. It was as if he could still smell the sweet scent of her young flesh. But instead of the girl, he'd been forced to take the foolish boy—Johnny, she'd called him—who had protected her.

Though not his first choice, the boy's heart would have satisfied him for a period of time. But he'd had to leave the boy behind in his desperate attempt to escape from Larkin—which had been successful by only the narrowest of margins. Had the faerie caught him she would have meted out the most terrible of punishments—her reputation was well known in the Otherworld. He shuddered at the idea of being staked in the depths of the forest again and left to a death that could take centuries.

Before being dumped, however, the boy had unwittingly provided a few tidbits of valuable information: the girl whose flesh the *liche* craved was named Fiona and she was somehow connected to Grosvenor Square in London.

That was where he would start. His hunger gnawed at him with a physical pain. He wouldn't be able to go long without feeding.

The *liche* straightened his top hat and gave a sharp tug to his lapels. He would find the girl—Fiona—and he would savor the taste of her young heart. And then he would find and kill the new Seelie queen.

Chapter Nine

"Happy birthday, Arthur," Leo said as he shuffled into his brother's office. He clutched a piece of parchment in one hand. "It appears Mother Nature has noted it's your special day and bestowed a gift upon us."

Prince Arthur swiveled around in his chair to watch his ailing brother's slow approach. Though it had been several weeks since Leo had been attacked by an unknown assailant while on his way to the royal mews, it was only in the last few days that his brother had felt well enough to be up and about on his own. A deep gash on his neck had bled persistently until Arthur had sought the help of Mamie, one of his mother's ladies-in-waiting, who had an uncommon knowledge, not only of the way of healing herbs, but also of the Otherworld.

"How's that?" Arthur asked. His shoulders sagged as if bearing a heavy load.

"Have you pulled your nose out of your books long enough to look outside? It was gorgeous earlier—like a mid-summer's eve. Mamie told me that today, May first, is a day of celebration in the Otherworld. A day they call Beltane—apparently the first day of summer." With a sigh, Leo sank into an overstuffed brown leather chair next to Arthur's desk. "And appropriately, this is the first truly nice night we've had in months and months." He raised his eyebrows. "Perhaps there's hope the battle in the Otherworld has taken a turn for the better." A wicked grin twisted one side of his mouth. "Or perhaps your birthday has special meaning—maybe you have a connection to the fey, yourself?"

"Always the jokester, aren't you, Leo?" Arthur shook his head. "If there is any connection to the fey in this family, I'm afraid it isn't with me." He motioned toward his brother. "What's that in your hand?"

"Oh, this?" Leo lifted the parchment he held. "I've remembered a few more things about my attacker and decided to document the details, so the guards have a better idea who to keep a watch for."

"May I?" Arthur stared down at the page. The charcoal-drawn image was of a dark figure, wearing a black top hat and clothed in a black cape. Clawed hands reached toward the viewer, but that wasn't the most notable feature in the drawing. It was the attacker's eyes: they were slitted like a cat's and glowing red.

"What is it?" Leo asked. "You seem out of sorts."

"There's been another attack."

Leo sat forward, his face slack with shock. "By this creature?"

"There's no doubt it was the same man. The victim's heart had been sliced from her chest."

Leo's face turned pale, making the scar on his neck that much more prominent. "Where? When? Who did he murder this time?"

"A young girl in Hyde Park. She was about sixteen years old—the same age as Marie Claire." Arthur heaved a heavy sigh at the mention of the murdered daughter of their good friend, Charles Bagley.

"And the same age as Baby," Leo said faintly, naming their younger sister, Beatrice.

"Good point. The girl must have been attacked sometime after midnight. Her body was found this morning not far from The Ring by a man out for an early ride. Because of the proximity to Buckingham, Scotland Yard thought it wise to inform us." He rubbed his forehead. "Just in case."

Leo sat back in his chair. "He's back." He raised frightened eyes toward his brother. "None of us are safe."

Chapter Ten

The clock chimed nine times as Tiki and Rieker entered the townhome. Several lamps were lit in the foyer and down the hallway, awaiting their return, the gas turned low to dim their light. Tiki removed her shoes and clutched them in one hand as she followed Rieker, her stocking feet silent on the wood floors.

What would she tell Fiona when the girl asked about Johnny? Tiki shook her head. How could she have forgotten to check on the welfare of the young boy? Guilt speared her stomach in an uncomfortable way. But so much had happened... It seemed she would have to return to the Otherworld sooner than she anticipated, if only to help Fiona find out how Johnny was faring. Plus, she couldn't shake the image of that starving faerie. How many others were in need like her?

Rieker paused outside a pair of large, carved walnut doors that led to his study. He fingered a strand of her dark hair, his smoky eyes fixed on hers. "I'm going to sit by the fire for a bit and absorb what we've learned today. Would you care to join me?"

Had it only been one day since they'd stared into the depths of the ring searching for answers? Was it only this afternoon that they'd talked with Arthur and been directed to the Coronation Chair at Westminster Abbey? Had it really been just a few hours ago that the Stone of Tara had cried out at her touch and the world of Faerie had accepted her as their Queen of the Seelie Court? A new sense of responsibility weighed on her. Was it up to her to save Dain? To feed the homeless and starving? If she didn't do it—who would?

Tiki shivered.

"Are you cold?"

She shook her head. "Just tired. And... and maybe a little scared."

Rieker brushed her cheek with the backs of his fingers, his eyes dark and serious. "I'll be here to help you."

Tiki nodded and forced a smile, a strange sense of foreboding making her chest tight. Were either of them strong enough to face what was coming? "I want to check on the others and then I'll be down."

Rieker nodded and reached for the brass door handle. "I'll stoke the fire and chase the chill from the room. Perhaps now that Larkin has finally got what she wanted, we won't have an unwelcome visitor in the middle of our conversations."

Tiki gave a wry smile. "One can only hope."

Her stocking feet were silent on the stairs as she climbed to the upper drawing room where they liked to gather at night. She rounded the corner and just as she'd hoped, Toots, Clara and Shamus were sitting before the fire. Shamus was whittling on a small figure he held in his hands, Toots was trying to build a tower with building blocks and Clara was turning the pages of a book.

"I thought I might find you lot here," Tiki said, "lolly-gagging about." As one, they lifted their heads in surprise.

"Tiki!" Toots and Clara bounded toward her and wrapped their arms around her legs and waist, clutching her tight. A slow smile spread across Shamus' face, making him look much younger.

"I was wondering when I might see you again," he said.

Tiki took Toots and Clara by the hands and dipped in a curtsy. "Home again and at your service, m'lord." Clara immediately copied Tiki's movement with a curtsy of her own.

"An' I'm here, too!"

Toots gave a gentlemanly bow. "Don't forget me."

Shamus laughed and nodded at them, his carving resting on his knees. "An' a beautiful sight you all are." He glanced at the open doorway then looked back at Tiki expectantly. "Not alone, are you?"

"Rieker's in his study tending to a few business matters." She gave Shamus a questioning look. "How's Fi?"

"Hasn't been out of her room much." He scratched his head, his brow pulled down in a worried frown. "Haven't seen her at all tonight."

"Did you find Johnny? Is he all right?" Toots asked. Death was a common visitor to London, especially if one lived on the streets, and Toots had seen his fair share. He was wise enough to know that Johnny was in dire straits.

"He's very sick." Tiki dodged the question. "I don't know much more than that."

"What about Dain?" Clara asked in her high little voice. "I haven't seen him for a long time. Is he sick, too?" She tilted her head, her blond curls swaying with her movement. "I thought he was going to come by and let me pet one of his pretty horses."

At the mention of Dain, a sense of loss filled Tiki, making it difficult for her to speak. How could she explain what had happened to Dain? That he needed them too, just as desperately as Johnny.

"Dain is...busy right now..." Tiki said, "with work. But you'll see him again soon, I promise."

Rieker rounded the corner, his tall frame and broad shoulders filling the doorway. "I see you've found each other."

Shamus pushed himself out of the chair and approached Rieker with his hand out. He was as tall as the young lord, but thin as a willow reed. His straight white-blond hair was a startling contrast to the dark locks that covered Rieker's head. Their features couldn't have been more different either: where Rieker's cheekbones and jaw were cut in sculpted curves, Shamus' features were long, and thin, much like his body. One wouldn't forget Rieker's handsome face, whereas Shamus could blend in with a crowd and disappear.

"Nice to see you again, Lord Richmond." Shamus dipped his head but there was a hesitant look on his face. "Grateful for your hospitality. Hope that you don't mind we're still here."

Rieker shook Shamus' hand and held tight until Shamus met his eyes. "Shamus, you are all part of Tiki's family, which makes you my family. You are welcome to stay as long as you wish."

Shamus bobbed his head with a relieved smile. "Thank you, sir." He motioned to the chair he had just vacated. "Would you like to sit?"

"Actually, I've got matters to tend to around here, so best get to it. I'll see you all in a bit."

Tiki looked at Clara and Toots. "And I've come to read you lot a bedtime story and tuck you in at a reasonable time, like good children." She eyed the two of them with a questioning look.

"How'd you know we stay up late sometimes?" Toots asked, a guilty grin on his face. "You're not here when we do."

"Just because I'm not here, doesn't mean I don't know things." She tweaked the ten year-old's nose. "And best that you don't forget it either, Thomas."

IT WAS ONLY minutes before Tiki, Clara and Toots were settled together comfortably on the couch with Clara's story book spread across Tiki's lap. Shamus sat in a nearby chair where he'd resumed his whittling, a content smile upon his face.

"Read it, Teek!" Clara cried. "Ol' Potts gave me this story about lep'reecons a long time ago and I still haven't heard it!"

"It's only been a few days," Tiki said, "and you could've asked Mrs. Bosworth."

"I did, but she can't read." Clara pouted. "An' Toots wouldn't even try."

Tiki looked down at Toots, who was leaning against her left arm. "Is that true, Toots?"

"I wanted to wait for you, Teek." He gave her an innocent look, his orange freckles bright against his pale skin. "It's better that way. You're the best storyteller *ever*."

Tiki snorted. "I don't know about that, but let's take a look. Mr. Potts seemed to think that Clara would like this one." She smoothed her hand over the cover and read the title: "The Field of Boliauns." She looked down at Clara then over at Toots. "Do you two know what a boliaun is?"

The children shook their heads, their gaze locked on Tiki.

"A boliaun is also known as ragwort. It's a green plant that grows about knee-high in fields around here and in Ireland."

"I've heard of that—it's bad for horses," Toots said with an important air. "Dain told me."

"Exactly." Tiki turned the page and began to read, affecting an Irish brogue. "So the story begins on one fine day in harvest—it was indeed Lady-day, that everybody knows to be one of the greatest holidays in the year—and clever Tom Fitzpatrick was taking a ramble. He went along the sunny side of a hedge; when all of a sudden he heard a clacking sort of noise. *Clack-clack-clack, clack.*"

Clara watched Tiki with wide eyes. "D'you think it's lep'reecons?"

"Hush, Clara," Toots hissed.

"'Dear me,' said Tom," Tiki read on, "'but isn't it surprisin' to hear the stone chatters singin' so late in the season?' So Tom stole on, going on the tops of his toes to try to get a sight of what was making the noise. But the noise stopped."

Toots and Clara watched Tiki with baited breath.

"Tom looked sharply through the bushes, and what should he see in a nook of the hedge but a brown pitcher and by-and-by a little wee teeny tiny bit of an old man, with a little motty of a cocked hat stuck upon the top of his head, and a leather apron hangin' before him."

"That's a lep'reecon," Clara whispered.

Tiki nodded. "As Tom watched, the little man pulled out a little wooden stool, and stepped up upon it, and dipped a little mug into the pitcher. Then he put the full cup beside the stool, and sat down and began to work at putting a heel-piece on a bit of a brogue just fit for himself."

"What's a brogue?" Clara asked.

"A type of shoe." Tiki continued with the story. "'Well, by the powers,' said Tom to himself, 'I've often heard tell of the Leprechauns, and, to tell the truth, I've never rightly believed in 'em—but here's one of them before me now. If I catch him, he'll be forced to give me his gold. But they say a body must never take their eyes off 'em, or they'll escape.'"

"Gold," Toots said, his eyes glowing.

"Tom stole on a little further, with his eye fixed on the little man just as a cat does with a mouse. When he got up quite close, he said, 'Bless your work, neighbor.'

The little man raised his head, and said, 'Thank you kindly.'

'I wonder you'd be working on the holiday!' said Tom.

'That's my own business, not yours,' was the reply. 'It would be fitter for you to be looking after your father's property than to be bothering decent quiet people with your foolish questions. There now,' the little man pointed down the field, 'while you're idling away your time here, the cows have broken into the oats, and are knocking the corn all about.'

Tom was taken so by surprise with this that he was just on the very point of turning round when he recollected himself; He didn't dare look away, or the little man would escape. Afraid that the like might happen again, he made a grab at the Leprechaun—" Tiki made a grabbing motion— "and caught him up in his hand."

Clara squeaked with excitement.

"Hush," Toots hissed.

"He then swore that he would kill the little man if he didn't show him where his money was. Tom looked so wicked and bloody-minded that the little man was quite frightened; so says he, "Come along with me a couple of fields off, and I'll show you a crock of gold."

So they went, and Tom held the Leprechaun fast in his hand, and never took his eyes from him, even though they had to cross hedges and ditches, and a crooked bit of bog. At last they came to a great field all full of boliauns. The Leprechaun pointed to a big boliaun, and says he, "Dig under that boliaun, and you'll get the great crock all full of guineas."

Tom in his hurry had never thought of bringing a spade with him, so he made up his mind to run home and fetch one; and that he might know the place again he took off one of his red garters, and tied it round the boliaun. Then he said to the Leprechaun, "Swear ye'll not take that garter away from that boliaun." And the leprechaun swore right away not to touch it.

"I suppose," said the Leprechaun, very civilly, "you have no further occasion for me?"

'No,' says Tom, 'you may go away now, if you please, and God speed you, and may good luck attend you wherever you go.'

'Well, good-bye to you, Tom Fitzpatrick,' said the Leprechaun, 'and may you do much good with what you find.'

So Tom ran for dear life, back home and got a spade, and then away with him, as hard as he could go, back to the field of boliauns. But when he got there, lo and behold! every boliaun in the field had a red garter, the very model of his own, tied about it."

"The lep'reecon tricked him!" Clara exclaimed, clapping her hands together in delight.

Toots sat back and let out a low whistle. "Clever bloke."

"Tom dug to the east some, then he dug to the west, but he found no treasure. He tried digging to the north as the harvest moon rose and it set as he dug to the south. Exhausted, he leaned on the handle of his shovel and looked around. Digging up the whole field was all nonsense, for there were more than forty good Irish acres in it. So as the sun came up, tired Tom Fitzpatrick came home again with his spade on his shoulder, a little cooler than he went, and many's the hearty curse he gave the Leprechaun every time he thought of the neat turn he'd been served."

Tiki closed the book. "And that's the story of clever Tom and the Leprechaun and their field of boliauns."

"Mr. Potts said those lep'reecons are tricky sorts," Clara said with a grin.

"Do you think the gold is still buried in that field?" Toots asked.

"Could be, but you'd have to be able to outsmart a leprechaun to find it." Tiki stood up. "Up to bed with you two, now. I'll be up in a minute to kiss you goodnight."

Toots and Clara scampered out of the room, chatting excitedly about leprechauns and gold.

"It's nice to have you home, Tiki." Shamus paused in his whittling. "But if you need to leave again, I'll watch the children," he said in his measured way. "They'll be safe here. You go do what you need to and hurry home."

Tiki nodded at Shamus' gaunt face. Even though he ate three good meals a day now, he had yet to gain an ounce of weight.

Mrs. B. said it was because he had a hollow leg where he stored all the food he ate, but Tiki wondered if it was because he was still making up for all the years he'd gone hungry.

Clara and Toots would be safe here with Shamus and the Bosworth's to watch over them. She needed to focus on saving Johnny and Dain. "Thank you, Shamus."

TIKI HURRIED UP the stairs to the third floor, checking first on Toots, and then across the hall to where Clara and Fiona shared a bedroom. Clara was snuggled into bed with her little arms clutched tight around her stuffed Doggie. Tiki smoothed a blond curl from her forehead and bent to kiss the tender skin. She inhaled Clara's sweet scent that was like a combination of fresh flowers and a summer breeze, and a sense of peace filled her. She was home and her family was safe. An image of Dain's battered face floated before her eyes and like a snuffed flame, her sense of well-being evaporated. "I love you, little mouse," she whispered to the girl.

"I love you, big mouse," Clara said with a happy smile.

Tiki straightened and glanced at the other bed. Fiona was buried under a mound of blankets with her back to the room. Tiki hesitated. She didn't want to wake Fi, and in truth, was hoping to delay telling the other girl that she'd forgotten to check on Johnny until the morning. Deciding to let her sleep, Tiki was almost at the door when something made her pause and look back over her shoulder.

She stepped toward the bed and peeled back the top blanket, just enough to see Fiona's dark wavy hair. But instead of hair, there was a mounded-up pillow.

Tiki's heart skipped a beat.

She gently lifted a corner to see under the linens, but there were only more sheets and blankets. A terrible fear ignited in Tiki's stomach and she yanked the covers back, desperate now to see Fiona's slim figure asleep under the blankets.

But instead of Fiona, there were more blankets, wadded up to look like a figure sleeping. Tiki yanked the remaining covers away as a terrible realization sank in.

Fiona was gone.

Chapter Eleven

Tiki flew down the stairs, her feet barely touching the steps as she raced for Rieker's study. She pushed the door open with a crash, causing the young man to jump to his feet in alarm.

"Fiona's gone!" Tiki skidded to a stop in front of him. "There are sheets and blankets in her bed—wadded up to look like her. Where do you think she could be? Do you think she was taken?" Tiki panted as she stared at him wild-eyed.

Rieker put his hands on her arms. "Calm down, Teek. Take a deep breath. There's no reason for anyone to take Fiona."

"But where is she?" Tiki's voice rose with panic.

"I don't know." Rieker returned to his seat, pulling a nearby chair out for Tiki. "Sit down. Let's figure this out calmly. Why would Fiona need to sneak out, anyway?"

"That's just it—she doesn't need to sneak—" Tiki froze and stared into the distance, a stricken look on her face.

"What is it?"

"I think I know where she's gone," Tiki whispered.

"Where?"

Her gaze riveted on Rieker's. "The Goblin Market. She's gone to save Johnny."

"Teek." Rieker shook his head. "What are you talking about?"

Tiki jumped up to pace in front of a long row of bookcases that covered one wall in Rieker's study. "The Goblin Market. Dain told me about it when he brought me back to London. He said the Goblin Market is at Covent Garden—it's one of the gates—one of the intersections between London and the Otherworld."

"Covent Garden?" Rieker's voice echoed with disbelief. "A *goblin* market? Are you daft?"

Tiki rubbed her hands together as she paced. "He said it opens at midnight and closes at the first light of dawn." She stopped and looked at Rieker. "I mentioned the market to Fi when we were looking for you." Tiki held her hands out. "Don't you see? I'm afraid she's gone to ask about the Cup. That was the angriest I've ever seen her this afternoon. She didn't want me to leave, she wanted to go look for Johnny…to save him…but I left anyway…" Tiki's voice faded.

"Tiki." Rieker's tone grew stern. "You had to go. You had to claim the throne, there's no two ways about that." He pushed out of the chair and came to stand near her. "I understand that Fiona is distraught, but you can't blame yourself."

Tiki whirled to face him. "But I do blame myself. Don't you see? If I'd stayed, she'd be here now, we'd be making a plan together to save Johnny. She'd be safe."

A clock chimed out the quarter hour.

"It's only 12:15," Rieker said. "If the Goblin Market doesn't open until midnight, and if that's where Fiona has gone, then she's only fifteen minutes ahead of us."

Tiki's eyes widened with hope. "You're right. Maybe we can catch her before anything happens." She scrambled to the door to collect her shoes, anxious to be on the way. "Should you wake Geoffrey?"

"Tiki." Rieker's voice was soft. "There's a faster way."

She glanced over her shoulder as she shoved her feet into the silk slippers. "What's that?"

Rieker straightened. "We can go the same way we came home."

Tiki stared at him for a long moment. "You're right. There's no reason it wouldn't work—but we just can't be seen suddenly appearing."

"It's night and it's dark." Rieker shrugged. One side of his mouth lifted in a grin. "Perhaps when you visualize where you want to transport us, you can picture shadows, too?"

Tiki didn't return his smile. "Do you think we should tell anyone we're going?

Rieker strode across the room toward her. "Rather than that—probably best to go immediately, find Fiona, and get back before anyone knows we've gone."

THEY ARRIVED IN the shadows under the portico along-side Theatre Royal in Drury Lane, just a short walk from where the costermongers hawked their fruits and vegetables at Covent Garden. Tiki was used to being out at night. There had been many times when she'd snuck into pubs in the wee hours of the morning to pick the pockets of unsuspecting drunks, then disappeared back into the dark night. But it was with an unfamiliar apprehension that she walked toward the strange glow of light that emanated from Covent Garden in the distance.

At Rieker's insistence, they'd both changed their clothes before departing, slipping into their old familiar street clothes: worn pants, an oversized coat that hid the fact that Tiki was a girl, caps that shadowed their faces—clothes that made them invisible as they mingled among London's underbelly.

A strange sense of familiarity filled Tiki's chest as she peeked at Rieker from the corners of her eyes. Dressed as he was, he'd once again become the rakish pickpocket she'd first met at King's Cross more than a year ago. Then, she hadn't believed she could trust him, but now—she trusted him above all others. He, alone, knew her secrets. And for once, she believed that she might know all of his.

Tiki slid her hand into his and he gave her a sideways grin, squeezing her fingers. For that instant, it was if they were the only two people in the world and they shared a secret no one else knew. Longing tugged at Tiki's heart and part of her wished the moment would never end.

"William Richmond," she whispered softly in a disapproving tone, "I believe you're enjoying this."

A wicked grin twisted one corner of Rieker's mouth. "Always had trouble saying no to a bit of adventure."

As they approached from Drury Lane, the night carried the normal sounds of the City at rest: the sporadic clack of carriage wheels across the cobblestones, accompanied by the jingle of coach rigging; the cries of the night people coming and going.

They rounded the corner to the open mall where the fruit and vegetable vendors parked their carts each day and Tiki stared in amazement. Before them stretched a scene beyond her wildest imaginings. The plaza was awash in bright light: candles blazed, grease lamps glowed, flares flickered with red tongues of flame, orange fires radiated from the barrels of chestnut roasters and blue-white shafts of moonlight shone over it all, creating a wash of illumination.

"Bloody hell," Rieker muttered under his breath. "What is *that?*"

In a macabre imitation of the costermongers and vendors who populated the market during the day, carts stretched in a line along the cobblestones. But these carts were very different from the straining wooden two-wheeled versions Tiki was used to seeing. These sturdy carts appeared to be made of gold, gleaming beneath their precious loads. Luscious fruit, plump and dripping with juice, were piled high in cart after cart, like candy waiting to be plucked from the piles. The fruit sparkled in the fire light, as though coated with a sugary layer that would melt on one's lips at first bite.

As the market came into view, a tantalizing melody filled the air, pulling Tiki forward. She had heard the enchanting music of the faerie court before: the mournful cry of the bagpipes, the lofty notes of a harp and the laughing trill of a panpipe—but this music was different. It murmured in her ear like she imagined a lover might: breathy promises of a clarinet, the seductive strums of a guitar, the yearning notes of a pianoforte—yet there were no musicians in sight.

"Can you hear the music?" Tiki whispered, tightening her grip on Rieker's fingers.

Rieker stared at the glowing lights. "Yes."

As they drew closer, a succulent smell filled the air and Tiki's mouth began to water. A hunger started in her stomach and grew into a burning craving with each step. She scarcely noticed the ugly, small men who hawked their wares in sing-song voices, their calls blending with the melody of the instruments.

"Git yer fruiiit…special and sweet," one beak-nosed goblin sang, "just one bite, you'll never want meat."

"Three a lock, such a small price to pay," cried another, "hurry now, we'll be gone by day."

"A lock?" Tiki repeated, pulling Rieker to a stop. "What type of lock, do you s'pose?"

A little man lifted a glowing orange melon from the pile and held it out, balanced in his long fingers. "Take a taste, sweet, see for yourself if the price is fair…"

Though the market was filled with bright light, his body was oddly encased in shadows, making his eyes appear to glow with a malevolent light. His back wore a slight hunch, giving the impression he might spring at them at any time.

Tiki reached out, but Rieker stayed her hand.

"What is the price?"

A smile tweaked the corners of the little man's mouth and he squinted in a shrewd expression. "All I ask for is a simple lock of hair—surely you can spare a strand or two..."

Tiki hesitated, torn between her desire for the fruit and trying to remember why they were there. She took a deep breath, trying to concentrate.

"Yes, I've a lock right here I can give you." Rieker reached into his pocket and pulled out a small glass jar with a cork shoved in the top. Inside, black strands of hair glistened in the moonlight.

Tiki closed her eyes and the music stopped. Startled, she blinked her eyes open and the haunting melody filled her head again, tugging at her like greedy hands. She closed her eyes again and the music was gone, as if the entire Goblin Market was nothing more than an illusion. Her urgent need to find Fiona came rushing back along with a sense of panic. How much time had they wasted drooling over the fruit?

Without opening her eyes, she tugged at Rieker's arm. "Close your eyes."

Rieker ignored her. "Here are four strands—" he held out several small chunks of the black hair— "for four pieces of fruit."

The goblin let out a low hiss. "Take it away! I won't touch such a thing."

Tiki jerked her eyes open. "What are you talking about?"

The firelight reflected off the sharp pointed teeth that protruded from the bottom jaw of the goblin as he snarled at them. "Who do you think you're dealing with? We do not trade for the hair of the *liche*."

Chapter Twelve

"*The liche?*" Tiki repeated in surprise, peering closer at what Rieker held.

"Remember?" He held the small glass container up for Tiki to see. "Leo gave it to me a few weeks ago. Said he pulled it from the head of his attacker. I must have left it in the pocket of my jacket." He turned to the goblin, his voice turning petulant. "I don't understand why you won't..."

Tiki grabbed Rieker's arm and forced him toward her. "Close your eyes."

"What?" His brow scrunched in consternation. "But Teek..."

"Close your eyes," Tiki commanded.

With a sigh Rieker accommodated her and closed his eyes. After a second, his lids jerked open again to stare at Tiki in surprise. "The music..."

"Close them," she said. "Remember why we're here." Tiki closed her own eyes and focused on what she knew to be true. She was here to find Fiona. She needed to find a way to rescue Dain. To keep her family safe. Another voice whispered in the back of her head: *you are the queen of the Seelie Court with responsibilities to many people now.* Tiki opened her eyes and faced the goblin, who watched them with a wary gaze.

"How is it you have the hair of the *liche?*" he asked, holding his hand up as if to ward them off. Long, tapered nails were filed to razor-sharp points on each finger. "Rumour says the *liche* returned to hunt in the Wychwood. Have you killed him?" There was a note of hope in his gravelly voice.

"No, but we are trying to stop him before he kills again," Tiki said. "We're looking for a young girl, about fifteen human years. She came here tonight seeking information about a magical cup that is said to be held by your people." The music swelled on the night air, the fluttering call of a flute wrapping them in the magical notes. Tiki closed her eyes again to regain her focus. Each time she opened them, the music and smells seemed fainter. In the distance, the cries of the other goblins echoed through the night.

"Be on time, be on time, you'll never find fruit so fine."

"Ho ho, hi, hi, taste the fruit, you'll want to buy."

The goblin stroked his pointed chin. "A magical cup, you say?"

"One that can cure the ills of those who drink from it." Rieker said.

"Oh," the goblin said with sudden understanding. He returned the melon to the stack and seemed to dismiss them, surveying the market for other potential buyers. "Three a lock...." he called out.

Tiki frowned, confused by his perplexing behavior. "Do you know of the cup?" she persisted, taking a step closer. "Have you seen the girl?"

The goblin turned a cold stare on them. "I haven't seen your friend, and everyone knows of the cup. It's one of the Four Treasures, but you won't find it among this lot."

"Why not?" Rieker asked.

"Because the Redcaps have it." He motioned at them with his long fingers. "Now, move along."

The Redcaps. In that instant Tiki remembered Dain telling her of the vicious goblins who dyed their caps red in their victim's blood. She tried to remember what else he had said about them.

Rieker pulled her away from the goblin interrupting her thoughts. "Let's see if we can find out more from another one."

"I've heard of the Redcaps before," Tiki said. "There's something..."

"I have, too." Rieker eyed the row of golden carts strung across the plaza. "Dain has mentioned them." His lips tightened at the mention of his brother. "Said not only are they vicious, but greedy and clever. If they have the cup, they won't just give it up. They'll expect a trade at the least."

"What would we trade?"

"That's my point. We've got nothing to trade."

Tiki frowned. "How else would we get it?"

Rieker raised his eyebrows. "We might have to steal it."

"Wouldn't be the first time," Tiki muttered. "Do you see Fiona anywhere?" She continued past the line of carts ignoring the cajoling cries of the goblins. "She wasn't that far ahead of us—she must be here somewhere."

There were a few people bargaining with the otherworldly vendors while others appeared to be pleading as they negotiated for the magical fruit.

"Why do they want it so bad?" Tiki whispered as she watched one man drop to his knees before the crooked little goblin, begging for a shiny red apple.

"When mortals eat faerie food, they develop a craving—like a scratch that can't be itched—they forever want more. Mortal food doesn't satisfy their need and they'll waste away to nothing, always longing for a bit more."

Memories of faeries tales she'd been told as a child, as well as some of the stories she'd read to Toots, Clara and Fiona with borrowed books from Mr. Potts, ran through Tiki's mind. All were laced with warnings to never eat fey food or suffer an insatiable desire for more.

"You don't think Fiona would have…"

A harsh whisper sounded in the darkness behind her. Tiki jerked around and peered blindly into the shadows, blinking to help her eyes adjust to the change in light. A shadow darted up to her and Tiki jumped back in surprise.

"It's me, Teek." Fiona's small frame was like a wraith among the shadows. Her wavy hair was tucked inside her cap and she wore oversized garments like Tiki, hiding the fact that she was a girl. "What are you two doing here?"

Tiki threw her arms around the other girl and hugged her tight. "Fiona," she said in a ragged voice, "don't you ever scare me like that again." She pushed away from the other girl, still holding her shoulders. "You haven't eaten any of the fruit, have you?"

Fiona shook her head. "Do you take me for daft?" She linked her arm through Tiki's and pulled her into the shadows that surrounded the market. "I climbed the hollow columns—remember? I told you about them before—and hid in the roof of the arcade until I could figure out who to talk to about the…" she stopped abruptly and bit the corner of her lip.

"The cup," Tiki finished for her. "I know why you're here, Fi, but why would you come by yourself? Why couldn't you wait for me and Rieker to help you?"

"I didn't know when you'd be back…" Fiona wrung her hands together, glancing nervously over Tiki's shoulder toward the goblins who continued to hawk their fruit to other passersby who had wandered into the market. "Johnny needs our help. He sacrificed himself to save *me* and now I need to help him…" Her voice began to rise.

"Shh…." Tiki said, rubbing Fiona's arms. "I understand and we're here to help." She tilted her head and gazed at Rieker with a puzzled look. "Can you still hear the music?"

"You can barely hear it when you're in the dark." Fiona said in a matter-of-fact voice. "It's only when you're out in those strange lights that you can hear it." She motioned toward the wash of illumination that made the golden carts and their spectacular loads glow as though imbued with magical powers.

She gave Tiki a guilty look. "I learned that by accident. When I arrived here I was drawn to the carts of fruit just like that pied piper in the story you read us, Teek, but one of those horrible little men tried to grab me and I still had enough sense to run. Once I was out of the light and back in the shadows I realized the music was dangerous."

"Very observant of you, Fi," Tiki murmured. There had been many times over the last few years that Fiona had amazed Tiki with her street smarts. Though Tiki had been educated in conjunction with the middle-class up-bringing she'd known before the deaths of her parents, Fiona's education had been earned in the course of survival. Even without the benefit of 'book learning', Tiki was hard-pressed to ever find a time when she felt she knew more than Fiona. Often, it was the other way around. It had been Fiona who had taught her how to survive by picking pockets and had brought her home to live with Shamus in the abandoned clockmaker's shop they'd found at Charing Cross.

"What are we going to do, Teek?" Fiona shivered, stepping closer. "I'm afraid to even talk to those creatures..." She curled her nose in distaste. "Let alone try to track down some magical vessel or whatever Larkin called it."

"This might not be the best place to start," Tiki said. A soft whooshing noise filled the air around them, making the night seem to shimmer. Callan and the two other Macanna who had identified themselves as her bodyguards earlier flickered into view.

"Majesty." Callan's tone was a mix of relief and reproach. "For your own good as queen, you shouldn't leave without telling us." He scowled at Rieker, his thick dark brows pulling low over his green eyes. "We are the best trained to protect you now." His gaze slowly perused her outfit but his face remained impassive.

"I'm sorry, Callan," Tiki said, hoping the man wouldn't question why she was dressed like a boy and out in the middle of the night. "I only planned to be gone a short time…"

"Teek." Fiona's brow scrunched in a perplexed look. "Who are you talking to?" She looked around in confusion.

"*Any* amount of time is too long," Callan interrupted. "And to be around *goblins*…" he spat the word out as if he could think of nothing more distasteful to say.

Behind them, Tiki heard a slow murmur building, like a wave growing as it drew near to shore. She glanced behind her and was alarmed to see that a number of goblins had gathered and watched them with what appeared to be a combination of anger and curiosity. Were they reacting to the presence of the Macanna? Unseen to a mortal eye, it was obvious the goblins could see the other faeries. These men immediately caught one's eye, with their wild hair, bulging muscles and bevy of weapons that hung from their belts.

"Yes, well, thank you for checking on me, but as you can see, I'm quite fine and I'll be returning home shortly. No need for you to stay."

"Perhaps you haven't heard, Majesty?"

"Heard what?" Rieker asked.

Callan's eyes narrowed ever-so-slightly and his nostrils flared as if he could smell a foul odor as he faced Rieker. There was an underlying antagonism in his manner that Tiki didn't understand. "It's the *liche*. He's been spotted in London. In the vicinity of Grosvenor Square."

Chapter Thirteen

Tiki's heart plummeted into her boots. "Where?" Clara and Toots were unguarded back at Number Six. Could the *liche* be headed there?

"Majesty!"

Tiki jerked around to see who had called her. At her movement, a cry erupted from the group of goblins watching them. Whispers and hisses exploded at the same time crooked fingers pointed their way.

"I told you that's what he called the boy!"

"Is it a boy or a girl? It must be a girl if she's queen."

"What could *she* be queen of?"

"Why is she dressed like that?"

"Who is she with?"

"Do you think she's spying on us?"

Their heated whispers and grumbles sounded like an approaching thunder storm.

"Majesty," Callan said in a low voice, moving to stand between Tiki and the group, "we should go now. Goblins are an unpredictable lot."

"Teek," Rieker murmured, "we should listen to them."

"Yes," Tiki said, "I think you might be right."

Fiona's eyes were round moons in her face as she looked from Rieker to Tiki. "Have you two gone mad? What are you on about?"

Her eyes got even wider as she looked at something over Tiki's shoulder.

Tiki reached for Fi's hand. "I'll explain when we get home. I want you to know we did talk to one of these...er... men..." she tilted her head toward the goblins, "about the cup and he said it's not here. These aren't the ones who have it."

With a squeal of fright, Fiona darted behind Rieker and clutched at the back of his coat, hiding.

"Fi." Tiki's jaw dropped in surprise. "What's wrong?"

Rieker tried to glance back over his shoulder, then lifted an arm, twisting, trying to see Fiona behind him.

Fiona pointed a shaking finger.

Tiki turned on her heel to see a tall, well-dressed man approaching. He wore a top hat cocked over his black hair and he was swathed in a long black coat that swirled about his knees as he strode through the market, oblivious to the succulent fruit displayed around him. The goblins had become aware of him too, some scuttling to the far side of their carts as he passed. Like a flame that had been snuffed, the cries of the goblins and the music of the market became muted.

Tiki's heart clanged a warning in her chest.

Rieker straightened, eyeing the man with a frown. "Who do you suppose that is?"

"It's the man who took Johnny," Fiona cried in a strangled whisper.

"It's the *liche*," Callan said in a grim voice.

Tiki swayed on her feet, her breath hitching as though her throat had suddenly become constricted. The dapper gentleman walking toward them was the *liche?* How was it possible? He didn't look anything like the monster Tiki had imagined. In fact, he looked quite the opposite. Some of the costermongers in Covent Garden were more frightening to gaze upon than this man.

"Fiona..." His voice carried toward them, not as if the words floated on the wind, but as if they *were* the wind. "There you are, my dear. I've been looking for you since we last met in Hyde Park."

Tiki froze. There was something so elemental—so disturbing in the timbre of his voice—like death coated in sugar. In a rush of insight she realized the *liche* had been near Grosvenor Square not because he'd been looking for Clara or Toots or even herself—he'd been there looking for Fiona. Had she and Rieker led him straight to the girl?

"Don't let him take me," Fiona cried, as she huddled behind Rieker.

"We should leave, Majesty," Callan said in an urgent tone. "Don't let him get too close."

Tiki's mind raced. This attractive man, who appeared to be an upper-class gentleman, was the creature who had taken Johnny and injured him so gravely he lay dying in the Otherworld. He was the killer who had murdered five people of which they knew, including a sixteen year-old girl, and had cut out their hearts. He was the murderer of the Seelie King. He was the creature to whom Donegal intended to feed Dain's heart—and now he was after Fiona. What power could she draw upon to stop this madman?

"We need to fight," Tiki said in a low voice, clenching her fists by her sides.

"No, Majesty," Callan cried, taking a step closer. "Their magic is different than ours—it isn't simply a battle of wits or controlling the weather..."

"I can smell your sweet skin from here, Fiona..." The man's voice was silk—undulating, mesmerizing. "Come to me..." He stopped ten feet away and held a hand out. "Come to me now...."

Fiona peeked from behind Rieker's back. She slowly straightened. The fear that had twisted her features seconds ago had been replaced with complacency—she moved as though she were in a daze. To Tiki's horror, she stepped from behind Rieker as if she intended to walk over to the man.

"No!" Tiki jumped in front of Fiona and stretched her arms wide to stop the other girl from moving forward. "You can't have her," she shouted.

The man snarled and for a second Tiki swore his eyes glowed red and become slitted like a cat's.

"Get out of my way, urchin boy. You're not part of this."

Fear was so heavy in Tiki's chest she could barely breathe, but anger made her voice strong. *"I AM part of this and you will not—"*

The blow hit her from the side, knocking her off her feet. Strong arms wrapped around her waist and everything around her began to shimmer. At the last second, Tiki reached out and grabbed Fiona's wrist.

THEY LANDED INSIDE the Palace of Mirrors in a room Tiki had never seen before. Though the soaring walls were white, intricate gold trim glittered from every inch of the walls and ceiling, making the room appear to have been spun from gold.

Callan's strong arms braced Tiki's fall as their momentum carried them forward upon their arrival. With no one to catch her, Fiona sprawled awkwardly on the floor, landing on her side with a painful *thump*. Before Tiki had time to react, Rieker and the other two Macanna arrived, as well.

Tiki jumped to her feet and jerked around to face Callan. "How dare you! What right do you have to treat me like that?"

"Majesty." Callan bowed his head, several braids of his brown hair falling forward. "I apologize, but you were in grave danger. The *liche* has powers that could harm you, and I couldn't take that chance."

She propped her hands on her hips and glared at the huge man. "What powers?"

"Mind control, for one." Callan motioned toward Fiona. "Did you not see your friend's reaction? It's why the *liche* targets young girls. They are the easiest to bend to his will."

"Teek." Rieker's voice had a calming influence on Tiki. He stepped close and ran his hand down the back of her arm. The three Macanna shifted their positions and glanced at each other, unsmiling. "Remember what you said the Dryads told you and Dain? To kill the liche you have to burn his body on a stake of Ash. I don't know what that means, but we weren't in the best position to defend ourselves there. We didn't even know what we were up against, plus, we were surrounded by goblins who didn't sound too friendly." His voice softened. "The first rule of war is to know your enemy."

Tiki hesitated, her anger melting away. Rieker was right. She couldn't just go barging forward against magic she didn't understand. Especially when she didn't even know what she was capable of doing herself.

"You're right." She glanced over at Callan. "I'm sorry. You did the right thing. Thank you."

The relief in the room was palpable. All three of the Macanna visibly relaxed and a broad smile broke across Callan's face. "It is my job, Majesty."

"Where are we?" Fiona sat on the floor gazing around the opulent room with her mouth ajar.

Tiki whirled toward the girl. She hadn't had time to process the fact that she'd brought Fiona into the Otherworld.

Fiona looked up at Tiki, comprehension dawning in her eyes. "We're here, aren't we?" She pushed herself to her feet, her voice becoming more excited. "We're in Faerie." There was a note of awe in her voice. She raced to Tiki and grabbed both her hands. "I want to go see Johnny, right now!"

Chapter Fourteen

"I thought that was you I heard." Larkin marched into the room, her golden hair swirling about her hips. Her gaze raked over Tiki. "And dressed to impress, I see." She curled her nose in distaste. "You're back sooner than I thought. Did you miss me?" She bit the corner of her lip and batted her lashes at Tiki in a coy expression.

"Hardly," Tiki muttered, releasing her dark hair from her cap.

"Ah, guttersnipe, you'll come to love me one day." Larkin's striking blue-green eyes narrowed as she spied Fiona. "You've brought more of your little rag-tag band of thieves here?" She planted a hand on her hip and cocked her head at Tiki. "Or perhaps you've come to your senses and realized she is the bait we need to lure the *liche* to us?"

"Bait?" Fiona echoed, looking from Larkin to Tiki.

"Don't start on that again, Larkin," Tiki snapped. "I'm not in the mood for your twisted humor." She hardly drew a breath. "We want to see Johnny, the boy the *liche* brought here when he ran from Hyde Park. Where is he?"

"In the zagishire, of course." She crossed her arms and gave them an appraising gaze. "Are you sure you want to see him? He is very sick."

"Yes." Tiki and Fiona spoke at the same time.

"Very well." She motioned toward the Macanna who stood at attention nearby. "Callan or Toran can take you. After you see the dying mortal I need to speak to you about some other matters."

"Dying?" Fiona squeaked.

"Larkin, could you be civil for once?" Rieker said in a disgusted voice.

Larkin lifted her chin in an arrogant fashion. "The truth is the truth, William. One grows stronger facing the facts rather than living in a world of make-believe." She swept toward the door. "A hard lesson for some, but necessary." She paused, a breathtaking snapshot of beauty and elegance. "A lesson I fear you're soon going to have to learn for yourself."

There was a note in the faerie's voice that Tiki struggled to define. Could it be regret?

"Always the riddle." Rieker growled under his breath.

Larkin stared at him for a long moment before she answered. "We've located Dain."

"You have?" Tiki stepped eagerly toward the faerie. "Where is he?"

"Donegal has taken him to the White Tower—deep within the Wychwood Forest." Her expression soured. "It is probably the most difficult place from which to try and rescue him." She yanked the door open. "Come find me when you're done with the mortal and we'll discuss the situation." Her voice drifted back through the open portal. "And change your clothes before the Court sees you looking like a guttersnipe!"

THE WALK TO the zagishire led them down a hallway that ran adjacent to the Great Hall. Even Tiki was impressed by the grandeur of the palace now that the Seelies were back in control. No longer were the rooms filled with shadows and darkness, but instead, bright light reflected off gold and gems that seemed to line every surface.

"I feel like we're in Buckingham Palace," Fiona whispered to Tiki as they walked along. "I've never seen such a place in my life."

Tiki had taken Larkin's advice, as much as she hated to do anything the faerie suggested, and removed the familiar glamour she'd grown up wearing in London. She'd tried to warn Fiona first, but to her surprise Fiona had shrugged away her explanation. "I think I'll know it's you, Teek."

But even Fiona's jaw had dropped when Tiki removed the glamour and revealed her natural image. Her black hair hung in a great braid down her back, framing skin that was a creamy ivory, making her eyes glow like two emeralds. She wore a gown the color of crushed cranberries, embellished with threads of silver that glittered in the light of the torches that lined the walls. Fiona had hurriedly looked away, sneaking peeks at Tiki from the corner of her eyes.

"Are you all right, Fi?" Tiki asked, distressed at her friend's strange reaction.

"It hurts to look at you," Fiona said in a whisper. "You're so beautiful. I'm afraid I'll never be able to look away."

"Don't worry, Fi," Rieker said in an oddly strained voice. "You're not the only one who feels that way." Even Callan and Toran seemed affected by Tiki's new appearance, dropping their eyes when Tiki looked at them and bowing their heads in a subservient way.

"I'm the same person underneath," Tiki replied, not sure if she were pleased or irritated by their reactions. "I think we should change your clothes, as well, Fi." Whispering familiar words, Tiki had run her hand near Fiona and the girl's dirty, oversized jacket and trousers had melted into a stunning gown of royal blue. Her wavy hair was pulled away from her face in a crown of soft curls and she looked every inch as regal as a young blue-blood in London.

Rieker also had changed his outfit, donning clothes similar to what Tiki had seen others wear to court—tight brown trousers the color of bark, a spotless white shirt with an embroidered brown jacket. Used to seeing Rieker dressed as Lord William Richmond, in London, his transformation wasn't quite as shocking.

They passed many hallways in the Palace that turned off in different directions and on any other day, Tiki would have itched to go explore where they might lead. But today, she was focused on finding Johnny, so they could assess the state of his health. Because after that, she needed to learn what had become of Dain and how they might save the young man. And underlying those concerns, she desperately wanted to keep her promise to Clara and return to London.

Shafts of sunlight streamed through open windows and the sound of birdsong carried on the wind as they drew near the entrance. A soft, summer breeze blew through the portico as they stopped beneath the grand entry arches and gazed out at what had previously been the Night Garden.

Rather than the dark, shadow-laden thicket of bare branches and sharp brambles that had housed predatory, nocturnal plants, this garden was well-tended and overflowing with abundant blossoms in every color. Healthy, green vines stretched in wild abandon, and a tantalizing fragrance filled the air. Nearby the sounds of a brook running over stones babbled, and laughter could be heard in the distance.

"I don't believe it," Tiki breathed.

Rieker stood by her side, a look of wonder on his face. "It's hard to imagine it's the same place."

Callan stood with his hands on his hips, a proud smile stretched across his face. "It's how the gardens that surround the Palace of Mirrors should look all the time." He pointed to the left. The horizon in that direction was dark and filled with black clouds.

"And the UnSeelies should stay in the Plain of Starlight where they belong."

UNLIKE THE PALACE, the zagishire had an earthen floor and walls, with a ceiling made of thatch. A quiet hush hung over the building like a misty fog, almost as if the earth itself had wrapped its healing arms around the sick and dying who were lodged there.

A faerie greeted them at the entrance, her surprise at seeing the new queen evident as she bobbed her head and said, 'Welcome, Majesty.'

"We'll wait out here," Callan said in a gruff voice, positioning himself on one side of the door and motioning for Toran to stand on the other.

Tiki, Rieker and Fiona followed the woman down the hallway, their feet silent on the hard-packed dirt floor. For a fleeting second the healing sense of the place reminded Tiki of another spot she'd visited in Faerie—the underground hall where the Macanna had gathered in the Plain of Sunlight, waiting for their opportunity to overthrow the Winter King. It had been there that the Macanna had bowed to her and first shouted 'TARR-UH'. It was there that she'd shed the glamour she'd worn all of her life and become someone new.

Johnny was the only occupant in his corridor. Tiki rounded the corner with the others and stared curiously into the shadowed room. Small, rectangular windows lined the upper reaches of the walls, letting in streaks of sunlight. Dust motes wafted in their shafts while the rich, fragrant scent of heather filled the air. Fiona let out a cry of dismay as she spotted Johnny's limp form and rushed toward him.

The young pickpocket was lying on his side in a bed that appeared to be constructed of white and purple heather. Fiona dropped to her knees and reached for one of his hands.

"Johnny," she said softly, "it's me, Fi." There was no response from the still form. "I've come to help you get well." Fiona's voice cracked. "Please open your eyes."

But even as Fiona whispered the words, Tiki wondered if there was any way to save the young boy. He was but a shriveled shell of his former self—his cheekbones protruding from a face that was a macabre caricature of the charming boy she'd known.

Johnny's head lolled to the side as Tiki gently rolled him onto his back. A white bandage covered his neck but a long scratch descended below the wrap and stretched down the center of his pale chest, red blood oozing from the wound. His brown hair hung in greasy strands, partially covering his face. Tiki smoothed the bits of hair out of Johnny's eyes and was shocked at how hot his skin was.

"He has a fever." Tiki looked up at the faerie for an explanation.

"Yes, Mum." She dipped her head and gave a little curtsey. "He's been like that since they brought him in. And he's getting worse. Larkin won't let us give him food or drink." Her voice dropped. "He's just a mortal, you know. I think he's given up."

Chapter Fifteen

Donegal raised his hands, the sleeves of his black robes falling back, revealing arms that seemed to lack any skin—covered instead with a macabre combination of black veins, white sinew and red muscle. The Winter King and his closest advisors were circled around the bound body of the Seelie spy.

"A seventh year is upon us again. In payment of our tithe to the Seelie ruler to allow the noble UnSeelies to remain a separate Court—we shall provide a sacrifice at Samhain."

The Winter King reached inside a bag of woven ferns that Bearach held and drew out what appeared to be a handful of brown feathers. As he turned the item in his hands, the feathers fell back, revealing a white face partially covered by a golden eye mask. The lips were painted gold and what looked like three hinges were positioned on both sides of the jaw and centered on the chin.

He spoke in a guttural voice. "As a symbol of our commitment to this obligation, we affix this mask to our sacrifice and dub thee the Seven Year King."

Dain jerked his head to the side as Donegal leaned toward him, but with his arms and legs tied behind his back, it was impossible to fight. The UnSeelie leader forced the mask over Dain's bruised and bloodied face—the eerie facade replacing his natural features.

The mask tightened against Dain's skin as if permanently attached.

The Winter King straightened. "Your new queen must care a great deal for you." Donegal's voice was questioning, as he peered down at his prisoner. "She wanted to trade for your release."

Though the probability of escape was non-existent, Dain had searched for any opportunity. The idea that someone might try and rescue him had not occurred to him. When agreeing to infiltrate the enemy Court one accepted the risks and with that, the knowledge that capture was considered a casualty of war. He was doomed and he knew it. Even Larkin wouldn't try and free him from Donegal.

"I've never heard of a queen who cares so much about a *spy* that she would negotiate for his release." Curiosity echoed in his words as Donegal nudged Dain in the ribs with his boot. "Most leaders deny all knowledge of such things. Why would she care about you, I wonder?"

Beside the Winter King, Bearach pulled a whip from his belt and unfurled it with a cracking snap of the leather against the stone floor. "I can get him to tell us who he is." A laugh rumbled deep in his chest. "No one but the hobgoblins will hear his screams here."

Dain stared at the far wall, willing himself to be strong. Just the sound of the whip made the lashes that already marked his back start to throb with pain again.

"It's not just who *he* is," Donegal murmured, his hand braced against his chin as he contemplated Dain. "I wonder if our prisoner can't tell us who his queen might be? For that's what we need to know: where has this new Seelie queen been hidden and by whom?" He nudged Dain again, harder this time. "And most important—what are her weaknesses?"

"WHAT IS YOUR TRUE NAME?" Bearach shouted.

The first strike of the whip was like flame being laid to his bare skin. Dain surged against the iron cuffs that suspended him from the ceiling by his wrists, trying to escape the bite of the lash, but the iron seared his flesh creating a different sort of pain.

"WHAT IS YOUR RELATIONSHIP TO THE QUEEN?"

Dain closed his eyes and tried to picture his favorite parts of the mortal world that he'd come to know—Piccadilly Circus, King's Cross Station, Covent Garden. He imagined the myriad mix of people who went about their business every day: the flower girls, the coal porters, the bankers and the shop girls; crossing sweeps and the gentry in their finery—all of them unaware of the fey who walked in their midst. But one face rose to the surface with each memory: green eyes, fair skin, dark hair.

The second strike whistled through the air in a macabre warning before the thin leather cracked against his back. A small groan of pain escaped his lips as he sagged against his bonds.

"THE QUEEN IS A MACLOCHLAN—WHERE HAS SHE BEEN HIDDEN ALL THIS TIME?"

Dain inhaled through his mouth, his eyes squeezed shut, trying to breathe through the excruciating agony. He would never willingly reveal any knowledge that could possibly harm Tiki or her family. He imagined William's face. So familiar—yet so unknown. A twinge of regret mixed with the pain. He'd not had long enough to sort out his feelings for the brother he'd just discovered. He felt curiosity and respect for William certainly, intertwined with a new emotion: jealousy. Had he lost the chance to know him?

At the third strike, flashes of white light danced before Dain's eyes. He ground his teeth together and prayed he would lose consciousness soon.

DAIN'S LIMP BODY hung from the chains that bound his wrists, his masked face pointed toward the stone floor.

Nearby, Bearach finished wiping his whip clean and re-attached it to his belt. "He is stronger than most, not to utter a word." There was a grudging note of respect in his voice.

Donegal's face twisted with barely suppressed rage. "We've got six months to make him talk." He snapped his cape behind him and walked to the door. "We'll leave him here without food for a few weeks—" his lips curled in a snarl— "and then we'll see what he has to say."

Chapter Sixteen

F iona insisted that she stay with Johnny. Tiki realized she
wasn't going to be able to get the other girl to change her
mind, so she returned briefly to Grosvenor Square and came
back with bread, cheddar and several jugs of water. After warning
Fiona not to eat or drink anything but the mortal food, Tiki had
asked Toran to stand watch over the girl while Fi visited the sick
patient. Tiki needed to return Fiona to London for her own safe-
keeping, yet she didn't dare as long as the *liche* hunted her. Along
with her fear for Fiona, another chilling prospect had occurred
to Tiki. Larkin had said that Donegal plotted to claim the Seelie
throne again. Had the Winter King sent the *liche* to hunt her, as well?

LARKIN'S STUDY WAS in a room behind the Great Hall,
not far from where they had returned with Callan. Though graced
with soaring ceilings and spectacular arch-topped windows that
flooded the area with light, the room was surprisingly bare of
adornment and grandeur. Larkin sat at a simple table hewn from
a giant slab of tree, in a chair that appeared to be constructed of
willow branches and moss. A small dried gourd rested on the desk,
wrapped with a lock of Larkin's hair.

The faerie motioned to two similar chairs across the table from
her. "Sit down. We've much to discuss." Callan, who had escorted
Tiki from the zagishire, took a stance near the door, a blank look

on his face as he stared at the far wall. Larkin gave a questioning glance as Tiki and Rieker were seated. "You've seen the mortal?" At their nods, she said, "It doesn't appear he has long to live."

Anger flared in Tiki's chest at Larkin's callous attitude. "A goblin at the market said the Redcaps have the magical cup that you mentioned could help Johnny." She wasn't going to argue with the faerie, she simply wanted answers. "How does one find the Redcaps?"

"The Goblin Market?" Larkin's voice echoed with surprise. "You dared to visit the goblins?" At Tiki's nod she tapped her long fingers on the table. "You are either braver than I gave you credit for, or more foolish than even I knew." She continued to tap, her beautiful face scrunched in a quizzical expression. "I wonder which it might be?"

"What does it matter?" Tiki snapped. "Where do we find the Redcaps?" No matter how hard she tried, it was difficult to keep her patience with Larkin.

"They live on the northern border of the Wychwood, but you take your life in your hands if you go there." She shifted her gaze to Rieker. "Along with anyone else's who is foolish enough to accompany you." She held up a slender finger. "I warn you both—do *not* go there. The chance that you might actually recover the cup is so infinitesimally slim that there is no justification for the risk your journey would entail."

Tiki worked to keep her voice level. "But if we don't go, how else are we to save Johnny?"

Larkin raised her eyebrows. "Perhaps he isn't meant to be saved."

Tiki's jaw sagged in disbelief at the faerie's callousness.

Rieker sat forward, focused intently into Larkin's face. "We understand your concern about the Redcaps and appreciate your warning. Thank you." He barely took a breath. "Where is Dain being held?"

Larkin leaned back in her chair and crossed her legs, every movement graceful and effortless. "It is a top secret location. We believe he's being held in the White Tower. No Seelie knows the exact location and it is said that among the UnSeelie's, only Donegal's inner circle is privy to the information."

A conversation she'd had with Dain echoed in Tiki's ears. *The town has a prison called The White Tower there. It's hidden in the very heart of the Wychwood—where the damned and demented are held...It is said to be a place of no return.*

"Dain said the Tower was in a town in the heart of the Wychwood."

"We have looked there. It is not to be found. We now believe the information was a lie to mislead us."

Rieker's voice was low and intense. "There's got to be some way to find him—to free him."

Larkin's lips twisted in a bitter smile before she pushed away from the table and paced to the far side of the room. "If only it were that simple. The White Tower has been controlled by the UnSeelies for a very long time. It is old and steeped in enchantments. " Her words sounded oddly detached, drifting over her shoulder. "It's where Donegal held me after I was captured last winter."

Tiki imagined the scene in Rieker's bedchamber. Two of Donegal's men had clamped Larkin's wings with iron and taken her away. For months afterward, the faerie's cries for help had echoed in Tiki's ears with a damning resonance. But Larkin had escaped from Donegal eventually, tearing off her own wings in the process.

"But you escaped," Tiki said. "Can't you find it again?"

Larkin stood with her arms crossed, gazing out the window. "When I escaped I was wounded and bleeding heavily. I transported from where I was being held prisoner to a place of safety. I never saw the exterior location of the Tower." Her voice dropped. "I only saw the inside of the stone cell where they tortured me."

She turned to face them, her lips pressed tight, her eyes hooded. "Dain does not have the same ability to travel through our world as I do. Our spies tell us that after my escape, the Winter King went a step further and hid the White Tower behind a glamour that only he recognizes."

Tiki gritted her teeth with frustration. "What do you suggest?"

"I'm not sure, yet." Larkin returned to stand near her chair. "I need to give the situation further thought. Our task is complicated by the fact that Donegal has named Dain his Seven Year King."

Rieker clenched his fists and rested them on the desk. "What does that mean exactly?"

Larkin's face became expressionless and in a flash of insight Tiki wondered if it was because she was trying to hide the fact that she actually cared for Dain.

"The UnSeelies are obligated to pay a tithe—a sacrifice—every seven years to retain their sovereignty. They name a Seven Year King as a way of mocking the Courts. One normally associates being a king with power, glory and ultimate dominion. Because they hate the fact that they are obligated to make payment to avoid servitude to the Seelie throne, they mock the very stature they seek. The UnSeelies name their Seven Year King and then torture him until Samhain at the end of October, almost as if he were an effigy of Seelie royalty—before he is sacrificed and offered to the ruler of the Seelie Court.

Chapter Seventeen

"There's been a sighting." Arthur stormed into the library where Leo sat with Queen Victoria and their younger sister, Beatrice, who at fifteen years of age, was still fondly called Baby by the Queen. They were playing cards by the fire.

"A sighting of what?" Baby asked, looking up from the cards. She was Queen Victoria's youngest and last child and the Queen doted on her. After the death of her husband, Albert, the Queen had insisted that Baby spend most days by her mother's side. "Not a traveling fair or something interesting like that, I'm sure." She looked hopefully at her elder brother.

"Oh, hello, Baby." Arthur's tone changed. "Didn't know you were in here with mother." He raised his eyebrows at Leo. "I need to talk to you. It's about... that horse we were discussing."

Leo laid his cards on the table and pushed back his chair. "Probably for the best," he said, ruffling his sister's hair. "Baby was giving me a licking, anyway."

Queen Victoria's gaze shifted from one to the other. "Baby and I will be returning to Windsor tomorrow. Perhaps you should join us?"

"That is a splendid idea, Mother," Arthur said. "I think it's an excellent time to leave the City."

Leo frowned. "I'm afraid the journey would be more than I could bear, right now, but I'm relieved you and Baby will be going. You'll be safe at Windsor."

"Safe from what?" Baby asked, looking from one brother to the other. "Are you expecting trouble of some sort?'"

"Nothing to worry about." Arthur slipped his hand under Leo's elbow and led him toward the door. "A few rumours about a cough that's going 'round. Wouldn't want either of you to catch it." He led his brother from the room.

"What have you learned?" Leo asked in a low voice.

"Were you aware that Charles Bagley has formed a brigade of sorts?"

Leo frowned. "No. What sort of brigade? I thought he was still in mourning."

"He is. Grief-stricken over the death of his beloved Marie Claire at the hands of that murderous butcher." Arthur grimaced in distaste. "It makes me sick to think of that poor girl in the hands of someone so depraved. Sixteen years old and to have her heart cut from her chest…" Arthur shook his head. "Charles has formed a vigilante group to hunt the man down. Of course, he has no idea what he's dealing with, nor do we really, but several of the chaps swear they spotted the murderer last night."

Leo gasped. "You're joking. Where?"

"At Covent Garden, of all places. Apparently, there was a gathering of some sort, the details are a bit muddled, but two of Charles' men spotted someone who fit the description of Marie Claire's attacker. They gave chase and here's the part I wanted to tell you—" Arthur put his hand on Leo's shoulder— "they say the man had glowing red eyes, just like your drawing."

"I knew he'd be back." Leo said with conviction. He rubbed the wound on his neck that had just begun to heal as he stared at the floor in thought. "But how do we stop him?"

"That's not the worst of it."

Leo jerked his head up in alarm. "What else?"

"They swear they followed him to Grosvenor Square."

"You don't think...."

Arthur's lips were pressed in a thin line. "They said he disappeared into the coach house of Number Six."

Chapter Eighteen

Tiki pushed herself out of the chair, as much in frustration at her inability to help either Johnny or Dain as her desire to take action. "We've got to save Dain," she cried. "Samhain isn't for six months! We can't let Donegal torture him for that long."

Rieker was already pacing, his hands on his hips, a troubled frown darkening his face.

A flicker of emotion crossed Larkin's face. "We are continuing to search for a way to help him. In the meantime, life must go on." She crossed her arms and nodded at Tiki. "You need to address the Court before you leave again. There are matters which require your attention, plus you should greet them simply out of respect. They have waited and hoped for your return, along with everyone else."

"All right," Tiki said doubtfully, looking at Rieker for his opinion.

"They gather each day while we rule Faerie," Larkin continued, "and oversee the governing of many parts of our world." She gave a soft snort. "If you want to feed all the beggars in Faerie, you'd better start by convincing the Court that it's in our best interest."

"Fine. Where do we go?"

Something shifted in Larkin's eyes. "There is no 'we'. You are the queen—*you* need to attend."

"But I want Rieker to attend with me."

Larkin put her hands on the table and leaned forward. She spoke softly, as if she didn't want the Macanna who guarded the door to hear. "William is not your equal here. It would be inappropriate for him to attend Court as your consort."

"My con—" Tiki's mouth dropped open as she looked to Rieker for an explanation. He had stopped pacing, his gaze steady on Larkin. Tiki whipped back around to face the faerie. "What are you talking about?"

Larkin's lips twitched as if she found their conversation amusing. "Surely you realize he's a half-breed here in Faerie." Her eyes skimmed Rieker with a mocking light. "Barely trustworthy, and really only qualified to be a servant to those in Court. Certainly not good enough to serve the queen." She straightened and gave Rieker an appraising once-over. "William must prove himself in our world, though even if he does, he'll have a terrible time ever convincing anyone that he's a match for a royal."

"But that's absurd," Tiki protested.

Larkin arched her eyebrows. "Really? Don't you find it amusing that your roles have been reversed? In London as a *pickpocket*—" she sneered the word— "you were an incomprehensible match for Lord Richmond. Even as a middle-class orphan the two of you moved in worlds that rarely intersected. Here, William is an equally inappropriate match for you." She heaved an exaggerated sigh. "It never ends well for star-crossed lovers, does it?"

"I don't care what society here thinks about any of this," Tiki spat out. Anger bubbled in her veins and she clenched her fists. "I am the queen and if I want Rieker with me then I'll bloody well have him."

Larkin laughed out loud at Tiki's temper. She waggled a finger at her. "Tsk tsk, guttersnipe, do you really want to start your reign like this? Having Donegal seeking revenge isn't enough? Now you want to do battle with your own Court?"

Rieker spoke up. "Tiki, she might be right. Now isn't the time to make an issue of what class I'm considered here. We've got bigger problems to worry about."

Tiki fought the urge to stamp her foot. Was he agreeing with Larkin *again?* "Fine," she snapped. "I will ignore this ridiculous conversation for now because I need to return home as soon as possible and take Fiona with me—" she pointed her finger at Larkin— "but mind my words, Rieker will join me at Court." She reached for his hand. "Because he is the one and only person I know I can trust here."

"You may think you can trust him," Larkin snapped, her mood shifting yet again, "but *I'm* the one who gives you answers and the knowledge you need to survive here. You need *me* to command and control this kingdom." Her eyes narrowed. "I would suggest you don't ever forget it."

RIEKER WENT TO check on Fiona while Larkin led Tiki in the opposite direction. Behind them, Callan trailed at a discreet distance. His constant presence was wearing on Tiki's nerves and she began to look for ways to escape his watchful eye.

"Court meets in the High Chamber of Ladies and Lords each day." Larkin gave Tiki a sideways glance. "This will be a pleasant surprise for them. They've been especially curious about you."

"Majesty." A voice squeaked from behind them.

Tiki glanced over her shoulder but no one was in sight. As she was turning away, a small figure emerged from the shadow of one of the great columns. Tiki recognized Ailléna's hunched form.

"Thank you for the food, your Grace," she said in a hoarse whisper.

Tiki paused, and squatted down so she was eye level with the ugly little creature. Ailléna's bottom teeth were razor sharp and protruded up over her upper jaw, but she was in such a pathetic state,

Tiki found it difficult to be afraid of her. "You're welcome. Are you feeling better? I see you're able to walk on your own now."

"Yes'm." Ailléna bobbed her head. "Most I've had to eat in more years than I can count."

Tiki tried not to react, though the idea that anyone had gone hungry for so long was upsetting to hear. "I struggled to find enough food myself for a few years," she confided. "It can be very difficult to be hungry all the time."

Ailléna gasped. "You, Majesty? But how can that be? You're a queen. You have everything."

Tiki bit back a laugh. If only the little creature knew the truth.

"I don't think anyone has everything," she murmured, "even if you are queen. But from now on," she put her finger gently on Ailléna's chest, "you will have enough to eat." Nearby, Callan cleared his throat in warning.

"Come along." Larkin tugged at Tiki's arm. "You've more important things to do."

Tiki stood. "I'll look for you in the Great Hall at supper."

Ailléna fell to her knees. "Your Grace is the kindest queen we've ever had. Blessings on you, Majesty."

"Enough already." Larkin's lips curled in disgust as she tugged Tiki away, mumbling under her breath. "Nothing more than the scum of the earth, and you treat her like she's a bloody relative. '*I'll look for you in the Great Hall*,'" Larkin mimicked.

"Not every heart is as cold as yours," Tiki replied, nonplussed by Larkin's reaction.

"Be careful," Larkin snapped. "Or she'll bite the same hand she pretends to kiss."

They continued down the hall, their dresses flowing behind them, creating a shushing noise as they walked. The faerie steered them around a corner and stopped before a pair of mammoth plank doors. Two red-coated guards stood on each side, clutching razor-sharp spears. A variety of other weapons glittered from their belts. Larkin spoke in her normal, arrogant tone. "Queen Tara has arrived for Court. Please announce us."

With a sharp salute, the guards jumped into action, simultaneously sweeping the doors open to provide an unencumbered view of the High Chamber. Tiki's eyes widened in surprise. She'd been expecting to see another opulent room with grand columns and gold-filigreed walls, but instead, the room that stretched before them looked like an enchanted wood—there were no walls, only forest in every direction as far as the eye could see.

The floor was covered in moss, making Tiki long to kick off her shoes and run barefoot across the spongy ground. In the distance, the sound of a brook singing over stones drifted toward Tiki, along with the voice of the forest—birds chattering, animals scuttling through the undergrowth, the rustle of the leaves in the wind. Shafts of sunlight beamed down through the branches of the trees and Tiki had an overwhelming sensation that they'd somehow been transported to the Wychwood Forest.

As though in protection, a giant tree stretched its leafy canopy over a great wooden table filled with faeries of every shape and size. At the far end of the table an elaborately carved chair sat empty.

"Why, it's the Queen," a familiar voice cried.

Before Tiki could connect who the voice belonged to, someone sprang up to land gracefully on the table. Tiki recognized the Court Jester, his gaudy outfit impossible to forget. Yellow streaks stretched from his eyes, making them look like miniature suns and the bells on his three-point hat jingled as he artfully pranced down the center of the table.

"I thought he was with Donegal's court," Tiki whispered from the side of her mouth.

"The Fool knows only one court—that of Faerie," Larkin said. "He has no allegiance to a Seelie ruler or an UnSeelie ruler. He knows only the truth, which he shrouds in wit and puns, for fear we will realize how truly perceptive he is."

The Jester began to chant in a sing-song voice, striking a pose with each stanza:

"At long last the faerie queen shows her face
An unequaled beauty with effortless grace
Crowned by the cry of the Tara Stone
Will she stay long enough to grace the throne?"

Tiki frowned at the gaudily-dressed man. How had he known she wanted to leave? Had Larkin told him?

"Or will she seek an impossible quest
A treasure not to be possessed
And when the weak to death concede
Will the long-sought prize answer those in need?"

Tiki glared at Larkin. Had she put the Jester up to this? Riddles and puns and secrets hidden in layers. There seemed to be some veiled message in the Jester's verse, but what? Why couldn't anyone just speak plainly in this world?

"Queen Tara Dunbar MacLochlan," the guard cried and both men stamped the staffs of their spears on the hard floor.

By now, everyone who had been seated at the long table had risen to their feet and faced where Tiki stood by the door, their faces etched with curiosity and expectation. They each wore a crimson cape, the color of the wine her father used to drink, the rich fabric shot through with gold thread.

The Jester held his arms out wide and bowed. "Welcome back, Majesty."

Tiki gave a stiff nod of acknowledgement and followed Larkin, not sure what to make of the Jester's verse. With little fanfare, Larkin swept along the length of the table introducing lords and ladies as they went.

"Conrath, Morgan, Flaherty and O'Donoghue, they live..." her explanations blurred into a drone of information that Tiki couldn't possibly retain. They reached the far end of the table where the lone chair sat. Larkin snapped her fingers and a second, almost identical, chair joined the first. She motioned for Tiki to take the seat, and pulled up her own chair.

"Let the meeting be brought to order," she said in an imperious tone, as though she were used to running the Court. The other faeries took their seats and the order of business was discussed.

THOUGH THE TOPICS were interesting and the members of the High Court intriguing, Tiki struggled to follow the conversation. Thankfully, Larkin directed much of the meeting.

While she listened, a nagging sense of urgency tugged at Tiki with unrelenting persistence. Where was the *liche*? How could they track him down and stop him once and for all? Where was the cup they needed to find to save Johnny and how much time did the young boy have left? And where was Dain? A sick feeling twisted in Tiki's stomach. Was Donegal torturing him even now? A pang of longing speared her chest as she thought of Clara, home alone at Number Six. Tiki squirmed in her chair, fighting the conviction that she needed to be multiple places at once.

After what felt like hours, Tiki nudged Larkin under the table with her toe. The first time Larkin ignored her, continuing to verbally spar with some Lord about the consequences of regulating the water use of the Avon river.

The second time, Tiki wasn't as gentle. She trod hard on Larkin's toes while she stared at the faerie's face, hoping to catch her eye. A grimace of pain shot across Larkin's features and she turned to glare at Tiki.

Tiki stood up abruptly.

"Thank you all so much for your hard work and dedication to our Court. I must leave you now, but please do carry on with your much-needed efforts." She flicked a hand at Larkin as if commanding a dog. "Come Larkin."

Tiki swore she heard Larkin growl behind her, but the noise was lost as everyone at the table scooted their chairs back and jumped to their feet as Tiki swept by. She practically flew up the steps, reminded of the time she'd run from Buckingham Palace, having just returned the ring she'd stolen.

As if magically sensing her approach, the guards pulled the doors open and Tiki walked through with her head held high, trying not to sprint toward the entry that would lead outside to the zagishire. Callan, who had been waiting impatiently outside the door, hurriedly fell into step behind her.

"Where are you going?" Larkin snapped from behind her as Tiki marched down the hallway.

Tiki didn't slow, but turned to answer over her shoulder. "I've got things to do."

Larkin's eyes became shrouded. "Such as?"

Exasperation made Tiki's voice sharp. "I'm worried about Johnny and Dain and my family and where the *liche* might be and—" she jerked around, her hands on her hips— "why there are faeries starving in a palace overflowing with opulence."

The faerie's jaw tightened and she raised her nose with an imperious air. "There are centuries of history at play here of which you have no grasp. I couldn't possibly explain it all to you while we stand here."

"You don't need to explain it to me," Tiki snapped. "I can see for myself what is happening. There are faeries within the Seelie Court who are starving while others feast." She and her family had gone hungry too many nights while the wealthy in London had more food than they could possibly eat in a lifetime. She would not let such inequity occur in Faerie if she had any control over the circumstances. "I plan to make sure there is food for all."

TIKI FOUND RIEKER and Fiona in Johnny's room. She could see at a glance that Fiona had been crying and Rieker's face was tight with concern.

"Any change?" Tiki asked gently.

"I think he's worse," Fiona sniffed. "It's like he's sinking into himself and disappearing." She turned and clutched at Tiki's hand. "What can we do, Teek? I can't let him die. Besides our family, he's the only good thing that's ever happened to me in my life."

Tiki slid her arms around the frail girl and held her tight. Over Fiona's shoulder Tiki's eyes met Rieker's. "We're going to go find the Cup of Plenty."

Fiona jerked back, her overflowing eyes searching Tiki's as if she were afraid to hope. "When?"

"Now."

Chapter Nineteen

In the coach house of Number Six, Grosvenor Square, a man who seemed to be wrought from the darkest shadows sniffed the air as though a tantalizing aroma wafted beneath his nostrils.

"Ah," he whispered to himself. "I smell children." He licked his lips in anticipation.

Chapter Twenty

After discussing the situation, it was decided that Fiona would stay with Johnny while Tiki and Rieker would go to the northern border in search of the cup. As they approached the exit of the zagishire, Tiki pulled on Rieker's arm. "It might be best to gather our things and go from here. I don't want Larkin to know where we've gone and though I know he means well, I don't want Callan following me everywhere."

"Good point," Rieker said. He glanced around the entry foyer but the nurse who had greeted them before was nowhere in sight.

"I'm going to dress like a wood nymph," Tiki said, remembering her trek with Dain through the Wychwood and how difficult it had been to maneuver in the dress she'd worn. Plus, she'd left a trail and they'd been followed by Bearach, putting themselves at great risk.

Rieker raised his eyebrows. "A wood nymph?"

"With my top half covered," Tiki added in a hurry. She'd forgotten that wood nymphs rarely covered their breasts. "To blend with the forest."

"Not only to blend with the forest, but to blend with those who inhabit the forest," Rieker said. He muttered Gaelic under his breath and swept his hand along the length of his body. As Tiki watched, his clothes seemed to dissolve to be replaced by garments that appeared to be made from the fabric of the Wychwood, greens and browns, looking like leaves, bark and shadows.

Tiki reached up and traced a finger across a faint scar that lined his jaw. "You remind me of Sean, the glamour Dain used when undercover in the UnSeelie court."

Rieker caught her hand in his, and brought her fingers to his lips. "Dain's bravery is my inspiration. I won't rest until we set him free."

Tiki's heart ached at the thought of Dain being tortured. The image of his battered face was never far from her mind, nor was the constant worry of what new abuse Donegal might impose on his prisoner.

"We'll find him," she whispered. Her fingertips lingered on Rieker's skin as if soaking up the essence of him. She ached to hold—to keep him safe, as well. "I promise."

Rieker slid a hand behind her neck and pulled her toward him. His lips covered hers with a hunger Tiki knew all too well. Their breath mingled and became one, their tongues meeting in an explosion of sensation. His other hand slid around her waist, crushing her against him.

A soft groan escaped from Rieker as he kissed the corners of Tiki's lips, then her cheeks, his lips and tongue leaving a trail of fire everywhere they touched. Tiki closed her eyes and let her head fall back as his lips moved below her ear, down her neck to the hollow at the base of her throat. His hand moved up to cup her breast—

A strangled cough broke the spell. Tiki opened her eyes to see the faerie nurse staring at them with an open mouth and a shocked expression. Her gaze went from Tiki to Rieker, then back to Tiki again. She seemed incapable of speech.

Instead of trying to explain the situation, Rieker simply nodded at the woman, who mumbled something unintelligible and rushed back out the door. A giggle rose in Tiki's chest and she covered her mouth to keep it from breaking loose.

"Did you see the look on her face?"

"Apparently she doesn't approve of half-breeds snogging the queen," Rieker said with a chuckle.

Tiki frowned at his choice of words, but since he didn't seem upset, she let it go.

"But the queen likes it." She gave him a shy smile and squeezed his hand.

"And so does the half-breed."

Tiki's cheeks warmed with pleasure. She tightened her grip on his hand as they exited the zagishire and headed toward the Palace of Mirrors to prepare for their departure.

LATER, THE TREES of the Wychwood Forest swayed and moaned above Tiki and Rieker, almost as if in warning not to proceed. Tiki shivered, not only from the cool air, but also at the thought of seeking out such savage creatures as the Redcaps. They'd made a plan to go north to the border and find the goblins, but it was hard to know what to do beyond that, neither of them having been there before. The end goal was to recover the cup, but there were so many unknowns, it was impossible to plan much beyond finding those who were said to guard the cup.

"We'll just have to go and see what we can find," Rieker said, "and hope common sense and a little help from Lady Luck will serve us well."

THEY'D LEFT AT dawn, wanting the light of daybreak by which to travel. Tiki's heart had soared when Rieker had met her at the zagishire leading a great white mare with red ribbons and brass bells threaded through her mane. When the horse moved, a musical jingle filled the air.

"I asked Larkin several days ago about a horse if I wanted to ride," Rieker said as he approached, "and she told me to take this one."

"Aeveen?" Tiki reached out to rub the beast's velvety nose. A sudden rush of tears burned in her eyes and she buried her face in the horse's neck. "You're alive." She inhaled the fragrant scent of horse hair, torn between laughing and crying.

"You know this horse?"

"Yes, she's Dain's." Tiki smiled at the beautiful horse, which stood with her ears pricked forward. "Aeveen is the horse Toots rode." The ten year-old had been enchanted by the beautiful beast, bragging often that he'd ridden a horse that could fly. "When Dain and I escaped from Donegal and the Palace of Mirrors, we went through the Wychwood. Dain led me out of the forest through the fields by O'Donoghue's farm and Aeveen was there with several other horses. He whistled for her and she ran so fast, she looked like she was flying. That's how we returned to London." Tiki stroked the horse's elegant neck. "I was so afraid she'd died when Donegal slaughtered those horses from the Seelie Court."

"Obviously not. Apparently, Larkin has been having her cared for while—" Rieker hesitated— "Dain's away." He stroked Aeveen's mane. "We'll need to take these bells off but she should be able to get us to where we need to go."

After they'd removed the bells, which Tiki tucked in a pocket, Rieker pulled her up behind him. She was careful not to bump the variety of weapons that Rieker had hung from the leather saddle, including a sabre, a dagger, a coiled whip and even a broadsword.

"Are you holding on?" Rieker asked over his shoulder.

Tiki slid her arms around his trim waist. "Ready."

THOUGH THE SUN was a brilliant orb in the blue sky, only filtered light breeched the dense canopy of the magical wood, casting strange shadows that moved with the wind. Tiki had the uneasy sense they were surrounded by half-seen creatures. She remembered the spriggans, kelpies and dryads they'd encountered the last time she'd gone through the Wychwood and watched their surroundings with a wary eye.

"I don't know how far the northern border might be," she said, "but that's where both Dain and Larkin said the Redcaps live." She had dressed as Rieker had, to blend with the forest in bark-colored trousers and a dappled green jacket that melted into the shadows. Her hair was braided and tucked inside her coat, much like she'd worn it when picking pockets in London. Knowing she would need all her senses to protect them here, she'd shed the glamour she'd grown up knowing, feeling less encumbered and stronger without it.

Tiki adjusted her grip on the thin branch she'd brought from her bedchamber in Grosvenor Square. It was the stake of Ash that Dain had carved for her when they'd traveled through the Wychwood before. A painful twinge tweaked her heart as she imagined Dain's face. She could remember his words clearly: *"A stake of Ash—for the liche. There's no telling where he is now. He could be in London or he could be in the Otherworld. You've attracted Donegal's attention. We don't know how much control the UnSeelie king has over the liche, or who the next target might be, but you've got to be prepared to defend yourself. I don't know how to burn someone on a branch of Ash, so aim for the heart if you have to use it."*

"There appears to be a path here," Rieker pointed, pulling Tiki from her reverie, "and it heads north."

THE MILES FLEW by as Aeveen galloped effortlessly through the wood. Bushes rustled as animals made their way along unseen paths. Birds chirped, hopping from branch to branch, cocking their heads to watch as Tiki and Rieker passed, but no one tried to stop them. Occasional hammering could be heard, but the cobblers remained well hidden. The trees grew closer together and the shadows thicker as they continued north. Rieker alternately urged Aeveen into a canter, then slowed her to a walk, dependent upon how straight the path was.

"Where do you suppose the *liche* is now?" Tiki asked, swatting at some low-hanging branches with the thin stake.

"Donegal must have some way of forcing him to follow orders," Rieker replied, lifting a branch as they rode under. "If we can eliminate the *liche*, we eliminate part of Donegal's power. It's just figuring out how to stop him."

Tiki held up her thin, pointed stick. "That's why Dain carved this for me." She swatted at another branch. "We're supposed to burn the liche's body on a stake of Ash, but I don't know how you burn a body on something this size. Seems like you'd have to stab them instead."

"It is curious," Rieker agreed. "I wonder how Donegal raised the *liche* in the first place. I heard the dark magic he used required him to give over something of his own body. Do you think it was blood?"

"I don't know, but we have to do something. The idea that Donegal might feed Dain's heart to that horrible creature…" Tiki shuddered. "It's unthinkable."

DAY TURNED INTO night as they wound their way through the forest. Many of the creatures who inhabited the wood during the dark months while the UnSeelies ruled had moved closer to the Plain of Starlight at Beltane, when control in Faerie had shifted to the Summer Court. The Jack-in-Irons, with severed heads of their victims tied round their waist, had lumbered to the east, along with the Kelpies, ridden by the river hags—though the púcas, those wicked-minded black, shaggy colts with the golden eyes who could entice riders onto their backs to be taken for a wild ride, still wandered the forest in small packs.

The creatures who supported the Summer Queen could be as intimidating as the monsters of the UnSeelie Court, but they were often more benign to look upon. Once, Tiki thought she saw a leprechaun, merrily working on a single shoe beneath a hedgerow. As dusk began to descend the bushes rattled with unseen bodies and Tiki was taut with nerves.

"Dain knew of an abandoned stonecutter's cottage where we stayed one night." She shivered and scanned the area before them. "Do you suppose there might be another?"

"I wouldn't plan on it," Rieker replied in a matter-of-fact voice. "Was it by water or a particular tree? Some sort of marker where you could find it again?"

"Actually, now that you mention it," Tiki said, "the cottage was completely hidden behind a thicket. I'd forgotten about that. Dain used some kind of magic to clear a path to the door for us."

"He was probably the one who hid the cottage in the first place." Rieker steered Aeveen around a tree stump that had been cut down long ago. The forest was changing, the further north they went. The trees had thinned and the ground had become rocky. "We'll find a spot up near those ledges," he pointed ahead, "where we'll be more protected and can light a fire."

RIEKER WAS SURPRISINGLY adept at building a fire.

"Where'd you learn to do that?" Tiki asked, as she held her hands out to the warmth of the flames.

"Living on the streets of London, of course. Some nights I thought I'd freeze to death." He stacked a few more pieces of wood to the blaze. "Luckily, I'm good with fire."

"When I traveled with Dain, he blew on his hands and a ball of flame flew through the air and lit the grate." She squatted down next to him. "Do you think we have the power to create fire like that?"

"Probably. You especially. Given who you are, I suspect there's little you can't do." Rieker sat on a rock and locked his arms around his knees. "Which is why I think Larkin only reveals snippets of information—she's afraid to give you too much power."

"Well, so far she's been successful at keeping me in the dark. What do you think about the Four Treasures she mentioned? The goblin at Covent Market said something about them, too. Do you think they're real?"

Rieker shook his head. "It's hard to say. They both said the Cup is one of the four, but what are the others? And what do they do?" He lifted his hands. "Just one more mystery to be solved. I wish now I could remember all the things Kieran told me. I suspect there was a greater purpose to him finding me."

"Can you remember anything?"

Rieker ran a hand through his dark locks. "Bits and pieces— nothing that makes obvious sense." He sighed and stared up into the trees that formed a canopy over their heads. "I'm hoping Dain can shed some light on Kieran's intent, as well as some information about our mother," he said. "It's a strange reality to find you're not who you think you are."

Tiki slid her hand into his warm fingers. "That I know."

THE LEDGE WHERE they camped was made of unyielding rock, which made it difficult to find a comfortable position to sleep. It was hard to relax while being so exposed within the forest and Tiki found herself scooting closer and closer to Rieker during the night. Dawn was just breaking when she opened her eyes to find she was snuggled next to him with one of his arms draped possessively across her stomach, his breathing soft in her ear.

Tiki exhaled slowly. Though shocked to find herself in such an intimate position with him, she was reluctant to move. The heat of their combined bodies warmed her against the frigid air and she felt oddly secure with him so close by her side. The fire had burned to coals covered in grey ash, and there was little heat reaching her from their orange hearts.

She searched the surrounding area for what had awoken her, but the forest was quiet at this early morning hour. Her thoughts turned to Johnny and Dain. Would the Cup of Plenty save Johnny if they could find it? Or were they wasting precious time searching for something not meant to be found?

A noise sounded from the ledge beyond—as if a rock had been dislodged by a careless step. Tiki shifted to look in that direction. Hidden among the underbrush, a pair of eyes stared back at her.

Chapter Twenty-One

Tiki froze.

"Don't move." Rieker's voice was so soft it sounded like the faraway sigh of the wind among the trees. Beneath the cover of his jacket, she could feel him shift enough to grasp the long dagger that he'd placed by his side when they'd laid down for the night.

Covered by bushy brown eyebrows, the eyes stared at them without blinking and Tiki tried to judge their expression. Was the gaze one of mere curiosity or was there a more malicious intent?

Rieker slowly sat up, his arm clutching the dagger still below his coat. "Let me get in front of you, before you stand up," he said in a low voice. His movements were swift and graceful and it seemed Tiki blinked and he was standing in front of her, clutching the knife.

She scrambled to her feet, positioning herself behind Rieker. Remembering how the spriggans had snuck up behind her and Dain, she glanced over her shoulder to make sure they weren't being ambushed.

"Who are you?" Rieker called out. "Come out and talk to us."

Tiki reached for the slim knife she'd shoved down her boot and clutched the wooden handle. She hoped nothing got close enough that she would need to use the ten inch blade, but if they did, at least the knife was some small way to defend herself. She peered around Rieker's shoulders. They were still being watched.

"Walk with me toward Aeveen," Rieker muttered to Tiki. They worked their way over to where the horse stood grazing on bits of grass that grew on the forest floor, oblivious to the tension in the air.

Rieker grabbed the reins and turned the horse so he could face their visitor. He kept his voice low so only Tiki could hear him. "I'm going to get on and reach down for your hand. Be ready."

In a seamless move, Rieker threw a leg over the horse's back, keeping his dagger pointed in the direction of the bush where their visitor still watched them, and pulled himself up. He thrust a hand down for Tiki and yanked her up to sit behind him.

Tiki wrapped her arms tight around his waist, and clutched her knees to Aeveen's sides, braced for the horse to bolt. Could whatever was watching them run as fast as a faerie horse?

Aeveen snorted and turned to the left, stamping her feet.

"Careful—we've got company," Rieker said in a low voice as he reined Aeveen in.

Tiki peered around his shoulders. Gathered in front of them, stood four little men. Their noses were like beaks, their chins long and jutting, and their hair was pulled back in long tails that hung down their back. They were as ugly as any creature Tiki had ever seen. But that's not what sent chills down her back. It was the red stocking caps they wore.

"Are you lost?" One of them called in a deep voice. He glared in an unfriendly way as he readjusted his grip on the spear-like hatchet he clutched. A quiver of arrows was slung across his back and a short bow hung from his belt. Thick fingernails, an inch long and filed to razor sharp points, protruded from the tips of each finger.

"No, we're headed north, to the border," Rieker replied in an even tone.

"You're going the wrong way." He pointed over their heads. "North is that way."

Rieker glanced over his shoulder as if contemplating the information. "Hmm, I thought we were headed in the right direction." Behind him, Tiki clutched his jacket, as she watched the four strange creatures warily.

The little man snorted. "The right direction would be to go back to wherever you came from."

"What do you want up north?" One of them asked. "Nothing but Redcaps up there."

Rieker eyed the hats the men wore. "You're not Redcaps?"

Hisses and gasps of disgust erupted from the group. The man in front, who appeared to be their leader, straightened his shoulders. "We most certainly are *not*. We're hobgoblins, a completely different, more *noble*, sort of goblin than a…" he emitted a small hiss… "*Redcap*." Two of the other creatures straightened their shoulders as well, nodding vehemently.

The fourth hobgoblin, who stood in the back partially obscured by the others, seemed oblivious to their conversation. He leaned far to the side, revealing the odd hump on his back as he tried to get a peek at Tiki. Their eyes met and Tiki recognized his bushy eyebrows. This was who had been spying on them. The hobgoblin immediately shifted his gaze and began whispering in another's ear. Both hobgoblins in the back leaned far to the right to catch a glimpse of Tiki seated behind Rieker.

"We've been told that the goblins of the north have a special cup," Rieker said.

"A cup, you say?" The leader ran a finger over his long curved nose. "What sort of cup?"

"It's said that to drink from the cup can cure all ills. We have a friend who is very sick."

From the corners of her eyes, Tiki watched the curious antics of the two goblins in the back. This time she made eye contact with the second goblin. His eyes widened, then he hurried over to whisper in the ear of the third goblin. An uneasiness twisted in her stomach as she wondered what they were talking about. She tightened her grip on Rieker's waist as Aeveen shifted positions beneath her as if she too, were suddenly wary of the strangers.

"Sounds magical to me." The hobgoblin said. He considered Rieker for a long moment. "Why do you think the Redcaps would let you even look upon such a thing, let alone touch it?"

"That's what we're going to find out. For our friend's sake." Rieker said. "Perhaps you could tell us who to speak to when we get there."

The hobgoblin cackled. "No Redcap wants to speak to the likes of you, I can tell you that much. More likely they'd want to eat you." He pointed a clawed finger toward Tiki. "Starting with her." He nodded at Aeveen. "Where'd you get your horse?"

"She belongs to my brother. Do you live in this part of the wood?" Rieker asked.

"Such curiosity." The little man's eyes narrowed. "You wouldn't be fey, would you?"

Behind him, one of the other hobgoblins leaned forward and whispered in the leader's ear, staring at Tiki as he talked. The leader cocked his head to listen, his gaze shifting to squint at Tiki.

"You don't want to linger in this part of the wood," another one of the hobgoblins called. "There's some in these parts what don't like strangers about." For the first time Tiki noticed he had an arrow threaded against his bow.

"He's right. The Redcaps are especially dangerous," the leader agreed. "They don't like visitors and they don't like strangers. It's not their way to share their possessions. You will come to harm if you go to the north border seeking them."

Larkin's words of warning whispered in Tiki's ears.

"Then we'll be on our way," Rieker said, nudging Aeveen toward the trail. "Thank you for your time. Good day." He turned his head to the side and whispered to Tiki. "Hold on."

Tiki tightened her grip as Rieker kicked the horse into a gallop and they headed north again. She glanced over her shoulder once, but the hobgoblins were gone. Aeveen seemed to enjoy the opportunity to run and she stretched out, her long legs pulling at the air until Tiki wasn't sure if the horse's feet actually touched the ground.

IT WAS MANY hours later that the path they were following forked and Rieker pulled the horse to a stop.

"Which way?"

Tiki glanced in either direction. To the left the sky was lighter and the trees seemed to thin. Anxious to escape from the shadows within the forest, she pointed in that direction.

"Let's see what's over there," she said. "I've got to get off this horse and stretch my legs."

Rieker climbed down and held a hand up to help Tiki, who slid down with a groan.

"I don't know if I'll ever stand upright again or not."

"You have to walk it out." Rieker held his hand out. "Come along."

They followed the winding trail until they broke free of the trees and stood on a small rocky overhang. Before them stretched a long thin body of water formed between tree-covered cliffs like a highland fjord. Reflecting the myriad trees, the water was a deep green. Snow capped the tops of nearby hills and in the distance, a small village sat at one end of the lake. Tiki stopped to take in the sight.

"Oh, it's beautiful. It's reminds me of a picture in a faerie story my father read to me when I was little. " Tiki drew a deep breath. "The air is so crisp and clean, like we're a world away from London."

"That we are," Rieker said with a shiver, drawing his coat tighter across his chest and squinting at the sky. "It feels like it could snow."

"Isn't that odd?" Tiki murmured.

"Yes," Rieker said emphatically. "It's incredibly odd and just plain wrong, if you ask me. It's spring. The Seelies are in power. It should be getting warmer not colder—"

"No, I'm not talking about the weather." Tiki pointed at the lake. "Look at the ripples across the surface of the water like there's a wind, yet—" she looked up— "the trees aren't moving."

Rieker gave a disinterested grunt. "The lake is probably fed by an underground spring that creates a current. It's not uncommon." He nodded toward the village. "What town do you suppose that is?"

"Dain told me there were three villages in the Wood. Two on the borders and one in the heart of the forest. This must be the town within the Wychwood."

"Let's keep moving and see if we can find some shelter there for tonight or we might freeze otherwise. Maybe someone can tell us how far we are from the northern border, as well."

"I almost hate to leave this spot," Tiki murmured. "It's like a beautiful painting. So peaceful. Look at the spires reflected in the water." Rieker turned and headed back to the trail, but Tiki lingered a moment longer, soaking up the magnificence of the scene. The water mirrored the deep forest green of the trees, the purple shades of the snow-capped mountains and the stone buildings of the village on its surface. One-by-one she matched the watery images to the structures on the shore.

Rieker's call interrupted her musings.

"Teek! Come on!"

With one last glance, Tiki made her way back to the trail where Rieker waited. She'd tied a long strand of grass to each end of the

Ash stake and slung it over her shoulder like a bow, allowing her to grab Rieker's hand and pull herself up behind him on the horse.

They followed the trail as it curved through the trees. More than once, they found themselves on a crag above the scenic view of the water, where it had carved a path through the steep mountains. When they got to the town, the dirt streets were strangely empty. Though the buildings were a collection of oddly shaped stone structures, some larger with spires and turrets, while others were nothing more than rudimentary huts, they all had one thing in common: every window was dark.

"Where is everyone?" Tiki asked.

"I don't know," Rieker replied slowly. The breeze ruffled his dark hair as he surveyed the scene. "But it feels odd here, doesn't it?"

They followed the main street to where it ended in a grassy area. Three large standing stones stood in a circle and the lake stretched beyond, the surface of the water as flat and smooth as a mirror. Once again, Tiki began matching the reflections on the water with the buildings situated along the perimeter of the lake. Her eyes stopped on one image and she searched the shoreline again.

Just then, Aeveen let out a wild whinny, as if calling to another horse. She rose on her hind legs and pawed the air, repeating her cry.

"Ho, there, settle down, girl," Rieker said in a soothing tone, working the reins to bring the horse down on all fours.

Tiki clung tightly to Rieker, gripping the horse's sides with her knees in an attempt to stay seated.

"Settle, Aeveen. Easy now." Rieker looked over his shoulder. "Something has her spooked—but I don't know what. Do you want to use one of these abandoned buildings as shelter tonight or continue north?"

Tiki glanced around. The air was turning colder the further they traveled and sleeping within a structure would certainly be more comfortable, but there was *something* here—something unsettled. The idea of trying to sleep in this atmosphere was not appealing in the least.

"Better to go north, I think."

DUSK HAD JUST fallen when they stopped for the night. They'd found a small cave within the rocky terrain and after spreading their bed rolls and making a small fire, their accommodations were quite comfortable.

THE SUN ROSE and burned a path across the sky as they rode north the next day. The wood around them changed from dense evergreen forest to scraggly pine trees spiked with long deadly-looking needles. The ground became rocky, forcing their pace to slow.

"We must be getting close to the northern border of the Wychwood," Rieker said as he pulled Aeveen to a walk, angling toward a nearby river where they got down and stretched their legs while the horse drank her fill. "I've heard the Redcaps like to occupy abandoned buildings and castle ruins."

Tiki shivered as she splashed her face with the cool water from the river. "Is it true their hats are red because they dye them in their victim's blood?"

"So I've been told. When the color fades they look for their next victim." Rieker's voice turned grim. "I overheard something else when I was at the stables. I've been trying to decide if I believed it enough to mention it, but I think it's better that I do."

Tiki stood up and wiped her hands with some nearby ferns, pleased that Rieker was not keeping secrets from her. "What?"

"I heard one of the stable hands say that Donegal is blackmailing the outlying lords to send their men to the Plain of Starlight so they can prepare for battle."

Tiki's heart quickened. Even though she didn't feel ready to admit it out loud, she bore a new sense of responsibility for what happened in this world. "Do you think he'll attack during the summer months?"

"I don't know, but he's planning something." An uneasy frown creased Rieker's brow. "We need to be prepared."

THEY HAD RIDDEN most of the next day when they stopped on a bluff before the gaunt, imposing remains of what appeared to have once been an abbey. The sun was low in the sky and threw its last rays of light in their direction, turning the color of the stone to molten gold. Skeletal spires reached skyward, held upright by the few stone walls that were what was left of a pinnacled transept with vacant arch-topped windows.

"It's like looking at a ghost," Tiki whispered, staring at what had clearly once been an awe-inspiring building, but was now less than a shell. The few walls that stood gave the impression of a half-finished painting.

Rieker grunted. "If Redcaps like to inhabit the ruins of ancient buildings, then we must be getting close. I've heard the border has lots of ruins."

They slid off Aeveen and let the horse graze freely. Rieker took Tiki's hand and led her through one of the elaborate doorways that should have led to an equally elaborate foyer, but instead led to the grassy ruins beyond.

"It's like time is fractured." Tiki whispered, gazing at the towering remnants. "As if one foot is in the past, when this building was alive and full of people—and one foot in the future, left with only the memory of what has been." She walked close to a wall and ran her hands over the rough stone. "It's so quiet. It feels like if we stand still we'll hear the voices of those who have gone before us."

"I wonder what secrets they would share? What words of wisdom?" Rieker mused, following Tiki.

Her lips twisted in a wry grin. "They'd probably tell you to beware the girl with the mark on her wrist."

Rieker caught Tiki by the arm and pulled her toward him. "Why? Would they tell me she's dangerous?"

Tiki gave a derisive laugh. "Probably."

He slid his arm around her waist and looked into her eyes. "Or that's she's wickedly beautiful and I'll be trapped in her web?"

Tiki gently brushed a lock of dark hair from Rieker's forehead, her fingers tracing the side of his face. "If only I could be so calculating as to spin a web that might catch someone like you, William."

"Perhaps they'll warn me to beware the power of the Summer Queen for being the lowly half-breed that I am, I will forever suffer a slave in the hopes of winning her love?"

Tiki traced her fingertips over Rieker's bottom lip. "You've already won, Lord Richmond, and we will shock the world with our disregard for their societal boundaries and teach them that love has no limits." She stretched up on her tiptoes and kissed him, enjoying his breath mingling with hers, the taste of him upon her tongue.

"What have we here?" The voice was sandpaper and crushed glass. "Young lovers?"

Tiki and Rieker broke free of their embrace and jerked around to see who was speaking. But it wasn't just one man who watched them. It was twenty or more. Men, no taller than Tiki, wearing filthy brown tunics, belted around the middle, with a knife tucked under the leather. In clawed hands, each held a long pikestaff with a cleaver-like blade fixed on the end. Their hooked noses jutted like beaks over mouths filled with razor-sharp teeth protruding from their lower jaw. Grey stringy hair hung long and their eyes were narrowed and unfriendly. All of them wore tight red caps, some still dripping blood.

Chapter Twenty-Two

"Greetings," Rieker said in an easy tone. "We were hoping to meet you."

Tiki's crossed her arms and felt for her dagger. After their encounter with the hobgoblins, she'd started sliding a blade up her sleeve, just as she had when living in Charing Cross.

"How are you this fine day?" Rieker asked.

Tiki's gaze skimmed over the group, who watched them with unblinking eyes and spears clutched in their hands. Rieker could try and be friendly but these men didn't appear interested in making their acquaintance. Their intent seemed deadly, at best.

The leader held his pikestaff in both hands, ready to swing at any moment. His voice rasped as if each word was an effort. "Who are you and why are you here?"

"We've come looking for—" Rieker hesitated— "something a mutual friend told us you might have."

The goblin grunted. "What is ours, stays ours. Did your *friend* tell you that?"

Rieker raised his hands slightly. "I'm sure we can discuss this in a reasonable manner. We mean you no harm."

Another man, several feet away shifted his pikestaff from an upright position to point it at Rieker and Tiki. "You look Seelie to me."

"Or mortal." A bulky man pushed his way through the group to come stand at the front next to the first. His squinty eyes looked them up and down and he gnashed his teeth as if he were already chewing their flesh.

Tiki's gaze locked on his hat. The color was a dingy pink, as if all the red had washed away.

"But there's only one way to be sure—" his lips twisted in a malevolent grin, revealing more razor-sharp teeth— "cut 'em and see what color they bleed."

With a wild cry, he ran forward, swinging his blade from side to side.

"Damn it," Rieker muttered as he shoved Tiki behind him. He crossed his arms and yanked two knives from his belt, one in each hand. He flicked his wrist and threw the first. The knife spun so fast it was a blur of glistening metal before it sank easily into the goblin's shoulder, forcing him to drop one hand from his weapon.

The ugly little creature slowed and glanced at the hilt of the blade still vibrating from the impact with his flesh. A growl of rage ripped from his mouth and he readjusted his grip as he picked up speed again.

The second knife made a *whishing* noise as it cut through the air, sinking into their attacker's other shoulder with a quiet *thunk*. The goblin dropped to his knees with a howl of pain, his bleeding arms hanging limply by his sides as his pikestaff clattered to the ground.

"Anyone else?" Rieker asked in a menacing voice, two more knives clutched in his hands, ready to be thrown. "I assure you, I can throw faster than you can run."

The goblins muttered amongst themselves, pointing their clawed fingers in Tiki and Rieker's direction.

The first goblin spoke again. "You wound and threaten us, then tell us you want something of ours? What sort of mad man are you?"

"I simply defended myself," Rieker said. "We come in peace." He adjusted his stance and let his arms fall, though he didn't relax his grip on the weapons. "We're looking for a cup—one that's said to heal the ills of the sick. That's all."

A new round of whispers started, punctuated by a few menacing growls. The man with the scratchy voice, the apparent leader of this group, smiled and his features reminded Tiki of a feral dog.

"That's all?" he said in a mocking tone. "You've come because you want to take a magical vessel from us—one of our most treasured possessions?"

Rieker looked at Tiki, as if just realizing how unreasonable his request sounded.

Tiki spoke up. "We only want to borrow the cup, to help heal our friend, then we would return it—with payment, of course."

All eyes shifted to Tiki. The goblin leader took a step closer and sniffed the air. "A girl are you, now? Dressed like a man—how very strange." He placed one clawed hand over the other and rested them on the top of his staff as he contemplated Tiki. "How very strange, indeed. What sort of payment could you make that would tempt us to part with such a prize?"

Tiki was at a loss. What could they give that a murderous goblin might want?

"We have access to gold," Rieker said. "How much would you want?"

A titter of laughter went through the group.

"What do we look like—*leprechauns*?" The laughter grew louder. The leader adjusted the red cap that covered his skull. "We've no need for your gold. There's only one thing you might be able to give us." He paused, as if to give weight to his request. "Mortal blood." His eyes grew steely and cold. "That's the only payment we'll accept."

"Fine," Rieker said. "Lend us the cup and we'll be on our way."

Tiki looked at Rieker from the corner of her eyes. What had he just agreed to?

At that moment, a noose was thrown around her neck from behind and pulled tight. Tiki coughed and gagged, tugging against the rope. The Redcap leader had tricked them. While he had distracted them with negotiations, others had snuck up from behind.

Tiki's knees were weak with panic. It was hard to fight back when she couldn't breathe. Images of Dain standing in the Palace of Mirrors, bloodied, bruised and with a noose around his neck flashed before Tiki's eyes. Was she doomed to the same fate? Or perhaps something worse?

Chapter Twenty-Three

Next to her, Rieker struggled with another goblin, though Tiki couldn't tell if he had deflected a noose from settling around his neck or not. She pried her fingers under the rope crushing her throat, as she gasped for breath. She twisted around and found herself eye-to-eye with the gruesome face of her captive, his rancid breath hot on her face.

"Stop!" she rasped. "I can't breathe."

The Redcap tugged the rope tighter in response, his lips spread in a gruesome, leering grin. "No need to breathe when you're dead."

Like a flash fire, rage boiled through Tiki's veins. She was not going to be dead. Others needed her. Just like when she had lashed out at Larkin and drawn blood, it felt as though claws sprang from her fingertips. Tiki stabbed at the goblin's face, aiming for his eyes. She was surprised when she made contact, and with a growl, she ripped her fingernails across his skin.

Overhead, dark clouds boiled across the sky and thunder rumbled, as if in warning.

With a howl of pain, the goblin released the tension on the rope as he covered his face with one hand and stepped back. Seeing her opportunity, Tiki kicked him in the knee, then kicked him between the legs. This time, the goblin screamed and let go of the rope, sinking to the ground in a fetal position.

Tiki yanked the rope from around her neck and jerked toward Rieker. He was fighting two goblins, deflecting their blows, using his dagger like a sword. But he couldn't see the third goblin behind him, with his long-handled hatchet raised to strike. Tiki jumped for the little man's arm, when someone grabbed her from behind, pulling her back.

"No!" she cried, struggling to break free. Thunder boomed so loudly the ground shook. A jagged bolt of lightning fractured the sky. In horror, Tiki watched the axe-wielding goblin's arms start to swing downward.

"NOOOO!" she screamed, reaching helplessly toward Rieker.

A whistling noise split the air and an arrow embedded itself in the attacking goblin's forehead. His eyes rolled skyward as if to look at the offending object, before he fell back—dead before he hit the ground.

Three more whistles sliced toward them, one so close Tiki felt the rush of air brush her cheek. The arms that gripped her around the middle suddenly relaxed and she turned to see her captor dead on the ground with an arrow through one eye.

Cries and shouts erupted as the goblins realized they were under attack. They ran this way and that in their confusion, not sure where this new enemy was positioned and trying to get out of the deadly line of fire.

"Run!" Rieker cried as he reached for Tiki's hand and pulled her away from the melee. He yanked a noose from around his neck as they sprinted across the grass toward one of the other vacant doorways. As they passed under its arched portal, Tiki glanced back. Arrows continued to be volleyed into the group of Redcaps from outside the walls of the ruins, keeping their benefactors a mystery. Who risked their own lives to help them?

"Blast it all," Rieker muttered under his breath. "Where's Aeveen? She must have been spooked by the noise."

Tiki scanned the horizon. The white horse was nowhere in sight. She closed her eyes and imagined she was standing with Dain on the edge of O'Donoghue's farm like the first time she'd laid eyes on the horse. Dain had been glamoured as Sean then and he'd blown a piercing whistle to call the horse.

Using all her concentration, Tiki put her fingers to her lips and blew, mimicking the sound she'd heard Sean create.

Beside her, Rieker jumped in surprise. "What are you doing?"

"Calling Aeveen." Tiki opened her eyes and searched their surroundings, but there was nothing besides trees and rock.

"Don't give away our location," Rieker snapped. "What makes you think…."

"There!" Tiki pointed. Aeveen came galloping from between the trees, so ethereal and effortless as to appear to be a creature molded from the frothy foam of sea waves. Her beautiful white tail arched and blew behind her as she flew across the rocky terrain. With a snort, she pulled up to a stop next to them. She jerked her head once, as if in acknowledgement of Tiki's call.

"You can explain this one later," Rieker said, admiration unmistakable in his voice. He grabbed a handful of mane and pulled himself onto Aeveen's great back then thrust his hand out for Tiki. With an easy yank, he pulled her onto the horse and they raced into the shelter of the trees and away from the Redcaps.

"WHO DO YOU think saved us?" Tiki asked, once they were sure the goblins weren't following.

"Most likely Callan or the Macanna," Rieker said. "It is their job, after all."

"Would Callan remain unseen, do you think?" Tiki asked doubtfully. "We left without telling him our plans and he doesn't seem too adept at following me. Usually he likes to give me a lecture when he catches up."

"Who else would risk their lives for us? No one knows who you are."

"That's true," Tiki mused. "What are we going to do about the cup, now? It's clear the Redcaps won't let us near it." She chewed on her bottom lip as they rode. "Once again, Larkin was right. She told me they would never give it to me."

"That's definitely a good question. Besides the fact that we don't know what it looks like, even if we wanted to steal it—where would we look? Every abandoned building and castle ruin within the Wychwood?" Rieker shook his head. "Impossible. We might just have to find a way to give them mortal blood."

THEY RODE UNTIL the moon had crested before Rieker pulled Aeveen to a stop.

"Time to rest," he said with a weary sigh. He slid off the horse and reached up to take Tiki by the waist and help her down. "That's enough adventure for one day."

Tiki rubbed her neck and nodded in agreement. She was tired and discouraged and her body ached from riding, as well as from being strangled. Immediately, a sense of guilt washed over her. What must poor Dain be experiencing? He'd been beaten and strangled and who knew what else? And where was he now? Being held under what conditions? And there was Johnny—attacked by the *liche* and clinging to life. She and Rieker were both Dain and Johnny's best chance of surviving—they didn't have time to be tired.

TIKI AWOKE TO the sight of four pair of leather boots, so soft and supple as to appear to be slippers, lined up in front of where she and Rieker slept. She jerked upright, startling Rieker awake in the process.

"Good morning." The leader of the hobgoblins stood on a nearby rock, the head of his spear-like hatchet resting on the ground. The other three hobgoblins stood next to him, along with five or six newcomers behind the others.

"We've got to stop sleeping," Rieker muttered as he slowly climbed to his feet. Tiki glanced around as she too, stood. They didn't appear to be surrounded, but there were more hobgoblins than before, and for the first time, Tiki noticed that they all carried bows, some cocked with arrows, and each had a quiver on their back.

"It was you!" Tiki cried, pointing at the hobgoblin with bushy eyebrows. "You saved us from the Redcaps, didn't you?"

To Tiki's amazement, the ugly little man ducked his head as if he were embarrassed and wouldn't meet her eyes.

The hobgoblin leader didn't deny or affirm Tiki's claim. "There's a rumour going about that you're the new Queen of the Seelie Court, herself. Is it true?"

The bushy-eyed goblin raised his head. "I seen her before. I was sellin' fruit in the market an'—" he pointed a shaking finger— "she was there, an' one of them called her 'Majesty'." He dipped his head and dropped to his knee. "Welcome to our part of the Wychwood, your Highness."

Tiki tried to hide her surprise. These were the men who sold fruit at that otherworldly goblin market during the dead of night in London? An image of that hunch-backed little man they'd talked to that night played before her eyes. As she considered the man before her she could see they were the same person. And they had risked their lives to save her? She hesitated. Should she acknowledge the truth? But then, what would they do? Instead, she nodded her thanks.

"Thank you for your kind greeting and for your bravery in saving us from the Redcaps yesterday. We are in your debt."

They ugly men nudged each other and smiled in delight.

"Perhaps we will seek repayment one day," the leader said in a cagey manner. "But you've not answered my question. Is the rumour true? You're beautiful enough to be a queen, but how do we know you're speaking the truth? Maybe you've been sent by the UnSeelies to spy on us. It wouldn't be the first time, given what goes on in this part of the wood." He watched her through narrowed eyes.

Tiki's mind raced. How was she supposed to prove she was Queen of the Seelie Court? She had little knowledge of the Otherworld as evidenced by her foolish question previously about the hobgoblins and she barely knew any magic.

Rieker spoke up. "She is marked with *an fáinne sí*—" his voice rang with confidence— "do you need more proof than that?"

"Finn's mark?" The leader asked in surprise. Then his brows pulled down. "Prove it."

Tiki slid her sleeve up to her elbow, revealing the black lines that swirled and arced around her thin wrist. "It's true."

The leader took a step forward to peer closely at her arm. Then to Tiki's surprise, he gave a deep bow and swept his red stocking cap from his head. "We are here to serve you, Majesty." Behind him the other hobgoblins dropped to their knees.

"Thank you," Tiki said. "It's a pleasure to meet all of you."

An excited titter went through the group and a few edged closer to get a better look. Rieker tensed and rested his hands along his belt, giving him easy access to a weapon, though they were sorely outnumbered by the hobgoblins.

The leader looked at Rieker as he nodded toward Aeveen. "That is a fine horse. One of the strongest I've ever seen. You say she belongs to your brother?"

Rieker gave a short nod.

"Where is your brother, that he lets you take such a magnificent beast? Why didn't he accompany you on this dangerous journey?"

Rieker frowned. "He's occupied with other matters at this time."

The ugly little man didn't move for a long moment, his brow furrowed in a frown. "I see," he finally said. He turned his attention to Tiki and inclined his head. "Majesty, why did you seek the Redcaps after we warned you of their danger? As queen, don't you have others to take such risks?" His eyes shifted back to Rieker.

The goblin who had recognized Tiki spoke up. "Besides, they don't have anything you want, Majesty."

Rieker searched their faces. "But what of the cup?"

A look of disgust crossed the leader's face. "The Redcaps *had* the Cup of Plenty, but they lost it. Everyone who lives in the Wychwood knows that." There was a question threaded within his statement.

"Lost it?" Tiki echoed.

"The one who was guarding it, got drunk and left it out. The cup was stolen."

"The mortals took it," another of the goblins added.

"The Redcaps were so angry they banished the one who was responsible," a third one said. "Came through here a few years ago, looking to join us but we said no."

"The Redcaps don't even have the cup?" Tiki said faintly. They'd risked their lives for nothing?

"Any idea where the Redcap who lost the Cup went?" Rieker asked.

The leader shrugged, holding out his clawed hands. "Didn't know then, don't know now. Could be anywhere. Probably dead."

Chapter Twenty-Four

Dain's arms ached from being suspended above his head and rivers of fire burned across his back from the beating Bearach had meted out. He struggled to stand upright, his head oddly unbalanced from the weight of the mask. The constant exposure to the iron shackles made him queasy and for a moment, he thought he would be sick.

The gloomy light that cast through the one window in the room told him it was day—but which day, Dain couldn't say. Though his memory of the last meeting with Donegal was blurry, he didn't think he'd revealed any secrets that might put others at risk. Hopefully, he hadn't revealed anything at all, but there'd been a time when the entire world was nothing but a red haze of pain and he wasn't certain if he'd spoken or not.

The circular shafts that bound his wrists were too small to pull his hands through. He gritted his teeth and yanked one wrist hard against the ring, trying to force his flesh and bones through the opening. Pain exploded like a starburst behind his eyes and a groan escaped his clenched lips. Panting, he centered his wrists within the suspended rings so as not to touch the poisonous metal, rocking on his toes to shift with the chains as they swayed from the ceiling.

There had to be a way out of these shackles—he just had to figure it out. Larkin had escaped from the iron clamp in which Donegal had imprisoned her by tearing off her own wings. Dain searched his memory for any details she might have shared about her imprisonment, but he couldn't remember the faerie speaking of the matter. He had, however, seen the wicked scars that marked her back now and knew her escape had come at a significant price— just as his would. If he could escape.

As the movement of the chains slowed and finally stopped, Dain's gaze measured the diameter of the ring that bound his right wrist and then the size of his hand. Slowly, he tucked his thumb into his palm to minimize the circumference of his hand. Even then, it was evident there was only one way to get his hand through the ring: he would have to dislocate his thumb joint.

It took many deep breaths before he built up enough courage to try. Behind the mask, sweat beaded and ran down his brow, burning his eyes. He ground his teeth together as he used the pressure of the shackle to force his thumb joint from its natural position. The pain increased with the pressure he applied, until the agony was so great he thought he might faint. The walls around him distorted in a strange way and he was just about to give up—when suddenly his hand was free.

With a gasp of relief, he dropped his throbbing arm to his side. He'd done it. Using his bound hand he pushed his painful joint back into position.

Dain rested for a few minutes before he used his free hand to dislocate the joint on his left hand. Once again, the pain built until it felt like his hand might explode, then the joint moved out of position and he was able to slip his hand free. With a sob of relief he sagged to the floor, his wounded limbs cradled against his chest—exhausted.

HIS DREAMS WERE vivid—as if his imprisonment somehow made that which he longed for even more desirable. He was dressed in an elegant suit of black tails and standing in a lavish ball room at Buckingham Palace, attending a mortal ball at Larkin's insistence. The music to a waltz swelled around him as he watched Tiki from across the room, the skirt of her emerald gown swirling as she danced with William. Her face glowed with love as she looked up at his brother.

A pang of jealousy as sharp as a dagger pierced Dain's heart until his entire body ached with pain, making it difficult to breathe. Unfamiliar emotions threatened to crumble the sardonic bravado that he'd built over his lifetime as his shield. How would it feel to hold her in his arms? To have someone look at him like that? To have *her* look at him like that?

His dream changed and Tiki stood before him, her small hand clutched in his, her green eyes dark and mysterious. "Have you kept my secret?" he asked.

"Yes," she whispered and in his dream, Dain drew her near. Her lips parted in the most tempting fashion, urging him to kiss her. Happiness like he'd never known flooded his chest and his heart pumped with joy. Just as his lips touched hers, he awakened.

DAIN OPENED HIS eyes and slowly focused on the iron shackles above his head. They swung gently from the ceiling as if moved by the wind. The glittery images of Buckingham Palace slid away as the chill from the stone floor sapped the warmth from his battered body. A sad bitterness filled him as he returned to full consciousness and he held his breath in an unsuccessful attempt to stop the pain that colored every inch of his body. He clenched his eyes closed, but not before a tear escaped, scalding his cheek. For the first time, he wondered if death might be a preferable escape.

Chapter Twenty-Five

Tiki and Rieker rode until they were well out of sight of the hobgoblins before Tiki spoke.

"If mortals took the cup and the Redcap who lost it is dead—how will we ever find the thing?"

"Who told us of the cup in the first place?" Rieker gritted out. "Who told us the Redcaps guarded it?"

"And then told us not to risk our lives trying to get it from them," Tiki added.

Rieker's voice was tinged with disgust. "Like normal, it seems the trail leads back to one person."

They spoke together. "Larkin."

THEY RODE HARD, barely stopping to rest. Aeveen didn't seem to tire and her hooves never seemed to touch the ground. It seemed only a few hours, rather than days, before they were climbing Wydrn Tor and entering the Night Garden, outside the Palace of Mirrors.

The guards pulled the doors open, alternately bowing as Tiki passed through and frowning at Rieker. Tiki and Rieker rushed through the grand entry foyer and down the hallway that stretched alongside the Great Hall, headed for Larkin's study. But their frantic knocks upon her door went unanswered.

Tiki whirled to face Rieker. "Where do you suppose she could be?"

Rieker shrugged. "She could be anywhere, Teek. Remember, it's Larkin we're talking about. Let's check the Great Hall."

They retraced their steps and passed under the arches that stretched between the towering gold and white columns to enter the Great Hall. Larkin sat on the glittering Dragon Throne as if she were born to rule. She looked regal in a dress of shimmering gold as she gave instructions to several workers.

Tiki told herself she didn't care—that she didn't want to rule a world she didn't understand, but as she watched Larkin dismiss the men with an imperious flick of her hand, she wondered if Larkin was a better choice.

"Back so soon? I'm sure it wasn't common sense that caused you to return." She clutched a sheaf of papers to her chest and looked Tiki up and down. "You look like a common forest faerie. What is it you want?"

Rieker stepped close enough so that he towered over the faerie. "Where you aware the Redcaps no longer have the Cup of Plenty?"

Instead of stepping back from his intimidating posture, Larkin stepped closer and ran her hand down the side of his whiskered face. "William, I believe this lifestyle suits you. Half-breed or not, you look more handsome than ever."

Rieker jerked his head away. "Answer my question."

"The Redcaps lost the cup years ago. Everyone knows that."

"Everyone who lives in Faerie. You knew perfectly well that we wouldn't have known."

Larkin's blue-green eyes flashed like a turbulent sea. "And I warned you not to go, didn't I? I told you it would be dangerous—" her lip curled as she sneered at Tiki—"and pointless. But you two think you know it all."

Tiki tugged at Rieker's arm. "Come away. There's no point in arguing. Let's go check on Johnny."

QUIET HUNG IN the zagishire like a mist as Tiki and Rieker tiptoed down the hallway toward Johnny's room. A shadow flickered in the far corner, catching Tiki's eye. She peered in that direction but could see nothing out of the ordinary. They reached Johnny's room and Tiki peeked around the corner to find Fiona asleep in a chair next to the bed.

The other girl woke as they entered and pushed herself upright. Recognizing Tiki, she jumped to her feet, her face alight with hope.

"Did you find it?"

Tiki shook her head, sorrow heavy in her stomach. "I'm sorry, Fi..."

Fiona's shoulders sagged and Tiki wrapped her arms around the other girl. "We tried," she whispered in her ear. "We just didn't have all the information we needed to find it. We won't give up though. We'll try again."

Fiona sniffed and ran her hand under her nose. "I know, Teek."

"How's he doing?" Rieker asked. They stood by Johnny's bed and looked down at his frail body. "Has the fever subsided?"

"He goes between fever and chills." Fiona smoothed the boy's sweaty hair away from his forehead. "He never opens his eyes though and sometimes," her voice caught, "I don't think he's breathing."

THREE HOURS LATER, Tiki dropped into bed with a heavy sigh. She was exhausted but there were so many things on her mind she couldn't imagine sleeping. She missed Clara and Toots, the comforting silence of Shamus and chatty Mrs. Bosworth. Were they getting on without her? Did they think of her as much as she thought of them?

How were they going to save Johnny without the cup? It was clear the boy wouldn't last much longer and yet, Tiki didn't know where to turn to help him. Who else would have knowledge of the Cup of Plenty that might help them find the vessel?

And finally, Dain was never far from her mind. The blurry similarity in his and Rieker's features kept him present at all times, almost as if part of him was with them. She was afraid to think of what Donegal might be doing to him, yet, she didn't know how to help him, either.

Tiki rubbed her fingers over the bruised skin of her throat and thought of the bravery of the hobgoblins in attacking the Redcaps to save them. Her lips creased in a small smile. It wasn't all bad here in the Otherworld.

LARKIN HAUNTED TIKI'S dreams. The faerie whispered and laughed, sneered and snubbed her. She chased her when Tiki dreamed she and Rieker were racing through the Wychwood on Aeveen. Larkin snapped at her with teeth that looked like the over-sized fangs of the Redcaps, causing Tiki to scream in her dreams until her throat ached. All the while, the faerie talked: *'I told you not to go. You two think you know everything. They banished the one who was responsible. There are matters that require your attention. They won't give it up—not even to the Queen of the Seelie Court.'*

WHEN TIKI AWOKE, Larkin's voice still echoed in her ears. She rubbed her forehead, wondering how they were ever going to find the cup. Still exhausted, she threw back her covers and climbed from bed.

LARKIN WAS AT the door to Tiki's chambers when Tiki headed out to get something to eat. The faerie fell into step with her as if they hadn't had a harsh word the day before.

"I was wondering if you were ever going to get up. I need a word."

Tiki sighed, fighting the feeling she was forgetting something while at the same time wondering how she could escape from Larkin and whatever plans she'd made for her. As they neared the Great Hall they met Rieker walking the other direction and stopped to greet him.

"Good morning, ladies." He bowed toward Tiki and kissed her hand. "You look beautiful, today."

Larkin's lips pursed in a peevish expression. "Isn't it a little early for such blatant flattery?"

Rieker smiled. "The truth is the truth, regardless of the hour of the day. A hard lesson for some but one grows stronger facing the facts, wouldn't you agree, Larkin?"

Larkin hissed in response. "Cheeky."

Rieker laughed and tucked Tiki's hand under his arm, turning to walk with them. He was clean-shaven and dressed much like the Macanna—trim dark trousers with a red and gold tunic. The contours of his muscled arms were revealed by the cut of his garments and Tiki couldn't help but admire his trim physique.

He leaned forward to address Larkin "Any word on Dain? On where the White Tower might be?"

"No," Larkin snapped. "We've got scouts scouring the countryside, and spies searching within the Plain of Starlight, but so far, Donegal has been successful in keeping the Tower hidden. I'm about to go looking for him myself," she muttered.

"What of the *liche?*" Tiki asked. "Has he been sighted?"

Larkin hesitated for a split second. "Nothing confirmed." She glanced at Tiki from the corners of her eyes. "He could be in London, but I'm not aware of any new deaths."

Rieker snorted. "Is that supposed to be reassuring?"

Tiki frowned. "Where in London?"

They passed through the towering archways and entered the Great Hall. Several of the myriad mirrors reflected rays of sunlight and cast them through the room in a prism of light.

"I don't know." Larkin said. "He could be here in the Great Hall with us for all I know. Now, as I was about to say before we were interrupted—" she glared at Rieker—"the queen is needed at Court today, and there are some details with the kitchens we need to discuss."

Tiki yawned and tried not to limp. She was still sore from so much riding. "Such as?" What she really wanted to talk about was what Larkin knew of the Cup of Plenty and if there was any other way to save Johnny. Fiona had told them that Larkin had made arrangements for her to continue to have mortal food and drink, but the girl's health was clearly deteriorating, and Tiki knew she couldn't allow Fiona to stay in Faerie much longer. But after Larkin's rude dismissal of the matter last night, Tiki was hesitant to broach the subject again.

"First." Larkin held up a slender finger. "We need some rules established on feeding the beggars. That creature you befriended has been wandering the halls ever since you left, looking for more free food, I suspect. It's got to stop."

An image of Ailléna's bone-thin face filled Tiki's head. There'd been too many nights when Tiki had wandered through London looking for food herself not to be sympathetic to the poor creature's plight.

"It's not too much to ask—" Rieker started.

"Second—" Larkin spoke over him— "There is a new lord to be inducted, Fintan McPhee—"

Tiki jerked to a stop, her mouth agape as she realized what had been nagging at her subconscious.

Larkin paused a few steps ahead and glanced back with a look of annoyance. "What is it now?"

"Where do we find Ailléna?" Tiki asked.

"Who?"

"The starving girl we met in the Night Garden. The one who…"

"Oh, the beggar." Larkin gave a dismissive shrug. "Why should I know or care?"

"You said she's been wandering the halls ever since I left. That means you've seen her."

"True. She's been underfoot much too often for my liking. " Larkin turned away. "You might find her in the encampment."

Tiki and Rieker exchanged glances. "What encampment?"

"It's one of the places where the homeless faeries gather."

"Lady Larkin." A trio of muscular faeries crossed the Great Hall toward them. "A word, please."

"This will have to wait," Larkin said to Tiki and Rieker. "As you can see, I'm needed elsewhere." She raised her chin with an important air and marched toward the men, her skirts twirling around her bare feet.

"Where's the encampment?" Tiki called after her.

"On the far side of the Tor." Larkin glanced over her shoulder. "And don't be late for Fintan's induction—it's at noon in the High Chamber." She gave Tiki a gloating grin. "I'll save you a seat."

"WHY ARE YOU so keen to find the beggar?" Rieker asked after Larkin had disappeared around a corner in the hallway.

"Really, William." Tiki sounded like an odd echo of Larkin. "She has a name."

"Sorry. Why are you so keen to find Ailléna?"

"Because." Tiki put her hand on Rieker's arm. Her eyes glowed with excitement. "Now that we've been to the border I've just realized she's a goblin. *A Redcap.* Perhaps kicked out by her own kind?"

"LIFE HERE ISN'T so different from what we've seen in the slums of London," Rieker said as they made their way through the gardens in the direction they'd been told to find the encampment. "Remember, Larkin mentioned there are those in need. How did she put it? *'The squalor behind the court.'*"

"Yes, but food appears to be bountiful here—at least in the Seelie Court—why would anyone go hungry?"

"I don't know the answer, Teek. Maybe it's gone on for so long, that those in power have forgotten to care." They followed the curving path through a dense section of bushes. "I'm quite sure Donegal wouldn't have done anything to help their plight. He likes to keep people at a disadvantage."

Rieker rounded a corner and came to an abrupt stop. Tiki joined him to find they stood on the crest of a small ridge. Below, perched on a shelf of rock that appeared to be cut from the side of the Tor, was a teeming congregation of faeries. They covered the entire outcropping and in some cases, disappeared over the side, like ants in a hill.

Tiki squinted at the sight. "What is this?"

Rickety lean-to's made of sticks and leaves dotted the outcropping, but most of the faeries sat out in the open, gathered in small groups. Some appeared to be lying where they'd dropped, apparently too weak to move. A few sat around small fires, wispy threads of smoke curling into the air, as if even the fires were too weak to burn properly. All were painfully thin, and dirty, nothing more than rags covering their bodies.

"I can't believe it," Tiki breathed. "Do you think Larkin knows of this?"

Rieker slid his hands into his pockets as he surveyed the scene, his voice oddly quiet. "She's the one who told us where to find this place."

"What can we do? We need to get food for them immediately." Tiki pointed to a crumpled form. "Doesn't that one look like a mortal?" As they surveyed the scene, a fight broke out in one corner of the camp and shouts echoed across the open air.

"Leave it, ya dirty scumbag faerie!" A familiar scratchy voice shouted. "I brought as much as I could—we 'ave to share! Stop it! Stop I tell ya!" The grunts, thuds and whacks of a struggle could be heard as two faeries wrestled over the prize they both wanted.

Rieker held his hand out to Tiki. "I think we've just found Ailléna."

As Tiki and Rieker picked their way through the edges of the encampment, the crowd began to realize there were strangers among them. Whispers started, as faeries nudged each other and slyly pointed. Movement ceased and one by one all eyes turned to the newcomers.

"Don' .. make ..me beat ya ..with this bread," Ailléna huffed as she pounded an old, frail man over the head with a stale bread roll. "I tol' ya we had.. to.. share." She gave one last resounding whack and straightened. At her feet, the whimpering faerie was on his knees with his hands clutched over his head for protection. "There. Now ya can 'ave a small piece and we'll spread the rest out as far as it will…oh!" The little goblin jumped when she saw Tiki and Rieker standing nearby watching her.

"Majesty." Ailléna dropped into an awkward curtsy, sweeping the crust of bread to the side as if it were part of a voluminous skirt. 'I did'na see ya there." She peeked from under her eyelashes, her large hooked nose still pointed at the ground, frozen in her pose. "What are ya doin' *here*?"

"I need to talk to you." Tiki held out her hand. "Could you come with us for a moment, please?"

Ailléna straightened with a frightened expression and handed Tiki the half-broken bread roll. "I did'na steal, Majesty, you said I could 'ave the food and I thought I might share my good luck with a few friends." She gestured at the open-mouthed faeries who stood circled around them at a safe distance.

"I don't want your bread," Tiki said gently. "It was the right thing to do to bring a loaf to share. We'll find more bread for your friends, too." She wiggled her fingers. "I meant to hold your hand."

A gasp went up in the crowd followed by a buzz of whispers.

"You'd touch me?" Ailléna whispered.

"Of course," Tiki said, trying not to sound impatient. "Why wouldn't I?"

"It's just that you're the queen and I'm a ..."

"Stop, Ailléna." Tiki cut her off. "You are whatever you choose to be. Now take my hand and come along, please. We won't be long."

The little goblin tentatively slid her clawed fingers into Tiki's warm grip. Tiki squeezed gently and a tremulous smile shook the corners of Ailléna's mouth. Another buzz of whispers swept the crowd.

"She's touchin' her."

"The goblin's holdin' the queen's hand."

"Are they *friends?*"

"Where can we talk privately?" Rieker asked, glancing at the wizened little goblin as he fell into step beside Tiki.

"There's a spot up there," Ailléna pointed, "on top of the Tor."

IT ONLY TOOK a few minutes to reach a secluded section in the gardens. Tiki marveled at how the landscape and atmosphere could change in such a short distance. Where they stood now was serene and lush, a beautiful garden where life was bountiful; the crag of the Tor where the homeless were camped was devoid of vegetation, nothing more than a rocky outcropping, covered by faeries in various stages of despair.

They found a stone bench and Tiki sat down, patting the spot next to her. Rieker remained standing, positioning himself on the far side of Tiki so as not to intimidate the little goblin.

"How can I serve you today, m'lady?" Ailléna asked, twisting her hands nervously together.

"I want you to know you're not in trouble," Tiki said slowly.

"I'm not?"

"No." Tiki shook her head. "We just need some information. It's very important that you tell us the truth, all right?"

Ailléna gulped as she bobbed her head up and down.

Tiki got right to the point. "We're looking for a magical cup the Redcaps used to have."

The little goblin's eyes widened in horror.

"We've been told you might know something about its current location."

She shook her head frantically from side to side.

"You're a Redcap, aren't you?" Tiki asked gently.

Ailléna hesitated then jerked her head up and down once. Her lower lip trembled, causing her oversized fang-like teeth to chatter.

Tiki tilted her head to look in the goblin's eyes. "Tell me the truth, Ailléna, were you the one who lost the cup?"

For a second the little goblin looked like she might burst from the agony of her indecision. "I didn't mean to do it," she croaked hoarsely, her hands clenched in front of her chest as if she were begging for mercy. "It were a terrible mistake, it were."

"Do you know where the cup is now?" Rieker asked.

Ailléna let out a terrified squeak, her eyes darting from side to side, as if looking for an escape route.

"You won't be punished," Tiki reassured her. "We need to find the cup to help a friend of ours, that's all."

A terrible sob erupted from her throat. "You'll never find it," she cried.

"Can you tell us what happened?" Tiki asked.

"It weren't my fault," she croaked— "well... not exactly..." She ran a clawed hand under her beak of a nose and gave a loud sniff. "We were just havin' a bit o'fun, playing in the well an' dancin' a bit on the green. I set the cup down to keep it safe when ol' MaGee brought out some wine..." she took a shuddering breath, "an' next thing I knew—some mortal was runnin' away with our cup. We chased 'im and screamed—I even tried to pull it outta his hands, but he held fast," she finished, looking downcast.

"Where was this at?" Tiki asked. "Do you recall the name of the well?"

"O'course I do. It was St. Cuthbert's well, up north," Ailléna whispered. "We used to play there often. The manor house where the mortal ran is called Edenhall."

"Edenhall?" Rieker said in surprise. "That's up in Cumbria. It's the Musgrave estate. My father knew the family well. As a boy, he used to spend summers up north. He and Sir Musgrave were fast friends."

The little goblin shook her head, a miserable expression on her face. "You'll never get it back. The mortals call the cup their Luck now. The Luck of Edenhall."

Chapter Twenty-Six

Tiki and Rieker left the next morning for Cumbria. They drove through Northhampton and Coventry, on to Birmingham and Stoke-on-Trent, the English countryside a serene mask that hid the volatile life on the other side of the veil in the Otherworld. On the third day, as they approached the north country, they stopped in Blackpool on the coast. It had been years since Tiki had seen the sea, having only traveled with her parents when she was very young. She took her shoes off and walked along the sandy beach.

"The water is so immense," she murmured, watching the waves rolling into the shore. "It looks like it goes on forever."

"That's the Isle of Man," Rieker pointed to an island in the middle of the Irish Sea. "Have you heard of it?" At Tiki's nod, he continued. "Loads of faerie stories over there. They've even got a faerie bridge or two." He was silent for a moment, staring across the water. "My father traveled up to this area as a boy and then, later, as a young man. I wonder if this is where he met Breanna?"

Tiki gazed in the direction Rieker was looking. The island was far enough away that it appeared to be a mountain rising out of the sea. It was the first time he'd mentioned Breanna, since learning the truth of his heritage—that he and Dain were the sons of the mortal father Rieker had always known and a faerie named Breanna. Upon Breanna's death at their birth, Rieker had returned to London with his father, while Dain had remained in the Otherworld to be raised by a faerie named Kieran.

"I'm sure we can find out more information about Breanna," Tiki said softly.

Rieker's lips twisted in a bitter smile. "From Larkin, no doubt."

IT WAS LATE afternoon when they reached Cumbria. Tiki ached all over from being jostled in the carriage for three days straight. However, they had agreed they wouldn't waste time checking into an inn when they arrived, but instead, would go straight to Edenhall. The faster they could retrieve the cup, the faster they could return to the Otherworld to help Johnny and then focus on how to free Dain.

"Edenhall is lovely," Tiki murmured as they drew near the estate.

A chuckle escaped Rieker's lips. "That's not Edenhall. That's simply the entrance lodge." He pointed. "The estate is still a mile up the road."

Rolling expanses of green lawns stretched before them as they drove and Tiki watched with a growing sense of amazement. "One family owns all this?"

Rieker shrugged. "It's not uncommon."

"Not uncommon for you," Tiki snorted. "Uncommon for the rest of us." Just then, they rounded a corner and the grand façade of Edenhall stood before them. "Good lord," Tiki breathed, "it's like a bloody palace. How are we going to convince them to give us something they consider to be their source of luck?"

"We're not going to convince them," Rieker replied. "We're going to steal it—" a smile twisted the corners of his mouth— "and they're never going to know."

"YOUNG WILLIAM? IS that really you?" Sir Musgrave entered the foyer, his smile a mixture of curiosity and disbelief.

"When Harold announced William Richmond for a moment I thought it was your father." He heaved a longing sigh. "How I miss the old chap—" he lowered his voice— "*and* the adventures we used to share. Middle-age is such a bore."

He shook Rieker's hand and beamed. "I haven't seen you since you were a boy and look at you now—a young man of the world. Handsome, just like your father." He tilted his head to the side as he appraised Rieker. "With a bit of a devilish streak, I daresay, if you're anything like old Will." He clapped Rieker on the shoulder and shifted his attention to Tiki. "And who might this delightful creature be?"

"Tara Dunbar, sir." Rieker slid his hand behind Tiki's back. "Someone of great importance to me."

Sir Musgrave raised his eyebrows as he took Tiki's hands. "That's quite an introduction. You must be a special young lady to have captured Lord Richmond's heart so steadfastly."

"That she is, Sir, more than you can ever imagine." Rieker's lips quirked in a half grin and Tiki's cheeks grew warm.

"Hmmm... how fascinating. I shall have to get to know you better, Miss Dunbar and perhaps I'll fall victim to your magical spell, as well." He proffered an arm to Tiki. "I'm afraid Mrs. Musgrave has taken the children and gone to London for a fortnight, so you two are stuck with me. Come along and join me in the drawing room and let's catch up. I'm dying to hear what you're doing in this neck of the woods. Cumbria is a fair jaunt from London."

THEY MOVED INTO an elegantly appointed drawing room and Sir Musgrave rang for tea. Within minutes a servant arrived with tea and biscuits, along with a pitcher of water and several beautiful crystal goblets.

As Tiki listened to the older man chatter on, her eyes strayed over the contents of the room. The walls were graced with paintings of English hunting scenes and lined with bookshelves full to the brim but there was nothing that resembled a magical cup. What if Ailléna had been mistaken? Were they wasting their time when both Johnny's and Dain's lives were at stake?

"The Luck, you say?" Sir Musgrave boomed in a hearty voice in response to Rieker's question. "I'm not surprised your father mentioned it. The two of us looked for those faeries who left it behind for more hours than I care to admit." He pushed his hefty girth from the chair and strode across the room. "I'm afraid the Luck's a well-known secret, but we keep it locked up, just to be safe." He turned and in a dramatic fashion, held one finger to his lips and Tiki had to work to hold back a giggle. "There are very few who I would trust enough to show our Luck—but since you're Will's son—come along."

He picked up a lamp and led them from the grand drawing room, through a lofty hallway, taking several turns until he reached a small, winding hallway toward the back of the mansion. Tiki followed, one of the crystal water goblets clutched in her hand and hidden within the folds of her skirt—just in case she had an opportunity to glamour the goblet to look like the cup and perform a switch. Their host led them down a back stairway to an even smaller hallway, talking the entire time.

"Quite a history with this Luck—it's said the faeries left it behind while they were playing in the well at St. Cuthbert's...." He held the lamp high to navigate the dark space. "They were startled when my ancestor's servants chanced upon them and they ran for it, forgetting the cup."

They wound their way through the dim light until the older man finally stopped before a plank door reinforced with iron ribs and supporting a great black lock. "By the time they'd realized they'd forgotten the thing, it was too late—the butler had picked it up and claimed the cup for his own. The story goes the faeries were spittin' mad. One of them even yelled out *'if this Luck should break or fall—farewell the luck of Edenhall.'"*

Sir Musgrave pulled a heavy round of keys from his pocket and carefully separated one long ornate key from the rest. "So we've been protecting it ever since—partly because we're afraid they'll be coming back for it." The older man laughed as he gave the keys a rattle. "I carry these with me every day." He lowered his voice to a loud whisper. "Even sleep with them under my pillow." He winked at Tiki. "I've already instructed my son to retrieve the keys first before reviving me should I keel over one day. One can never be too cautious with the mood of Lady Luck."

The old metal lock groaned as it gave way beneath the teeth of the silver key and Sir Musgrave pushed the door open. They entered a small room that reminded Tiki of a root cellar. Shelves lined the walls but they were empty save for one. Displayed alone, centered on an end shelf, stood a tall glass goblet. Sir Musgrove stopped before the glass cup and held up his lamp. Brilliant blues, yellows, and golden gilding reflected the lamplight in a dazzling display of color.

"Here she is," Sir Musgrave said, almost reverently. "The Luck of Edenhall. We've had her in the family for well over two hundred years now."

Tiki's heart skipped a beat. This was it. This was what Larkin had said they needed to save Johnny. Surely, the Musgrave's wouldn't mind if they borrowed the cup for a week or two? Especially, if they didn't know it was gone. But how could they possibly get the Luck out of this little room without being seen?

THEY DIDN'T STAY with the Luck for long.

"There you have it," Sir Musgrave said, ushering them back out again. "Safe and sound, she is. I'm glad you mentioned it, I hadn't checked on that little beauty in quite some time."

"Quite striking," Rieker said, making eye contact with Tiki over Sir Musgrave's back as the older man bent to lock the door. "Thank you for letting us see the cup. Are you the only one who can grant access?"

"I am. Most people don't even know where we've hidden her." He slid the keys into his jacket and patted the pocket. "Yes, indeed. You have to go through me to get to the Luck of Edenhall."

WITH LITTLE ARM-TWISTING, Sir Musgrave convinced them to spend the night at the estate. Over dinner he regaled them with stories of Rieker's father.

"That old Will," Sir Musgrave chuckled, a glass of wine clutched in his hand, "how he loved adventure." The older man's belly strained against the brass buttons of his white vest as he leaned back in his chair and sipped on yet another glass of wine. "He loved the faerie stories in these parts. 'Course we're thick with them here in Cumbria, as we've all grown up with tales of the *"tyl-wyth teg"* or fair ones. But for some reason, Will believed more than most. He was always keen to go up to Hardknott Pass and look for the rath of King Eveling and he'd spend hours exploring Elva Hill."

"Elva Hill?" Tiki asked.

"A faerie hill that's supposed to hide a gateway to the Otherworld." The older man sobered. "It's up near Bassenthwaite Lake, just north of here." He shook his head. "Couldn't catch me up there past dark, but Will loved that area. Said it made him feel close to something bigger than England. He'd disappear for days at a time."

"Did he ever tell you he'd met a faerie?" Rieker asked.

To Tiki's surprise, Sir Musgrave didn't laugh. Instead, he squinted at Rieker long and hard, as if debating something. He drained his glass of wine before he spoke.

"He did tell me something strange once. I've never forgotten it."
Sir Musgrave gazed into the distance, over Rieker's head. "He'd just returned from a 'jaunt', as he liked to call them. He'd lost weight but he had a glow about him, like I'd never seen him before—triumphant, almost. He said, '*I've found it, Harry. I've found the gate.*'" The older man paused as he refilled his glass. "He never told me what gate he'd found, even when I pestered him for more information. In fact, he never spoke of the matter again, but I've always wondered, what *exactly* he meant that day."

Chapter Twenty-Seven

"How are we possibly going to get those keys?" Tiki murmured while Sir Musgrave excused himself to use the facilities. "He bloody well sleeps with them under his pillow!"

"I know," Rieker said. They'd left the table and stood near the fire as the well-trained servants moved silently and efficiently in and out of the room, clearing their dinner dishes. Rieker turned his back to the table and faced the flames, keeping his voice low. "The answer hasn't become clear, quite yet. Do you think we could pick the lock?"

"Doubtful. I can pick pockets, but I'm not a lock pick by any stretch." Tiki peered up at him. "Are you?"

"Not really." Rieker propped his hands on his hips, pushing his jacket behind. His brow was furrowed in thought. "Do you think we could get him drunk enough to pick his pocket while he's asleep?"

Tiki snorted. "Not likely. Unless you're planning to get him to pass out here in the drawing room, otherwise, you'd have to get past his staff to reach his bedroom."

Rieker sighed. "You're right. That was a rather far-fetched idea. Besides," he added in a dry voice, "I get the sense Sir Musgrave is well-versed in wine consumption."

"If only we had some reason to bump into him, I could pick his pocket," Tiki muttered. She thought of some of her escapades as a pickpocket and an idea suddenly struck her. "I've got it—we could dance."

WHEN SIR MUSGRAVE returned to the room, Tiki and Rieker were waltzing, none-too-gracefully, about the room.

"What a brilliant idea." Sir Musgrave called out in a jolly voice as he trundled toward them. "I love to dance!"

"Tiki wanted to practice her waltz," Rieker said, as he twirled her in a circle around their host. "Before we dance in public."

Tiki gave the other man a tremulous smile over her shoulder, her cheeks a bright pink. What Rieker had said was the truth. Though she had been versed in dancing at a young age, she'd had no practice for years and it took all her concentration not to step on her partner's feet. She stumbled and Rieker slowed.

"Perhaps if she could practice with you, as well? She'll feel better prepared for her debut."

"Certainly, certainly." Sir Musgrave held his hands up to take Tiki's hand and waist. "I love to dance and we seldom get the opportunity. And to have such a lovely partner—" He beamed at her and Tiki tried to ignore the twinge of guilt that twisted in her stomach. "Are you ready, then?" At Tiki's nod he gave an exaggerated dip. "And... one, two, three, one, two, three..." He swept Tiki away and they began to waltz around the room.

TIKI DANCED WITH both Rieker and their host several times before she pleaded for mercy.

"Thank you for your patience with me," she laughed, "but I'm out of breath and really must rest." She dropped into a chair with a loud sigh. "Perhaps we can try again later?"

"Delightful," Sir Musgrave beamed. "Simply delightful. Another go in a bit would be wonderful. Now where is my wine?" He headed for the table where his glass sat.

Rieker raised his eyebrows at Tiki and she gave a brief nod. "William, would you be so kind as to hand me my bag?" Before Rieker could move, Sir Musgrave retrieved the purse from where she'd set the bag next to her chair at dinner.

"I've got it right here, my dear." He held it high above his head as if he'd captured a prized flag. "Allow me."

"Thank you so much." Tiki reached for the bag.

"And your wine." He held her glass out for her to take. "We all need a nip after that bit of fun."

Tiki froze. She held her purse in one hand and the keys were clenched in her other hand, nestled in the folds of her skirt. Could she release her tight grip on them without the metal jingling together? At that moment, Rieker went into a coughing fit—hacking and wheezing, even bending over as though he couldn't breathe.

"Dear me, boy—" Sir Musgrave stepped closer and pounded him on the back— "are you all right?"

Using Rieker's cover, Tiki quickly slipped the keys into the bottom of her purse. By the time Sir Musgrave and Rieker turned to face her, Tiki was standing next to them, the purse held demurely at her side, one hand reaching for her wine glass Sir Musgrave still held. Rieker's eyes were watering and his face was bright red. Tiki giggled, so relieved to have secured the keys they needed, she couldn't help but tease him a bit.

"Hairball, William?" she asked in a polite voice.

Rieker gave a half laugh. "Something like that."

Tiki pressed her lips together to hold back her laughter. "If you'll excuse me, gentlemen, I must use the facilities. Do carry on in my absence."

THE MOON HAD reached its zenith when Tiki slipped from her room. She and Rieker had agreed to meet at the bottom of the stairs at midnight. She was dressed in a silk robe covering her light blue night gown—a gift from Rieker. In one hand she clutched the handle of the small lamp, in the other, the crystal water goblet she'd brought from dinner. The ornate key that opened the locked room downstairs was safely hidden in her pocket.

In their last round of dancing, Tiki had been able to slip the key ring, sans the most important key, back into Sir Musgrave's pocket. They had counted on the fact that the wine would make the older man less observant when he retired and hopefully, he'd never notice one missing key on the thick ring.

Tiki wore a thin pair of slippers on her feet, which made her passage silent, though it was difficult to hear over the pounding of her heart. The shadows were thick at the bottom of the stairs and she descended cautiously, staying close to the wall so that she might remain unseen.

As she reached the bottom, one of the shadows shifted and loomed toward her, making her heart skip a beat before she realized it was Rieker.

"Oh, you gave me a fright," she said softly.

He held his hand out and she slid her fingers into his. "Not to worry," he said softly, "you're safe with me." He led her down the hallway past the drawing room where they'd dined with their host.

"Do you know where you're going?" Tiki whispered.

"I think so. I tried to map it in my mind when he took us down here earlier in the evening—hoping we'd have an opportunity to come back on our own. Since we didn't hear anything, I don't think he noticed the key missing when he retired to bed."

Rieker led her through the darkened hallways with a surprising confidence. They took the small back stairway, winding through the narrow corridors until Tiki felt like they'd gone deep underground. Rieker finally stopped before the wooden door.

"Do you have the key?"

Tiki handed Rieker the slim piece of metal.

It only took him a second before the lock snapped open and he gave Tiki a devious grin over his shoulder. "Voila." He pushed the door open and Tiki held her lamp up as they stepped into the small room. From its perch on the far shelf, the Luck sparkled in the lamplight as if full of magical secrets. Tiki stepped closer to admire the glass design. "Amazing it's survived all these years," she murmured.

"Can you glamour that water goblet to look like it?" Rieker asked, coming to stand beside her.

"I'll do my best. I've never tried to glamour an object before."

"Seems like it'd be easier than changing an entire person."

Tiki handed the lamp to Rieker and placed the water goblet on the shelf next to the Luck. She stared at the Luck, getting a mental image, then shifted her attention to the water goblet. She held her hands close to the glass and picturing the Luck in her mind, then whispered the words Larkin had taught her.

The fresh scent of clover filled the air and before their eyes, the goblet melted from one shape into another.

"Bloody well amazing," Rieker breathed.

Tiki looked from the real Luck to the water goblet she'd just glamoured. They were identical. "It is a bit shocking, isn't it?"

"Shh!" Rieker held up a hand to silence her, his head cocked toward the door. "Listen. Someone's coming." Tiki grabbed the Luck as Rieker twisted the small knob that controlled the flame on their lamp. They were plunged into darkness. Tiki yanked loose the tie of her silk robe and hid the Luck within its folds as Rieker led her out the door and into the shadows further down the hallway.

A voice grew louder as it approached, soon recognizable as Sir Musgrave mumbling to himself. "Don't know how it could've come off the ring...but where else could it be?" He was in a purple night robe, edged in gold, with purple slippers on his feet that slapped against the floor as he shuffled along. He held a candle within a hurricane lamp to light his way. "Know I locked the door...didn't I?...Getting old....can't remember my name half the time...

Rieker edged back further in the hallway, nudging Tiki along.

She stood on tiptoe to whisper in his ears, "Where is the key?"

She could feel rather than see Rieker's grin. "Still in the door."

They watched Sir Musgrave as he held his light aloft and bent over to peer at the lock. He straightened with an audible sigh of relief. "Of course, you're here, my little beauty, right where I left you..." The man put his hand on the handle and paused. "Could've sworn I locked this door, though." He slowly pushed the door open and lifted his lamp to light the interior of the small room.

With his face illuminated by the glow of the candle, Tiki could see his fearful expression. The old man really did believe in faeries. Tiki had to bite her lip to stop a giggle. And well he should, she thought, because hadn't a faerie just stolen the very thing he was trying to protect?

"WE'RE ON TO Edinburgh." Rieker said the next morning, as they bid farewell to Sir Musgrave. "Thank you again for your hospitality and for allowing us to view the Luck. Quite a fascinating bit of history, there."

"Funny you should mention that, William. When I went to bed last night I found I'd misplaced my key to the door where we keep the Luck. Don't know how it came off the ring. Could've sworn I'd locked that door and put the lot in my pocket but when I went to check—there it was—stuck in the lock with the door open." The older man shook his grey head. "Can't quite explain it..."

"How curious," Tiki murmured. "Was the Luck all right?"

"Yes, thankfully." The old man smiled. "Right on the shelf where she belongs, though seemed a bit off-center. . . ." He scratched his head. "Gave me a bit of a fright, I have to admit. Decided today I'd best find another secret hiding place for it, you know—just to be on the safe side."

A FEW MINUTES later Tiki and Rieker were back in the carriage and Geoffrey was driving them away from Edenhall. Rieker sat close to Tiki as she carefully unwrapped the item hidden within her cloak and held it up for Rieker to see. The cup sparkled in the afternoon light as if pleased with their deception.

"The Luck of Edenhall," she said softly. "Let's return you to Faerie."

Chapter Twenty-Eight

"I still think you should have stayed home," Arthur said as he let the brass knocker drop against the strike at Number Six. "You're barely well enough to venture out. I can talk to Wills on my own."

"I know, I know," Leo replied. "I felt compelled to come. To see him with my own eyes and know that's he's all right. Wills can be so stubborn, at times." He shook his head and glanced warily up and down the dark street again. Fog was settling low against the cobblestones, muting the orbs of light cast from the row of gas streetlamps. "I suspect Tara is cut from the same cloth, but I'm not going to take no for an answer. Given his importance, not only to us, but also to the monarchy, I will insist they be protected until this monster is either captured or destroyed."

"In theory, Leo, that is a good plan, but I suspect Wills might have something to say about the idea."

The door swung open. Charles, the butler, blinked in surprise at the guests on the doorstep before his gaze flicked to the ornate coach that waited on the street, surrounded by four liveried footmen. He gave a stiff bow.

"May I help your royal highnesses?"

"Is Lord Richmond about?" Arthur asked.

"I'm sorry to say he's not here, sir." Charles gave a sharp tug to the bottom of his vest. "Was he expecting you?"

"No, no," Arthur waved his hand, "he didn't know we were coming. Tell me, did he say when he would return?"

Charles pulled his shoulders back and lifted his chin. "Unfortunately, your Highness, he did not."

"What about Miss Tara?" Leo spoke up. "Is she here?"

The butler shook his head. "Gone with Sir, I'm afraid."

A small face peered around the butler's legs. Leo blinked in surprise at the little girl. "Who are you?"

"I live here," Clara said. Her blue eyes surveyed the two men who stood on the doorstep. "Who are you?"

"Shush." Charles reached down and tried to shoo Clara away. "Watch your mouth, young miss. Run along now."

"You live here with Wills?" Leo couldn't hide his surprise as he squatted down so he was eye-level with her. "But who are you?"

"I'm Clara," she said in a matter-of-fact tone. "Clara Marie. What's your name?"

"Clara Marie," Leo echoed faintly. He turned to look at his brother. "Charles Bagley's daughter was named Marie Claire...the names are so similar..."

Arthur raised his eyebrows at his brother. "Indeed." He shifted his gaze back to the butler. "Who is in charge during Lord Richmond's absence?"

"In charge of what, sir?" Charles asked, shifting his stance in an effort to block the little girl from view.

"In charge of the household." Arthur nodded at Clara. "The child."

Leo reached around the butler and took Clara's hand, drawing her back into view. "Are there other children here?" he asked gently.

"Just Toots," she said, then leaned forward and said in a conspiratorial whisper, "but his real name is Thomas. He's ten." She pointed at her chest. "I'm almost five. Fiona's gone right now, but she's quite a bit older, you see, almost sixteen. That's where Tiki and Rieker have gone—to get Fiona and Johnny. What happened to your neck?"

"Rieker?"

Clara clapped a hand over her mouth, her eyes growing wide. Then she giggled and gave Leo a sly grin. "Just a nickname we made up for Wills." She motioned to his neck. "Wills had scratches like that on his leg once." She cocked her head, her eyes bright with curiosity. "What happened to you?"

The butler coughed, clearly uncomfortable. "Miss Tara cares for the children."

"But when she's gone?" Arthur persisted.

"Mrs. Bosworth, our housekeeper keeps an eye on them and they've an older... uh.. brother... who watches them, as well." Charles tugged on his vest again and twisted his neck as if he found his cravat to be too tight.

Clara leaned close and whispered to Leo. "We used to be orphans, but now, we're a big family."

"I see." Leo rocked back on his heels. "Is William part of your family?"

"Of course." Clara grinned at him. "Wills and Tiki are going to get married."

Leo smiled at the little girl. "How fascinating. I knew Wills had secrets—but an entire family hidden here? He's pulled the wool over my eyes."

Arthur glanced at Clara then dropped his voice and directed his comment to the butler. "I don't mean to alarm you, but there has been a sighting in the vicinity of a man who—" for a second he seemed at a loss for words— "a man with evil intentions." He motioned toward Clara. "Children in particular, seem to be at risk.

We've come to warn Lord Richmond so he can take the necessary precautions, but now—"

Leo pushed himself to his feet. "Now, since William isn't here, we must insist—for the safety of all—that several of our guards remain here until Lord Richmond returns."

Chapter Twenty-Nine

Adark shadow stood hidden among the trees in the square across from Number Six as the red-coated Palace guards were being given instructions at the front of the townhome. The *liche* hissed in anger at the interruption of his plans, though he'd learned the one he sought—sweet Fiona—was not on the premises.

Earlier, he'd overheard a conversation between the housekeeper and the butler discussing the fact that the girl was caring for Johnny, though they weren't quite sure where. The *liche's* sharp teeth glistened as he smiled, for he knew exactly where to find the injured boy Fiona cared for—he was in the Otherworld—right where he'd left him.

THE SUN WAS setting as the *liche* approached the zagishire and sniffed the air. The breeze carried the succulent scent of Fiona's tender skin—he was sure of it. He'd changed his clothes to blend with the Seelie fey who worked around the Palace of Mirrors—a green tunic with tan breeches, his black hair braided behind his head.

"Can I help you?"

He turned to find a nurse staring at him, a basket full of cut herbs slung over one arm. He motioned to the building. "I was wondering about your patients…"

"We've only one at the moment."

"The boy?" He tried not to sound too hopeful. "Johnny?"

The nurse blinked in surprise. "You know the mortal?"

The *liche* tilted his head and knotted his brow in a concerned expression. "Is Fiona caring for him?"

"I believe that's her name." The nurse's lips pursed. "I've been instructed not to speak to her much." She lifted the basket with a sour expression. "Yet, I'm good enough to deliver these herbs."

"Someone doesn't appreciate your talents, do they?"

The nurse glanced over her shoulder, then spoke in a whisper. "It's Larkin. I swear she thinks *she's* the queen of the Seelie Court now."

The *liche* held out his hands for the herb-filled basket. "Allow me to take these to Fiona. She'll be pleased to see me and you can take a well-deserved break."

The nurse hesitated. "You wouldn't mind?"

"Of course not." He wrapped his hands around the handle and pulled the basket free from her arm. "Scoot off now, while you've the chance." Without waiting for her reply, the *liche* pulled open the door to the zagishire.

"Tell the guard I asked you to deliver the herbs to her," the nurse called after him.

The man paused. "The guard?"

The nurse rolled her eyes. "*Queen* Larkin insisted. Don't ask me who those two are, but she's keeping a close eye on them."

Chapter Thirty

Rieker had Geoffrey drive for several miles before dropping them off at the nearby Penrith Inn, where he advised the man they were going to travel back to London in a few days time with several business partners who lived in the area.

Once they'd dispatched the driver to return to the City without them, Tiki and Rieker walked through the inn and out a back door. Tiki held the Luck wrapped within her cloak and clutched in her arms. A copse was situated nearby with a beck running through the middle. They followed a footpath to the stream and crossed over a small bridge into the trees. Tiki glanced around, to make sure no one was watching, then held out her hand to Rieker.

"To the zagishire?"

Rieker clutched her fingers and smiled. "To save Johnny."

THE SUN WAS low on the horizon when they returned to the gardens that surrounded the Palace of Mirrors. They arrived next to the stone statue of Danu, the original goddess of Faerie.

Tiki gazed curiously at the statue. Larkin had told her that Danu was the mother of the *Tuatha de Danaan*, the first faeries of Ireland, but that she'd been captured by a human who was so besotted with her beauty that he'd torn off her wing to keep her in the mortal world.

During winter, while Donegal and the UnSeelies were in power, Danu's face had been etched with torment and she'd reached for the heavens as if she meant to take flight. One great wing had stretched from the left side of her back, while the other had lain broken on the ground.

Now, she wore a glittering mask, not unlike the one Tiki had worn to the masked ball at Buckingham Palace and her lips curved in a seductive smile. Instead of taking flight, the faerie appeared to be sliding her arms around the neck of an invisible dance partner, both wings arching gracefully from her back.

"Rieker, look. The statue has changed—how is that possible?" Tiki tapped on the carving, running her fingers along the cool stone, testing the rock. "One more thing that's different since the Seelies resumed control of the court. It's like there are two different worlds here. "

"You say 'the Seelies' as if you're not one of them," Rieker replied. "Don't forget it was because of you the Seelies were able to take control again on Beltane."

"I suppose that's true," Tiki mused, "but Larkin only needed me to find the Stone of Tara and claim the throne. She seems able to rule this world just fine without me." Tiki frowned. "Perhaps better without me."

Rieker slid his arm over Tiki's shoulders and pulled her close. "That remains to be seen. For now, let's focus on helping Johnny. Come along." Rieker set off down the path that led toward the zagishire.

The Night Garden glowed with a colorful luminescence from the nocturnal blooms of the plants, the blossoms swaying gently in the soft breeze as they made their way down the path. This time, the flowers were breathtakingly beautiful, rather than the blood-stained predators that had flourished when the Winter King ruled. A lilting melody whispered through the branches, as though borne by the wind.

They didn't pause to enjoy the beauty of the sight, however, hurrying toward the small building where Johnny was being treated. Larkin was exiting as they approached.

"There you are," she said, looking Tiki up and down. Larkin wore an elegant dress the same color as the summer sky, which, at this moment, matched her eyes, making Tiki all too conscious of the plain, brown clothes she'd donned in attempt to remain inconspicuous as they traveled. "Callan has been beside himself trying to find you." The faerie glanced around. "Have you seen a guard out here? He's supposed to be inside, but I can't find him."

"No, but we just got here. How's Johnny?" Tiki asked eagerly.

"I doubt he's going to make it through the night," she said in a flat voice. "Really, I'm amazed he lasted this long."

"Perhaps he's stronger than you think." Tiki didn't want to argue with Larkin, but the faerie's arrogance was too much to bear. "I believe he has a will to live that you're not able to see."

Larkin tilted her head. "Such confidence. I'm afraid it will take much more than even I'm able to offer at this point to save him."

Tiki held up her bundled cloak. A small triumphant smile tweaked the corners of her mouth. "Or maybe all he needs is a cup and a little luck." Beside her, Rieker let out a small chuckle.

The blond faerie frowned and eyed the rolled up cloak in Tiki's arms. "You didn't."

"I did."

Disbelief was thick in Larkin's voice. "You've found the Cup of Plenty?"

"It has been known as the Luck of Edenhall for several centuries now," Rieker said, "locked up tight in the cellar of the Edenhall estate up in Cumbria."

Larkin gestured at the bundle. "Let me see it."

"I'm not going to reveal it out here," Tiki said. "If you want to see it, come back inside."

Larkin yanked the door open and they stepped inside the small building. Tiki carefully unwrapped the glass goblet. Even in the dim light, the colors glowed with a mystic effervescence.

Larkin put her hands on the glass with an unusual reverence. "The Cup of Plenty," she breathed. "I don't believe it." She ran her long fingers over the colorful pieces of glass, as if by rubbing them, some of the magic might transfer to her. Her gaze shifted to Tiki, her blue-green eyes bright with an emotion Tiki couldn't identify. "Do you have any idea what you've done?"

Tiki's stomach clenched. "What do you mean?"

"This cup is one of the Four Treasures."

"Don't riddle us, Larkin," Rieker snapped. "Be specific for once in your long life. You've mention the Four Treasures before. What are they?"

Larkin shot Rieker a dark glare before she spoke softly as if revealing a secret. "The Treasures are the Ring of *Ériu*, the *Cloch na Teamhrach*—the Stone of Tara, and *Corn na bhFuíoll*— the Cup of Plenty." She traced her finger over one of the swirls of colored glass. "If this is really the Cup, then you've found the first three." She raised her gaze to Tiki's face. "That only leaves the fourth…"

"What is the fourth?" Tiki asked, her interest piqued.

"We need to discuss this further, but not here. Let's go to my study. There are other things I need to discuss with you, as well." Larkin's voice tightened in warning. "We can't let that cup out of our sight. It's sacred. I'll have Callan assign a guard to watch it immediately." She turned and swept to the door. "Come along."

"Wait!" Tiki cried. "We need to see Johnny first—that's why we risked our lives to find this bloody thing." The hours she'd gone without sleep were catching up with her and Larkin's imperious attitude made her blood boil. Tiki shouted after the faerie as she continued to walk away. "TO SAVE HIS LIFE!"

"Teek?" Fiona's worried voice called down the hall. "Is that you?"

Tiki jerked around. "Yes Fi, it's me." She hurried toward her friend, glad to leave Larkin behind. All the faerie ever did was create trouble. "Rieker and I are both here. How's Johnny doing?"

Tiki could tell by the drawn and exhausted look on Fiona's face that the boy was not faring well. Her hair was unwashed, her clothes rumpled and unkempt. Fiona's eyes were red-rimmed and bleary, as if she hadn't slept in days.

"I'm doing my best to keep him with us, Teek," Fiona whispered as they walked back to the room together, "but I'm afraid." Her voice broke and a small sob escaped. "I don't think he's going to make it."

"Yes, he is, Fiona." Tiki said, a surge of strength returning. She could go a few more hours without sleep if it might save Johnny's life. She held the Luck up for Fiona to see. "We've found a cup that will help him."

Fiona stared at the glass goblet. "It's very pretty, Teek, but are you sure it'll help?" She sniffed. "He's in a bad way."

JOHNNY'S CONDITION WAS shocking. The young boy had deteriorated significantly since Tiki had seen him last. He was so pale, blue veins showed through his skin and his eyes seemed to have sunk into his head. Fiona spoke to him, telling him Tiki was visiting, but there was no response—no indication that the boy was even still alive, save for the shallow rise and fall of his chest.

"See?" Fiona said, looking up at Tiki with tear-filled eyes. "I'm not sure how much longer he'll last. Larkin was here and even she didn't know what to do for him."

Tiki gripped Fiona's hand. "You have to believe, Fiona. *Believe* he can get well—with all your heart. We have the power to heal him. We need to tell him that—so he believes it, too."

Rieker joined them next to Johnny's bed and stared down at the young boy with a grim expression. "Doesn't seem like the same chap who was such a cocky pickpocket, does it?" he said softly. "I barely recognize him."

Tiki put her lips close to Johnny's ear. "I know you can hear me, Johnny, so I want you to pay attention." Tiki spoke slowly, emphasizing each word, as if to convince herself, as well as Johnny. "You're a clever boy. You've escaped from the bobbies too many times to count. Now, you're going to escape from Death, as well."

Tiki watched the boy's face and for a second she thought she saw an eyelid flicker, but then it was gone and he remained limp and unresponsive. She leaned close again.

"Listen to me, Johnny. I am a faerie queen and I'm going to save your life." As she said the words 'faerie queen' the Jester's impromptu recital when Tiki had first been introduced to Court flitted through her head. What was it he'd said? *Would the prize answer those in need?*

There was no response from the limp figure on the bed.

"What do we do?" Fiona cried.

Tiki motioned at the girl. "Help prop him up, Fi. I'm going to try something."

Fiona slipped her arm behind Johnny's shoulders and lifted his emaciated frame. His mouth sagged open as he hung limply in her arms. Tiki put the Luck next to his lips and tilted the glass goblet.

"What are you doing, Teek?" Rieker asked. "There's nothing in the cup."

"It's just a hunch," Tiki said. "Let's see what happens."

At first, there was nothing, then a trickle of green liquid poured from the Luck into Johnny's mouth.

"Look—" Fiona cried— "there's water... or...*something*..."

Tiki spoke in a confident tone. "It's healing—one of the essences of life. It pours from the cup for those in need."

Fiona looked at Tiki with a dazed expression.

Tiki smiled triumphantly. "The Jester told me." She leaned closer to the young boy's ear. "You're going to get better, Johnny. Drink from this cup and heal your ills. Do you hear me? You've got the power now—be well." She poured until the fluid spilled from the corners of his mouth.

Tiki straightened the cup and watched him intently, looking for a sign that the magic was at work, but Johnny didn't move a muscle. In fact, he seemed to quit breathing.

"Johnny." Rieker shook his arm and Johnny's head flopping back against Fiona's arm. "Wake up."

"Tiki—" Fiona's voice wavered with barely restrained hysteria.

Tiki reached for the young boy's hand and slipped her fingers around his. Her voice wavered. "Johnny?"

"It's too late." Larkin spoke from behind them. As one, they turned to look at the faerie, who stood just inside the door. "The Cup of Plenty can heal the ill, but it can't bring the dead back to life." She shrugged. "It was a gamble anyway. Mortals interact with the world of Faerie in different ways than the fey. Who knew if the cup would heal or kill him? I never dreamed you'd find it in the first place."

A whimper escaped from Fiona's lips.

"He's not dead," Tiki said, though her words were unconvincing.

"He's mortal—what did you expect?" Larkin's face was cold. "And even if he had survived, you realize by feeding him faerie drink you risk binding him to life in Faerie forever?"

"No!" Fiona cried. She grabbed Tiki's arm, a beseeching look on her thin face. "Tell me that's not true, Tiki."

"*Now* you tell us?" Rieker spat out.

Tiki straightened her shoulders. "A heart-breaking choice, but a risk worth taking. Better alive in Faerie, than dead forever." She tightened her grip on Johnny's hand, wishing she could impart some of her strength to him.

Larkin narrowed her eyes at Tiki and her lips turned in a mocking smile. "You sound like you've grown attached to our world. Not thinking of staying, are you?"

"My matters are my own affair, Larkin, and none of your business."

The smile slid off the faerie's face. Her lips pressed together as if trying to hold in words she'd like to say. "I'll send the nurse to take his body," she finally snapped. "William, if you want to know of your brother, come see me in my study."

IT TOOK ANOTHER hour before Tiki was convinced that Johnny was truly dead. It took longer than that to convince Fiona to leave his side. Tears streamed down Tiki's cheeks as she tried to console Fiona, her own exhaustion making it difficult to remain strong for Fi.

The faerie nurse returned and ushered them out the door. "Larkin's given me instructions to care for your friend," she said gently. "We have a special place where we let them rest through the cycle of the seasons—before nature reclaims their bodies. Don't you worry—we'll take good care of him."

RIEKER WAS THE one who insisted they go back to London.

"I'll talk to Larkin later," he said. "Right now, we need to get Fiona home to Grosvenor Square and care for her. The longer she stays here, the more she's at risk."

Tiki's heart jumped. Home—Clara, Toots, Shamus and Mrs. B—the familiar sights and sounds of London and the security of Grosvenor Square. Nothing sounded better at this moment. She was tired and discouraged. What had all their efforts to find the cup been for, if in the end they'd been unable to save Johnny? Life was as much a struggle here in the Otherworld as it was in London—just with a different set of circumstances.

"I'm sure no one will miss me here. I'm a failure as a queen—I can't even save those I love," Tiki said bitterly. "Grosvenor Square is where we all belong—not here." She slid her arm around Fiona's shoulders and reached for Rieker's hand. She whispered the words that would transport them to London and the zagishire shimmered from view.

Chapter Thirty-One

Behind the zagishire the *liche* licked the blood of the fey guard's heart from the corner of his lips. The tough flesh of the middle-aged fey was hardly satisfying, but he'd had to feed.

Voices carried through an open window from the room where Fiona cared for the mortal and the *liche* crept forward to listen. He smiled at the mention of Grosvenor Square. He knew exactly where to find Fiona in London. This time she would not escape.

He froze as a female voice said, '*I'm a failure as a queen— Grosvenor Square is where we all belong.*' Could he be so lucky?

Chapter Thirty-Two

They arrived back in London inside the coach house at Number Six to minimize any chance they'd be seen upon their return. Night had fallen in the City and the shadows within the small stable were deep and impenetrable. The horses snorted and shuffled in their stalls, spooked at their sudden appearance.

As Tiki, Rieker and Fiona stood in the shaded darkness of the building, chill bumps crawled up Tiki's arms like invisible spiders. She glanced around, trying to put a finger on what felt off, but everything was in its place: the carriages were parked, the horses were in their stalls, all the paraphernalia associated with buggies and animals was present and neatly organized. Yet there was something... Her eyes probed the gloom accumulated in the corners of the building—searching...but for what?

A dark shadow shifted in an unnatural way from the corner of her eye. One of the horses let out an alarmed snort and stamped nervously in its stall. Tiki searched the darkness. Had it been her imagination?

Rieker followed her line of sight. "What is it?"

"I thought I saw something move over there." She pointed to a far corner near the doors that led outside.

"Who goes there?" A voice called out. A man, dressed in the garb of a Palace guard, appeared at the door that led out to the alleyway, a spear clutched in his hands, pointed in their direction.

"William Richmond," Rieker said, walking toward the man. "Owner of this home. And you are?"

The guard peered through the shadows at him. Recognizing Rieker, he relaxed a bit. "Cunningham, sir."

"What are you doing here?" Rieker asked. "Are one of the princes visiting?"

"No sir. Been ordered to guard the property until your return." He snapped off a smart salute and lifted his weapon, his back ramrod straight.

"Guard the prop—" Rieker started. "By whose orders?"

"Princes Arthur and Leopold, sir. Hughes is out front."

"There are two of you?" Disbelief was thick in Rieker's voice. "What is the threat?" By now, Tiki and Fiona had joined Rieker and stood listening to their conversation.

The guard's eyes shifted briefly to the two girls, before he answered. "An unsavory bloke was seen in the area a few days back. We were ordered to make sure he didn't enter these premises."

Fiona clutched Tiki's arm. "It's him, isn't it? That man. The one who took Johnny."

Tiki grabbed Fiona's hand and raced for the back door. "We've got to check on the children."

Clara, Toots and Shamus were eating dinner in the kitchen with Mr. and Mrs. Bosworth, Juliette, the housemaid, Charles and Geoffrey. They all looked up in surprise when Tiki and Fiona dashed into the kitchen shouting their names. Tiki clutched the children in her arms. "You're safe," she whispered. "Thank God."

THE PALACE GUARDS remained outside, front and back. Callan had followed Tiki to London, along with Toran and Bith, and several other Macanna. For the first time Tiki was relieved to have the Otherworldly guards watching over them.

"You won't even know we're here, Majesty," Callan had said eagerly, so obviously relieved that Tiki was still alive. "We won't be botherin' you—just protectin' you—so no need to hide from us." He'd bobbed his head in a bow and vanished from sight before Tiki could reply.

FIONA SEQUESTERED HERSELF in bed, barely communicative. Tiki tended to her every day, Mrs. Bosworth made sure she got enough to eat, Clara pretended to read her stories, and Toots chattered on about the street children he'd seen, but none of it seemed the cure for her broken heart.

IT WAS SEVERAL days after their return when Rieker asked Tiki to join him in his study.

A sense of dread pricked along Tiki's skin as she followed Rieker into the study, knowing he was anxious to return to the Otherworld and find Dain. Every day she'd been struggling with guilt—she was desperate to find Dain, too—but Fiona's health concerned her and it was comforting to be home—familiar. Tiki hadn't realized how much Grosvenor Square had come to mean to her. But she could never push her worry for Dain far from her mind or the images frozen there—of him stroking her hand, asking if she'd kept his secret, or holding out his hand to pull her onto the back of Aeveen. The need to help him—to care for him—was ever-present, like a sliver under her skin. And to make matters worse, she battled with a newfound sense of responsibility for those homeless faeries on the Tor. If she didn't go back and make sure they got access to food—who would? But she was needed here, as well. There were times when she felt like she was being ripped in half.

Rieker pulled out a soft leather chair for Tiki and she sank into its depths, pulling her legs up beneath her. For the first time, she noticed the lines of exhaustion under his eyes. She'd been busy caring for Fiona, as well as Clara and Toots, and he'd been tending to the business of his estates, so they'd spent little time together. No doubt, Dain's imprisonment weighed even more heavily upon his shoulders.

"How's Fiona doing?" he asked, sitting in a chair next to hers.

"It's going to take some time," Tiki said. "I don't think she believes he's really gone. Even I'm having a hard time adjusting to the idea. I just can't imagine how someone as vibrant and full of life as Johnny, can really be..." She couldn't bring herself to say the word 'dead', heaving a long sigh instead. "You were right to insist we come home." She savored the word 'home'. Would Grosvenor Square truly be her home one day? "How is everything here?"

"The estate and all the associated businesses are fine. I have managers who do a splendid job of assisting me." Rieker leaned forward and rested his elbows on his knees. "However, there are other matters that aren't going as well. I've heard from Larkin. When we didn't come find her—she found me."

Tiki crossed her arms. Of course Larkin had found Rieker when Tiki wasn't around—now that the Stone of Tara had been located and the court returned to the Seelies, Larkin didn't need her as much. It was as if she wanted to divide Tiki and Rieker again.

"Did she have news of Dain?"

"We only spoke for a moment, but yes—there's been another development."

Tiki tensed. "What's that?"

Rieker's expression was grim, the muscles along his jaw clenched. "Donegal has declared that Dain will participate in the Wild Hunt this year."

"The Wild Hunt?"

Rieker toyed with the pieces of a chess set on a nearby table, not meeting Tiki's eyes. "An annual faerie celebration—if you can call it that—where the UnSeelies ride in pursuit of prey. It's usually around Samhain, the end of October, when the veil between the worlds is at its thinnest."

"Is it because of the army he is amassing? How does Dain fit into this?"

Rieker exhaled. "I've not heard any further on Donegal gathering troops. But what I have heard is this: Dain is going to be hunted this year."

Tiki froze, her brows pulled down in a frown. Surely, she couldn't have heard him correctly. "What did you say?"

"The Winter King is going to have his depraved and demented court hunt Dain like he was an animal."

"No." Tiki pushed herself out of the chair. "There's got to be a way to stop him."

Rieker tipped his head back against the chair and stared at the ceiling. "There's only one way: I've got to return to the Otherworld and find a way to free Dain before the hunt. Otherwise, he doesn't have a chance of surviving."

"You can't possibly be thinking of going alone," Tiki said, a new fear taking root.

Rieker leaned his elbows on his knees and gazed down at his hands. "I haven't really put together a plan yet. I'm still trying to absorb the shock of the idea."

"William Becker Richmond." Tiki's voice was adamant. "Look me in the eye and tell me you're not going to go alone."

Rieker raised his hands in surrender. "I won't go alone. But I have to go *now*."

THEY TALKED LONG into the night, discussing the best way to find and free Dain but the conversation always came back to Larkin.

"She's been in the White Tower—as a prisoner—" Rieker was pacing, one hand on his hip, the other on the back of his neck—"and escaped and lived to tell about it. She understands how Donegal thinks—the cat and mouse games he likes to play." He came to a stop in front of Tiki. "I don't think I can do it without her help."

As much as Tiki didn't want Larkin involved, she had to agree. Unbearably arrogant and hard to trust, the faerie was brilliant at the art of manipulation and as cunning as they came. Plus, she despised Donegal—a powerful motivator to find a way to successfully sneak Dain out from under the Winter King's nose.

"Do you think she'll help us?" Tiki asked. "She seems to enjoy her new role of being in charge... of everything."

Rieker gave a soft snort. "*Seems* to like it? She revels in it. I think Larkin's been plotting to be in charge for a very long time. But I do believe she'll help us. She has a special connection to Dain—"

"She has a connection to *both* of you," Tiki said. "Or maybe 'obsession' is a better word..."

"It's different with Dain, though. They've lived in the same world. He knows her for exactly what she is—there are no illusions between them. They've worked together as spies in the UnSeelie court for many years."

"He did mention once that he'd known her all his life," Tiki admitted, remembering the conversation she'd had with Dain while they'd traveled through the Wychwood. "To be honest, it sounded like he respected her."

"She is extremely clever," Rieker said, "and brave."

Tiki curled her nose and pressed her lips together in distaste. Being clever and brave still didn't make her like or trust the faerie. Even if Larkin was her aunt.

Rieker sank back into the chair opposite Tiki. "As much as we both hate the idea, I think I better talk to Larkin and see if she can help me."

Tiki ground her teeth together, already knowing her decision but reluctant to say it out loud. As much as she didn't want to leave Clara and the others, at least they were guarded by both mortal and faerie guards. She couldn't possibly let Rieker go alone and risk his life in the Otherworld when she could help him. When she spoke, it sounded more like a growl.

"Us."

"Pardon?"

"She's going to have to help *us*. You're not going without me."

IT WAS THROUGH a lump in her throat that Tiki informed Mrs. Bosworth, Shamus and the children that she and Rieker had to leave again.

"We'll only be gone a few days. We've got some out-of-town business to take care of."

"Why do you have to go?" Clara asked with a pout. "Why can't Rieker go alone?"

Tiki squatted down next to the little girl and put her hand on Clara's waist. "He needs my help with some matters. I don't want to go, but I have to go. Do you understand?" She lifted Clara's chin so she could gaze into her eyes. "It's the least I can do after everything he has done for us." She smoothed her fingers along the side of Clara's cheek. "Wouldn't you agree?" she asked softly.

Clara jutted her chin out in a stubborn way and traced a pattern in the carpet with the toe of her boot without answering.

"It's all right with me, Teek," Toots exclaimed from where he was laying on the floor in front of the fire, playing with one of Shamus' carvings. "We'll be just fine, won't we, Shamus? Mrs. B. will cook us good food every day and we'll get *fat* while you're gone, just like ol' man Binder." Toots laughed out loud at the idea. Across the room, Shamus shoved his hands into his pockets and nodded, though there was a worried frown on his face.

Clara lifted her head and looked Tiki straight in the eyes. "This is because of Dain, isn't it?"

Tiki's jaw sagged. "W..what?" she stuttered. "Why would you say such a thing?"

"Because he hasn't been around in a long time and Rieker is frowny all the time, like he's worried." She crossed her little arms, scrunched her eyebrows in a mad expression. "Besides, Larkin told me Dain can't go home. That a bad man won't let him." Her chin wobbled and she sucked in a deep breath as if she was trying not to cry.

"Clara—" Tiki started to slide her arms around the little girl's shoulders but Clara pushed her back. "I don't want Dain to be locked up." A big tear slid down her cheek. "An' I don't want you or Rieker to be locked up, either."

"We are *not* going to be locked up," Tiki said forcefully. "And Larkin should never have told you such a thing. Dain is very clever and can take care of himself—"

Clara interrupted. "But he needs you to help him." Another tear slid down her soft cheek.

Tiki hesitated. Should she lie to the little girl? Finally, she nodded. "Yes, he needs our help," she said softly.

"When you see him, you tell him I said to be clever like a lep'reecon and he'll be able to find his way home." Then she threw her arms around Tiki's neck and sobbed.

Chapter Thirty-Three

Outside Number Six a man dressed in a black top hat and a long black cloak stopped among the dense shadows beneath an elm tree, some distance from the townhome. Lit by the glow of a porch lamp, he watched the red-coated guard who stood at the front steps, his bayonet gripped in both hands. The man had already seen a similar guard at the back of the home leading into the coach house.

So the mortals were guarding the occupants of Grosvenor Square. But from whom?

Another movement caught his eye and he shifted his attention to the square. Though his ability to see otherworldly creatures who had not revealed themselves to the mortal eye was limited, centuries of living in both worlds allowed him to recognize the familiar shifting shadows that marked the presence of the fey. As he studied their indistinct silhouettes he counted two who appeared to be Macanna and two who looked like UnSeelie fey.

The man turned a contemplative eye toward the lighted windows of Number Six. Both mortal and otherworldly guards? Confirmation there was a prize greater than the delectable heart of a sixteen year-old being protected at these premises.

The *liche* did not have the ability to enter the townhome without being invited and it was too risky to try and bluff his way in with so many eyes watching. However, sated by the guard's heart, he could afford to bide his time and wait for the right opportunity to present itself...

Chapter Thirty-Four

Tiki was rigid with anger. Her rage at Larkin gave her strength, though, and she forgot to be intimidated when she returned to the Otherworld.

"I will have a word with her, *now*," Tiki snapped at the guard who stood outside Larkin's door. Tiki had removed her glamour upon her return to Faerie and donned the crimson gown she'd been wearing when she'd sat on the Stone of Tara for the first time. There would be no mistaking who was queen at this moment.

Rieker trailed behind her, followed by Callan, Toran and Bith.

Tiki stormed past the guard, who barely yanked the door open in time to allow her passage. Larkin was seated at her desk making notes on a stack of papers. She raised her head as though she'd been expecting Tiki.

"It's about time."

"You will *not* tell Clara anything about Dain," Tiki growled as she jerked to a stop in front of the desk. "And you will NOT visit her without my permission." Tiki slapped both hands down on the desk and leaned forward until she was only inches from Larkin's face. She was so mad it was hard to draw a deep breath. "*Is that understood?*"

Larkin didn't flinch as she coldly returned Tiki's stare—challenging her. A brittle silence filled the room until the air seemed to crackle with tension. Finally, Larkin leaned back in her chair and cocked her head at Tiki. "And how will you stop me?"

Tiki's mouth dropped open at the utter disrespect in Larkin's reply.

"Larkin—" Rieker stepped forward but Tiki stiff-armed him back from the desk without taking her eyes from the blond faerie.

"*Watch me.*" Tiki snarled at Larkin. She'd never felt such hatred for another person before in her life. Outside, a summer storm suddenly ravaged the daytime sky. A *boom!* of thunder cracked overhead as hail poured from the sky as though thrown from above.

Tiki whirled to face the Macanna who had followed her into the room. At her insistence, the other five Macanna had stayed behind in London to watch over Grosvenor Square. "Callan—you are here to protect and serve me, correct?"

The hulking faerie didn't hesitate. He bowed his head as he answered. "Yes, Majesty."

"I want you to keep her—" Tiki jerked her arm up to point in Larkin's direction— "under constant surveillance. She is to be watched at all times. She is not allowed to give orders to my staff. She is not allowed to attend Court. She is not allowed to go to London—under ANY circumstances." Tiki stared at the muscled guard, as if daring him to disobey her. "Am I clear?"

Callan dropped his eyes. "Yes, Majesty."

Larkin slammed her hand on the desk and jerked to her feet. "How *dare* you! You can't—"

Tiki cut her off. "I CAN and I HAVE because I AM QUEEN." She shouted the last words as she glared at the other faerie with pure loathing. "You have meddled in my affairs and with my family for the LAST time." Tiki raked her gaze over the faerie, her lip curled in disgust. "You're dismissed."

For a moment, Larkin seemed speechless. When she spoke, her voice was ragged with anger. "You've forgotten, this is *my* study."

"Not anymore." Tiki pointed at the door. "GET OUT."

LARKIN AND CALLAN left, leaving Tiki and Rieker alone in Larkin's study. Tiki stood at the window and gazed out at the panoramic view, trying to regain her sense of equilibrium. She fingered the soft braid of blond hair that was wrapped around a small brown gourd—the lone decorative item that Larkin had kept in the room. Tiki was tempted to throw the rattle through the window, but something held her back.

Larkin had provoked her to the point where she'd acted on impulse without thought for the consequences. From this perspective, perched high on Wydryn Tor, Tiki suddenly had a sense of the magnitude of her actions and the new responsibilities she bore as queen of a world she barely understood.

The Wychwood Forest stretched for miles before her, the tops of the trees creating a multi-layered canopy that hid the mysterious wood below. The creatures who lived in the forest answered to her now. In the distance, dark clouds gathered over the Plain of Starlight where the Winter King and the UnSeelies lived during the summer months. What threat would Donegal bring? When would the war between the courts that had simmered under the surface for so many centuries become reality? But even as she contemplated the evil that Donegal had done and could still do, Tiki wondered who was the biggest threat to her own happiness: Donegal or Larkin?

"I'm proud of you, Teek." Rieker spoke from behind her, his voice soft in her ear. He rested his hands on her shoulders and some of the tension seeped from Tiki's muscles at his touch. "I always knew there would come a time when you would stand up to Larkin—I just never knew when it would come. But you did and you were brilliant."

Tiki watched a large black bird with a crescent-shaped beak cut across the sky, its large fan wings sweeping the sky with mesmerizing repetition. She tried to ignore the guilt that weighed on her shoulders, perhaps even heavier because of Rieker's charitable forgiveness.

"We can't ask her to help us find Dain now," Tiki said quietly, wishing the sick feeling in her stomach would go away.

"No, we can't. But we didn't need her to find the *Cloch na Teamhrach*. We can find the White Tower without her, as well." He rubbed Tiki's arms slowly up and down. "You and I will find a way."

Tiki blinked back tears as she turned to cup his face. "My dearest William." She traced his cheekbone with her fingertip, marveling at the depth of her emotion for the handsome young man who stood before her. "I would be lost without you." Her finger dropped and gently traced the curve of his bottom lip. "You are everything to me." She placed her hand against his chest to feel the slow thud of his heart and raised her eyes to his. "I love you so very much."

Rieker slid his arms behind her back and pressed her close. He wrapped his fingers in the strands of her long hair as he gazed deep into her eyes. "Fear not, my faerie queen, for you will never be without me." He lowered his head and whispered against her lips, "I will be by your side for all eternity."

THE COURT JESTER was the first to approach when Tiki and Rieker entered the Great Hall some time later.

"Majesty." With a dramatic flair, the gaudily-dressed man swept one arm out to the side and bowed over his extended leg. "Your beauty provides inspiration for even the simplest of minds." He gazed up at her. "If I may be so bold?"

Tiki inclined her head. "Please. Is it too much to hope there will be another pearl of wisdom disguised within your wit?"

The jester straightened, the bells on his hat jingling. "Falsehood wears a mask that is concealed but from those who seek the hidden way." He pulled a reed flute from his pocket and played a haunting melody as his words echoed in Tiki's ears. The yellow sunbursts surrounding his black eyes made their depths seem bottomless and she wondered if it was wisdom or foolishness that he offered. His expression was sober as he raised an imaginary glass. "To your health, Majesty."

"And to yours," Tiki replied, pretending to lift her own glass.

He blinked in surprise and stared at her for a long moment before he inclined his head and murmured, "fear not the water, my queen, for it only appears to block our way." Then he turned and danced away, singing an Irish jig.

"A strange character," Rieker said, as he watched the Court Jester begin to juggle what looked like balls of white sparkling flame. "Did that mean anything to you?"

"Not in the least," Tiki replied. She slipped her hand through Rieker's arm and leaned against his shoulder as she led him in the direction of the High Chamber. "Larkin said the Jester's loyalty lies with neither Seelie nor UnSeelie, but with whoever rules Faerie. I imagine he's used to making up nonsensical sayings to amuse the royals."

"Think of the secrets that man must know," Rieker murmured, still watching the Jester in the distance.

"Half a step behind the queen, half-breed!"

The shout echoed across the Great Hall like a clap of thunder. It took Tiki a second to realize the insult was directed at Rieker. As the meaning sunk in Tiki jerked to a stop, searching for the speaker.

A hush fell over the room as the occupants waited for her reaction.

"Keep walking, Tiki," Rieker murmured. "Pretend you didn't hear him. This is not the time."

Tiki took a deep breath and nodded at Rieker, laughing up at him as though he'd shared a humorous tidbit. "It's Larkin's doing," she said through her forced smile. "I know it."

"It doesn't matter. You are queen. Remember that above all else."

Tiki could hear the whispers as they left the Great Hall and a slow burn began deep inside her chest. It would be just like Larkin to undermine her by trying to divide her relationship with Rieker here in the Otherworld. Tiki clenched her teeth. This was a battle Larkin wasn't going to win.

Chapter Thirty-Five

The next day, Tiki made preparations for a great table of food to be set up on the steps near the Night Garden for all to share.

"I want to make sure the faeries in the homeless camp know they can come eat," Tiki said.

"It's very kind of you, Majesty, but we're a bit short on supplies," one of the cooks murmured as Tiki made her request. "Larkin's givin' us instructions to ration what we put out."

"Short supply?" Tiki frowned. "Why would that be?"

"We get our fruit and vegetables from the hobgoblins, don'ya know?—they's the best gardeners we've got, but Donegal burned their fields and destroyed most their crops."

"Said it was because they was Seelies," another whispered, her eyes wide with a fright. "He wants to kill us all, he does."

THE SUN HAD crested the sky when Tiki and Rieker left the Palace of Mirrors. They gathered Aeveen from a nearby meadow where the Seelies pastured their horses while living on the Tor. The weather was sunny, with clear skies and just a hint of a breeze in the air—a perfect summer day. The murmured warnings from the cooks had stayed with Tiki, like a cloud blotting out the sun, and she wondered silently if Donegal would dare attack during the summer months.

The white horse had greeted them with a whinny, shaking her head, causing her white mane to fly. They had changed into their camouflaged garments and Rieker gave Aeveen her head to lead them off Wydryn Tor.

"It's like she knows where to go," Tiki said from where she sat behind Rieker, her arms wrapped around his waist.

"If only she could talk, maybe she could tell us where to find the White Tower."

"I've got an idea where to start. There was something strange about that village in the Wychwood. I think we need to investigate further." Tiki said. "Maybe this time I'll be able to see something I couldn't before."

THE BRILLIANT SUNLIGHT that had shone down on the Tor became diluted as they descended into the dappled light of the forest. The breeze was stronger here, rattling the leaves until they sounded like voices, whispering a message that Tiki couldn't quite understand. Once again, Rieker had loaded Aeveen with a variety of weapons: a broadsword, a whip, a sabre and several daggers that hung from his belt. Tiki had brought the stake of ash with her again, and scanned the surrounding trees and bushes as they rode, wondering what creatures watched their passage.

THE MILES PASSED as the sun moved from one horizon to the other. They stopped for the night in a thicket, and Rieker made a grassy bed for them, much like a deer would create. The air turned cooler at night and this time, Tiki put her bedroll close to Rieker's, knowing she would be grateful for the warmth of his body.

IT WAS PAST noon the next day when they reached their destination. They left the main trail a good distance from the village, hoping to avoid the hobgoblins they'd met before. When they'd reached the far side of the lake, Rieker steered Aeveen toward the town. The horse walked with her ears pricked forward, prancing in place at times, as they approached the vacant town.

"Do you see anyone...or maybe I should say *anything* out of place?"

Tiki searched the rocky ridges that rimmed the water's edge, but all was still. Even the surface of the lake was undisturbed by wind today, making the reflections of the village spires that much clearer. She surveyed the scene, looking for anything out of place, trying to pinpoint what felt off about this place.

"That's what's wrong." She pointed. "Look at the water—can you see that reflection of the tall tower off by itself? There toward the right side?"

"The white one?"

"*Exactly,*" Tiki said excitedly. "There's no corresponding building in the village to make that reflection. To create a reflection there—" she pointed at the water— "the building would have to be over there—on that side of the lake."

Rieker squinted in the direction she indicated. "There's nothing but forest over there."

Tiki gazed toward the cliffs of the opposite shore. "Nothing we can see. I wonder if the glamour Donegal created hides the White Tower but doesn't conceal the *reflection* of the tower in the lake?"

Rieker nudged Aeveen forward. "Let's get closer. Maybe there's something that will give us a clue."

They wound through the forest, the ground sloping upward, until they were close to the ridge they'd seen from the village.

"What do you think?" Rieker asked. "Can you see anything?"

Tiki shook her head, then realized Rieker couldn't see her sitting behind him. "I guess my ability to see through glamours only works with people—and even then, I only recognize their eyes and voice." Tiki's shoulders sagged. "I don't know how to find it. Maybe it's not here at all."

"I have one idea." Rieker reached into a pocket stitched into the side of the saddle and pulled out something flat.

Tiki peered around his shoulder. "What's that?"

Rieker opened his fingers. Resting on his palm was a triangular shard of glass.

"William, "Tiki breathed, "you're brilliant."

"I 'borrowed' it from Larkin." He grinned at her over his shoulder. "Now, if we hold this up and align it just right..." he nudged Aeveen around so they faced the water then lifted the mirror so it reflected the forest over his shoulder. "And get in the right position..." he made a clicking noise with his mouth and continued to nudge Aeveen with his knees, inching the horse around. A building flashed into view on the shard of glass and just as quickly disappeared.

"There! Did you see that?"

"Yes," Tiki said excitedly, "I saw it. It's right there!"

Rieker carefully maneuvered the horse until the tower was steadily reflected in the magical mirror.

Tiki squinted at the image. "It's not very large and it's awfully close to the edge of the cliff. How many prisoners do you think Donegal keeps in there?"

"I don't know," Rieker said. "I only see one window at the very top—can you see it?"

Tiki examined the tower through the mirror. "Yes. It has bars. Where do you suppose the door might be?"

"It must be on the other side."

It took almost thirty minutes to work their way around the entire tower, viewing it through the sliver of mirror. As they came full circle to their starting point, no entrance to the tower had become evident.

"There's got to be a way in," Tiki said, after they'd dismounted and stretched their legs. She stared at the clearing that she knew the tower occupied but there was nothing to be seen. "Do you think the door is glamoured within the glamour so no one can see it?"

Rieker was silently examining the tower through the mirror again. "That sounds too complicated, even for Donegal." He tilted the shard and stared at the reflected image. "There's got to be a way in."

"And out," Tiki added.

"You've returned."

They both jumped at the sound of the scratchy voice. Tiki turned to find the hobgoblin leader they'd spoken to before, standing in the forest not ten feet away. His clothing blended with the branches and leaves, as did his weathered skin. Only his red stocking cap made him visible. This time he appeared to be alone.

"Hello." Rieker said, nodding at the little man. "Nice to see you again."

The goblin stopped a good distance from them. His bow was slung over his shoulder and he appeared to be holding a crock. "Majesty." He tucked his head in a bow.

Tiki nodded. "Hello." The goblin stepped closer, his passage through the underbrush silent. He looked at Rieker with a curious expression. "What was that in your hand?"

Rieker feigned innocence. "I'm not sure what you're talking about."

The goblin carefully set the crock on a nearby stump. "Since I've found you in almost the same area for a second time, I assume you're not lost, but looking for something?"

There was a long silence.

"Is there something here to be found?" Tiki asked.

The hobgoblin rubbed his long pointed chin with his claw-like fingers. "Now, that's a tricky question in these parts."

"The answer seems simple enough to me," Tiki replied.

"That might be because you don't live here in the wood with us now, do you, Majesty? No disrespect intended," he added hastily.

"None taken. What do you mean? Are there troubles here?"

"There's troubles everywhere. Especially since Eridanus was murdered. Things got worse with O'Riagáin. People are starving, don't know who to trust—whispers of war getting louder all the time." He swept his arms toward the trees around him. "We do our best to survive but things have changed. People die—or their families disappear—if we don't do as we're asked. We used to answer to a Seelie king but now we walk a fine line down the middle and answer to the king of survival, if you understand my meaning."

Tiki kept her face blank. Everywhere in this world seemed to be on the brink of chaos. An assassin who hunted in both worlds, a homeless encampment of starving faeries, not enough food to go around and forest creatures who answered to whichever king would keep them safe. Donegal's evil influence had infected every corner of this world. Who was going to set it right? The Macanna were powerful, but they needed a leader to guide them. Could she trust Larkin to care for someone besides herself?

For the first time a new thought struck her: would her father—Finn—want her to entrust the survival of this world to a faerie from whom he and Eridanus chose to hide the truth?

"What's in your crock?" Rieker asked, motioning to the stone container balanced on the stump. "Are you feeding someone?"

The hobgoblin hesitated.

"Is it the prisoner?"

Tiki tried to identify the emotions that flashed across the goblin's ugly face: Relief? Fear?

"Once a day."

Rieker didn't seemed surprised by his answer. "Are there others?"

"No, he's the only one." The goblin glanced around, as if to make sure they were alone. He leaned toward Rieker and lowered his voice. "When I saw you riding his horse, I didn't know if you'd brought trouble to him. We were told to watch you, and keep you from harm if you found the Redcaps, but I knew nothing beyond that."

Tiki's breath caught in her throat. "Who told you to watch us?"

The little man's squinty eyes widened. "I swore not to reveal that information, Majesty."

Tiki ground her teeth together and took a step toward the goblin. Her words came out in a growl. *"I am the queen of the..."*

"It was Larkin," he said hurriedly. "Said she thought you might seek out the Redcaps and to make sure you didn't come to any harm." He took a step back and bowed his head. "She didn't mention it was the queen we were to protect."

Tiki's anger dissolved as quickly as it had appeared. Larkin had known they were going to go to the border to find the Redcaps. Instead of trying to stop them, she'd secretly had someone protect them?

"Where is the entrance to the tower?" Rieker asked.

"That I don't know."

"How'd you find him?"

The hobgoblin's face twisted in a pained expression. "I could hear them torturing him. Sound travels easily through the forest."

"Torture?" Tiki said faintly, her stomach doing a slow roll.

Rieker sucked in his breath in with a low hiss as the goblin continued.

"I followed his screams to this spot. After Donegal and his men left, I waited, knowing he'd need help."

"You're very brave to risk your own life to help him," Tiki said. "Do you know Dain?"

The hobgoblin nodded. "He traveled through the Wood often on his white horse. Always made time to visit with us." He motioned to Rieker. "It's obvious you're brothers, though he never spoke of you." His face lit up. "Sometimes he brought us seeds from the gardens around the palace to replant our crops.

Rieker turned and gazed up at the seemingly empty sky. "So he must be alone up there. How do you know where he's being held? Can you see the tower?"

"No sir. But I know where to come and I can see the rope when he throws it down."

"How did he get a rope?"

"I threaded an arrow through one end and shot it up to him." The hobgoblin propped his hands on his hips and puffed out his barrel chest. "Took a few tries, but we're the best shots in the Wychwood."

"You proved that with the Redcaps" Rieker said, admiration rich in his voice. "How does he know when you're here?"

"We used a signal to let the other know when we were in the area. It's the cry of a raven."

"Show us," Tiki commanded.

The goblin hesitated. "If we're caught…"

At that moment Aeveen gave a loud whinny. A heartbeat later a whistle split the air. Tiki and Rieker jerked their heads skyward toward the source of the noise, as the horse snorted and stamped her feet.

"Dain!" Tiki shouted.

"Shhhhh! Majesty." The hobgoblin held out his hands in warning, a panicked look on his face. "This forest has ears. You put all of our lives at risk."

Rieker pulled out the sliver of mirror and held it up so the shard reflected the tower. At the very top a pale face gazed out through the barred window.

"Tiki look." Rieker held the mirror so she could see. "It's him." His voice wavered with uncharacteristic emotion. "He's alive."

Chapter Thirty-Six

T iki and Rieker listened carefully as the goblin imitated the *caw caw* of the raven, then watched as he exchanged the full crock of food for an empty one. The only part of the tower visible during the entire transaction was the rope that dangled from what appeared to be thin air.

"Donegal left him to starve," the hobgoblin said.

Tiki didn't meet the little man's eyes. What would he think if he knew Donegal didn't intend to let Dain starve to death—that the Winter King had a more gruesome plan to end his prisoner's life.

"We need to find some way to write him a message," Tiki said in a low voice to Rieker.

"He's seen us now. He knows we're here. What we need to do is find the way in, so we can get him out." Using the mirror, Rieker walked toward the tower until he stood at the very base. He pulled a machete from his belt and notched a nearby branch. "Let's mark the perimeter." They worked their way around the base of the tower, drawing what amounted to an invisible line to define the shape and location of the tower.

"Do Donegal's men ever check on the prisoner?" Rieker asked the goblin, who followed at a safe distance, watching curiously.

"They'll be back, eventually," the goblin said slowly. "To torture him again, no doubt. It's whispered that they've put the mask on him." The hobgoblin slung the empty crock over his shoulder and threaded an arrow through the bow he now held.

"What mask?"

"The mask of the Seven Year King." His small eyes looked sad. "If they have, he's doomed. The mask can't be removed until he's been sacrificed."

"No," Tiki cried.

Rieker ran a hand through his hair, frustration evident in the frown that twisted his features. "Unless we can figure out how to get him out of this prison and away from Donegal."

The hobgoblin measured Rieker. "You're braver than most to even think to try. They say that prisoners in the White Tower are held there by the Winter King's magic. No one can release him but Donegal, himself."

Tiki spoke up. "Larkin was a prisoner here last winter. She escaped."

The hobgoblin's expression shifted. "She's the only one." He gave a slow nod. "It was a terrible time here in the Wood. Donegal's anger at her departure destroyed part of the forest—burned it to the ground. Much of it was the land where we grew our crops." He took a step back. "I don't know how Larkin escaped, but she is well known in both Courts. Only the most powerful faeries in our world can conjure the kind of magic that would compete with that of a king's." The goblin edged further back into the trees. "I shouldn't linger."

"Before you leave, can you tell us the name you go by?" Tiki asked.

"You can call me Gestle, Majesty."

"We won't forget your help, Gestle—or your need. We will work together to build a better life for all here in the Wychwood."

"Your words are the first spark of hope we've had in a long time. I will keep them close to my heart and share them with my brethren." The goblin bowed and in a blink disappeared into the forest.

THE HOURS CREPT by as Tiki and Rieker struggled to find a way into the tower. All the while, her guilt at losing her temper with Larkin built, like a cough in her chest, until she feared it might choke her. Why had she become so furious with the faerie at a time when they needed her most? But even as Tiki worried, part of her knew exactly why she'd taken the action she had. Someone had to protect Clara and her family from Larkin's manipulations. And somewhere in the back of her mind, a voice spoke in the quietest of whispers that someone had to care for the world of Faerie. For the sake of Dain's rescue should she apologize to the faerie upon their return? The idea made Tiki's stomach roil, yet, if she could help save Rieker's brother...

DARKNESS FELL AND they were no further in their search for an entrance to the tower than when they'd arrived. The air had cooled and Tiki shivered as Rieker walked up to her, having walked the perimeter, yet again.

"I don't know what to do, Teek," he said. He propped his hands on his hips and exhaled, his head tipped back to stare up at the sky, turning dark with the onset of night. "I don't know how to get in." Bushes rustled nearby as some creature made its way through the wood.

Tiki hesitated to speak. She felt the same frustration as Rieker, to be so close, yet unable to reach Dain—to help him—it was enough to make her pull her hair in frustration. Yet, every minute they stayed, exposed in the open as they were, in the vicinity of Donegal's secret prison, they put themselves at greater risk—especially at night.

"Do you think we should come back another day—now that we know where he is? It's still months until Samhain. There would be no reason for Donegal to move him before the end of October."

Rieker closed his eyes and hung his head. "Yes, that makes sense, but my gut tells me we don't have that much time."

"I know." Tiki stepped closer and rubbed Rieker's arm. "It's so frustrating not to be able to reach him. But at least we know he's alive. We know where he is, and maybe most important—he knows we're close and trying to help him."

SCOUTS MET THEM halfway back to the Palace. Four of the Macanna surrounded Aeveen to escort them back while one returned at a faster pace to inform Callan that Tiki had been found.

"Majesty." Callan swept a brown felt hat with a single feather from his head as he bowed low to Tiki as she and Rieker climbed the back steps into the Palace. "We have been looking everywhere for your Highness."

"Thank you, Callan," Tiki said, wishing there was some way she could dismiss the man from feeling the need to protect her all the time. "I'm fine, as you can see. No need to worry.

Besides—" Tiki spoke over her shoulder as she walked past him and entered the Palace— "I thought you were keeping track of Larkin now."

Callan straightened, his hat gripped with both hands. "Yes, Majesty, about that..."

Tiki stopped. "What about that?"

The man straightened his muscled shoulders and raised his chin. "I am bound to protect *you*, Majesty, so I delegated the responsibility to several of my men to... *observe*—" he said the word delicately— "Lady Larkin, as you've asked. However..." a red flush crept up his neck and burned his cheeks, "she has disappeared."

"IT WAS STUPID of me to ask the Macanna to guard Larkin," Tiki snapped, as she paced back and forth in one of an opulent set of rooms that were marked as the queen's chambers. Tall, multi-branched candelabras lined the walls, each holding a multitude of thick white candles that shivered with flame, like some kind of fiery trees. Their light reflected off the walls encrusted with gold-filigree, making the room seem to shimmer with magic.

"They've been following her for years—why did I think they'd change their allegiance just because I asked?" Tiki crossed her arms and paced the other direction, the train of her royal blue gown *shushing* quietly behind her. "Daft, daft, daft. Where do you think she's gone?"

Rieker sat in a beautifully carved chair, the seat and back covered in a rich brocade of greens and browns, shot through with glittering threads of gold. He leaned back, his head propped against his hand as he watched Tiki pace, his gaze distant.

"It's impossible to say, Teek, and useless for us to try. All I know is that it's up to us to save Dain."

Chapter Thirty-Seven

Over the ensuing weeks, Tiki and Rieker went back and forth between the Otherworld and London, trying to juggle all things. They returned to the White Tower on numerous occasions without being able to find a way in. They called out the raven signal each time, to let Dain know they were trying, and a shadowed face would appear behind the bars at the very top of the cylindrical tower. But they could hear no sound, and there were times when Tiki felt like they were trying to free a ghost.

Larkin's whereabouts remained elusive, though, thankfully, Clara and the others had not seen her in London. If the Macanna knew of the faerie's whereabouts, they didn't reveal her secrets.

Tiki requested that the kitchens set out tables of food for the faeries in need on a regular basis, even if they only had table scraps to share. "Something is better than nothing."

As July came to a close, Tiki celebrated her seventeenth birthday in London. She and Rieker, Clara, Toots, Fiona and Shamus all went to Hyde Park, as the weather was sunny and warm. Mrs. Bosworth packed a picnic lunch for them and they splashed in the water and sailed miniature boats on the Serpentine. Clara and Fiona made daisy-chain crowns and decided Tiki could be queen, but as much as she wanted to forget about the Otherworld, the flower crown just reminded her of the troubles there. Dain was constantly on her mind, as was Gestle, Ailléna, the homeless faeries, Larkin,

Donegal and the *liche*. Torn between two worlds, there didn't seem to be peace in either of them for her now.

SUMMER FADED TO Fall and Fiona slowly came back to life, though the sparkle was gone from her eyes and she lacked the enthusiasm she used to have. The sense of urgency to free Dain reached a fever pitch as frost began to breathe its icy breath over both worlds. Time was running out.

"THERE HAVE BEEN more sightings of Donegal's troops gathering," Rieker said one morning as Tiki returned from a meeting with the lords and ladies in the High Chamber. He'd been waiting outside the door for her to exit and walked beside her down the corridor to the Great Hall. "We've got to do *something* soon or Dain won't survive."

"I know." Tiki slid her hands into the fur muff that was stitched onto the front of her dress. The air had turned unseasonably cool and the lofty hallways and grand rooms of the Palace were chilly. Or perhaps the chill came from the fear that seemed to constantly ride her shoulders as each day brought her closer to the time when the Winter King would attack in his pursuit to gain control of Faerie. "The Court doesn't think Donegal will attack until Samhain has passed but I agree with you, he won't do what we expect of him. Plus—" she lowered her voice— "he knows I'm inexperienced. I'm sure he'll use that to his advantage."

They entered the Great Hall and the Jester greeted them with his usual fanfare, bowing low to both of them before striking a pose, forcing them to stop. He was one of the few who acknowledged Rieker's existence.

With a dramatic flair, the Court Jester breathed flame into his cupped hands, only to rub them together and release a snow-white dove, which flapped up to the highest reaches of the arched ceiling and disappeared.

"Have you heard the news, Majesty?" The Jester pranced by Tiki's side.

Tiki only half-listened as she walked up the steps to her throne. She rarely sat on the Dragon Throne, preferring instead to mingle, but today she was tired. They'd visited the White Tower yet again and the ride back had been long and exhausting. A cough had started in her chest and she had a terrible headache. What she really wanted was to be left alone, or, better yet—go home to London and read a story with Clara, Toots and Fiona. But she rarely got what she wanted anymore.

"Where is the second chair I requested?" she asked the guards who stood at attention. Days ago she'd asked that a chair be positioned next to her throne for Rieker to sit in, but her request continued to be ignored.

"Teek, it doesn't matter," Rieker said in a low voice, positioning himself next to her right arm. "Let it go."

The Jester leaned close. "The Lady Larkin has returned to Court," he whispered. "They say she has news of Donegal's army." He skipped away before Tiki could question him further and in a blink he was at the other end of the Great Hall.

She turned to Rieker. "Did you know Larkin had returned?"

"No," Rieker said, "but we both knew she wouldn't be able to stay gone for long. I wonder if she learned anything of Dain."

In the distance, the notes of the Jester's flute floated on the air. The familiar melody reminded Tiki of the words he had spouted some months ago. *'Falsehood wears a mask that is concealed but from those who seek the hidden way.'* Though she'd mulled the words over many times, she'd never been able to discern if they were wit or wisdom. Could there be meaning hidden within his mutterings?

Tiki repeated his words in her head. A mask—Gestle had said that Dain had been forced to wear a mask—

"Falsehood," Tiki murmured. Dain had been spying in the UnSeelie Court as Sean when he was caught—was that the falsehood the Fool had meant?

"What did you say?" Rieker asked, leaning closer.

Across the room, the Jester looked at Tiki over his shoulder. She could hear his voice as clearly as if he had whispered in her ear: *'Fear not the water...'* He gave her a cocky salute then started to dance an Irish jig. She jumped to her feet and grabbed Rieker's arm.

"Come with me."

She hurried out of the Great Hall as fast as she could without causing a scene, down the corridor and out the side door that Dain had revealed to her.

"Tiki—what's going on?" Rieker looked at her as if she'd lost her mind.

She pulled him through the gardens to a rocky outcropping at the very edge of the Tor so no one could possibly overhear their conversation. "I know how to get to Dain."

"You do?" He put his hand on her forehead. "How did you suddenly arrive at this miraculous answer?"

Tiki slapped his hand away. "I don't have a fever. It was the Jester, of course. He gave me a clue months ago. There's a secret passageway into the Tower."

Rieker's expression shifted to a thoughtful frown. "Where might the entrance to this secret passageway lie?"

"'Fear not the water, for it only appears to block our way.'" Tiki raised her eyebrows at him. When he continued to stare at her with a blank expression, she said in a slightly exasperated tone, "The passage is beneath the surface of the lake."

IT WAS HARDER to sneak away now that Donegal's threats had multiplied. Callan took his job seriously and seemed determined not to let Tiki elude him one more time. In the end, Tiki decided to invite the man to come with them, with the condition he be the only one who would accompany them.

"You take dangerous risks, Majesty." Callan protested after she'd made the proposal to him. "If we're attacked I might not be able to protect you alone."

"Rieker will be with us and I know how to use a knife." Tiki gave him a steely gaze. "It will have to be enough."

THEY SET OUT at mid-day. Neither she nor Rieker were willing to wait. Their ride through the Wychwood was uneventful, possibly due to the size and fierceness of the Macanna who accompanied them. Callan had not asked where they were going and Tiki hadn't yet informed him. The less he knew, the less he would be tempted to dissuade her.

DARKESS WAS SETTLING, on the second day, casting shadowy fingers through the trees, as they approached the far end of the lake. A frown settled across Callan's brow when they came in sight of the deserted village.

"We should not be here," he said in a low voice. "There's a reason this village is empty."

Like usual, Tiki rode behind Rieker and they both turned to look at the other man.

"Why's that?" Rieker asked.

"It's haunted."

"By what?"

"Many centuries ago this spot was home to a coven of witches. They had lived in these woods for almost as many centuries as the fey, celebrating Samhain, as we do, but for different reasons.

It is said three witches were dancing and chanting around a bonfire when the Wild Hunt rode through this part of the forest one Samhain. The legend says the witches were so outraged at being interrupted that they each pulled a rider down from their horse and turned them to stone." Callan pointed in the distance. "There they still stand to this day—frozen in time."

At the end of the road the three stones they'd seen before towered in the grassy area.

"You think those stones are faeries?" Tiki asked doubtfully.

"They aren't the first to be turned to stone. The Rollright Stones, on the border of the Wychwood, were once a king and his knights. They were foolish enough to bargain with a witch and paid the price."

"But this village is deserted," Rieker said. "What happened to the witches?"

"The UnSeelie king took his revenge in a different way—he used his magic to turn the three witches into trees: the thorny plum, the oak and the elder. They are trapped inside. That way he could torture them until the end of time."

"The Tree Dryads," Tiki whispered. She and Dain had encountered them during their trek to London. "I was told they were a deadly combination."

Callan nodded. "That they are, even after all this time. Beware if you see the three together, for they still roam these woods, seeking the fey who turned them into trees. The only way they can regain their original form is for someone to take their place within their woody trunk—thus, they try to lure passersby into their arms."

He gestured toward the stone buildings. "The other witches left, for fear they would be doomed to life as a dryad, but they cursed this place before they departed. None but those who cast the darkest magic would seek sanctuary here now."

THEY CONTINUED PAST the vacated town around to the cliffs where the White Tower was secreted. The cool air chilled Tiki and she fought to suppress the hacking cough that rose from her chest.

"This is the spot," Rieker said as he pulled Aeveen to a stop. He threw a leg over the horse's neck and jumped to the ground, then assisted Tiki. He pulled her cloak tighter around her neck and his fingers lingered. "You don't sound good. I'm not sure you should be here."

She put her hand over his, her fingers cold against the warmth of his skin. "This is exactly where I should be."

Callan remained on his horse, surveying the area. "Majesty," he finally ventured, "why *are* we here?"

Rieker pulled the mirror shard from his vest and stepped over toward the guard. "Because there is a prison here." He held the mirror up so Callan could see the tower in the reflection. "And we need to free the prisoner."

The soldier was silent for a long moment as he gazed into the mirror. "Only powerful dark magic can conceal an entire building," Callan said in a heavy voice. "It's the Winter King's doing, isn't it?"

"We think we know the way in." Tiki walked to the edge of the crag and looked down. The cliff was made of rough gray stone that offered a multitude of steps and handholds down the face of the precipice. "We need you to stand guard while we investigate."

Chapter Thirty-Eight

"**C**limb down the face of that cliff? You can't be serious." In a blink, Callan was off his horse and next to Tiki, ready to stop her from climbing over the edge. "With all due respect, Majesty, I can't allow you to do it."

Tiki didn't raise her voice as she stepped past him. "Callan, I command you to step away from me and remain with the horses." She gave him a sweet smile as she began to descend on a narrow trail. "I'm sorry, but you made me do it."

"But—" the muscular faerie's mouth dropped open in dismay. He stood there as if Tiki had frozen him in place like one of the standing stones.

"Sorry, old chap." Rieker clapped the man on the shoulder as he walked past. "I could've told you not to argue with her, though."

The narrow path was barely wide enough to traverse and Tiki clung to the jagged rocks as she moved lower down the face of the cliff.

"I think I see an entrance to a cave over there—"Tiki pointed— "that's only partially submerged. Do you see it?"

"Yes." Rieker followed more slowly, gingerly placing his larger feet on the slippery trail while gripping the rocks. "And it's close to where the tower sits on the cliff." They were dressed, once again, in the fabric of the forest: tight bark colored pants and dappled green jackets, allowing Tiki to move more freely than if she wore a gown.

Her boots were of the softest leather that allowed her toes to grip the little shelves of rock to secure her purchase to the cliff face.

The bluff was about twenty feet high and it didn't take long to reach the opening that Tiki had seen from above. She gripped a jutting rock tight with her hand and leaned out over the water to peer into the depths below.

"I think we'll have to drop into the water and swim in—what do you think?"

"I think you should let me go first and see what's down there." Rieker had already stripped off his jacket and dropped it at his feet. The well-defined muscles of his chest and stomach flexed as he kicked off his shoes. Tiki was surprised to see the ring of the truce hanging on a gold chain around his neck.

Rieker seemed immune to the cold breeze that came off the lake, though Tiki shivered and fought the urge to cough again. He dove neatly off the rocks and sliced into the water, barely making a splash.

"I didn't know you were part selkie." Tiki called down to him when he surfaced.

He flicked his hair out of his face and smiled. "I can't tell you all of my secrets now, can I?" His voice echoed off the rocks as he dove underwater and disappeared into the cliff.

Tiki said a silent prayer as she tugged her jacket tighter across her chest. How she hated to wait here helplessly. She'd barely finished the thought when she kicked off her own shoes and jumped in the water after Rieker. There was no reason he had to go alone. He might need her in there.

Though she had done some swimming in the lakes around London while growing up, she wasn't the best swimmer and panic rose in her chest at being in the cold, dark water. She kicked her feet as fast as she could and flailed at the water, trying to catch up to Rieker, sure she was going to drown. Her head went under once and she came up sputtering. There was too much water in her mouth to yell for help, and she began coughing and choking.

A firm hand gripped her arm and easily lifted her head above the water, steadying her.

"Take a deep breath and calm down," Rieker said. "Because I want you to be able to clearly explain what in *bloody hell* you're doing in the water."

Rieker's calm voice immediately soothed her fears, not to mention the seemingly effortless way he managed to support her in the water. Tiki gave him a wobbly smile, clenching her teeth together to stop them from chattering.

"I wanted to come, too."

He stared at her for a moment, an inscrutable look on his face, then he gave a small shake of his head. "I should've known. Can you swim?"

"Y..yes." Tiki said in a small voice. "I just needed to get used to the water."

"I'm going to take my hand away—" Rieker slowly let go of her arm— "but I'm right here if you need me, all right?" Tiki gave a shaky nod. "The worst thing you can do is panic. Now take small strokes with your hands like this—" he demonstrated a sweeping motion with his arms— "and kick your legs. There you go."

"I..I'm f..fine now," Tiki said. "I c..can d..do it."

Rieker frowned but didn't comment further. "Follow me."

A SURPRISING AMOUNT of light filtered in from the lake allowing them to navigate through the dim shadows of the cave. Tiki began to warm up as she swam, and became more relaxed in the water. Rieker led the way deeper inside the cliff, stopping and treading water as he waited for her to catch up.

"By my calculations, we should be just about under the Tower here." He turned a circle, squinting to see through the dim light. "Do you see any way we could gain entrance?"

Tiki swam closer to the rock wall, the little bit of light that reflected off the surface and the rocks, made it difficult to tell where one stopped and the other started. She reached out and blindly felt along the rock wall. After a few minutes she felt an indent within the face of the stone.

"Here," she called over her shoulder. "I think these are stairs."

They pulled themselves out, bracing their wet hands against the walls to steady themselves from slipping back into the water.

"You're right," Rieker said. The steps, hewn from the rock, were crude and small, but still effective. They wound up into the darkness and disappeared into the very cliff itself.

Tiki gazed up into the darkness. "Do you think this is it?" she whispered.

"Only one way to find out."

THE STEPS TWISTED upward like a spiral staircase, each circle a bit smaller than the last. The stairway was completely dark, unlit by any kind of light. The further up they went—the darker it got. Tiki moved by touch—one hand on each wall to balance herself.

Her breath was coming in short gasps when Rieker finally stopped. "It's a door," he whispered back to her. Tiki jumped in surprise when he pounded with both fists on the wooden panels.

"Dain!" he shouted. "Are you in there?"

"Yes!" Came the muffled reply. "But the door is locked."

Rieker felt around until he found the handle, then gave it a sharp tug, but the door held firm against the strength of a deadbolt. He ran his hands up the jamb until he located the locking mechanism and yanked the metal bar free. This time when he turned the handle the door opened with a rusty squeak.

Before them, the fading light of the day seeped through a barred window to illuminate a small room. Rieker moved to enter the room but jerked to a stop so suddenly that Tiki ran into his back.

"What are you—" but her words died on her tongue as she peered around Rieker's shoulders. Before them stood a young man, who at first glance appeared to be wearing a golden eye mask such as one might wear to a masked ball. Upon closer inspection, it became evident that the bottom portion of his face—the part that was exposed beneath the eye mask—was also a mask—a white face with golden lips. Around the porcelain face, great brown feathers jutted, like some wild ceremonial headdress. The Jester's words echoed in Tiki's ears. *Falsehood wears a mask...* "Dain?" she whispered.

"Yes, it's me," said his familiar voice. He started to reach for her hands, then seemed to think better of it and stepped back. There was a long pause and Tiki thought she heard him say, "I can't believe you came for me."

She turned her ear toward him. "I'm sorry—what?"

Muffled by the mask, it sounded like Dain cleared his throat. "I can't remove the mask—it's held on by magic."

It was a relief to hear his voice, but the porcelain facade made Tiki uncomfortable. She couldn't see his eyes through the sockets, giving her the eerie sensation there was no one behind the frozen face, but at the same time, she got the feeling he was staring at her with great intensity.

"Surely, there must be a way to get it off." She looked to Rieker for ideas, glad to turn away from his unsettling countenance.

"It's the least of our worries right now," Rieker said in a gruff voice. "Getting out of here is what we need to focus on."

A rueful chuckle came from behind the mask. "The mask comes off at Samhain—when I'm dead."

"Don't talk like that," Tiki said. She could see how thin he was. His clothes, which appeared to be the same garments he'd been wearing when she'd seen him tethered behind the throne in the Palace of Mirrors, hung on his frame. Brownish-red splotches covered the once-white shirt and Tiki had a terrible suspicion the marks were dried blood. Ghastly purple bruises covered his hands and Tiki wondered what they'd done to him.

Rieker stepped closer and motioned to the mask. "May I?"

"Be my guest." Dain put his hands behind his back as Rieker ran his fingers over the edge of the porcelain face searching for a release. No ribbons could be seen in the back nor was there any sort of connection at all. The mask was attached firmly to Dain's face as though it had grown there.

"Can you see to walk?" Rieker asked.

"I can manage."

"Then, let's go. We'll figure out a way to get the mask off later." Rieker reached for Tiki's hand and led the way out the door. "There's a winding staircase and then we actually have to swim for it," he said over his shoulder. "You can swim, can't you?"

A muffled grunt came from behind them followed by a loud *thud*. Rieker ran back up the steps as Dain picked himself off the floor.

"What happened?"

"When I tried to go through the doorway, it was as if I walked into a wall. It knocked me off my feet." Dain approached the doorway with his hands outstretched. "Can you see anything?"

"No, there's nothing," Rieker said, waving his hands through the open portal. On the other side, Dain stopped at the doorway and tried to reach through, but his palms appeared to be pressed against an invisible wall.

"It would appear that I'm locked in," he finally said. "There must be an enchantment around the room that won't allow me to leave."

Chapter Thirty-Nine

The moon hung high in the night sky by the time Tiki and Rieker accepted the fact that Dain could not exit from the room in which Donegal had imprisoned him.

"We'll figure out something." Tiki tried to project confidence, but inside she wanted to cry. How could they possibly save Dain if they couldn't even get him out of this room? A spasm of coughing hit her until she doubled over.

"Have you talked to Larkin?" Dain asked in a voice that was too casual. "She might have some ideas."

"Yes," Rieker replied. "We're working with Larkin to figure out the best way to free you. How often does Donegal have someone check on you?"

Dain gave a half-laugh. "He doesn't. He tried to beat information out of me and when I didn't give him what he wanted, he left me here to starve. If it hadn't been for a friend who lives in the Wychwood, I would probably already be dead.

"Gestle showed us your system. We can bring food too."

Dain turned his sightless eyes toward Tiki. "That's nice of you, but I'm sure as queen you have better things to occupy your time."

"But I don't," Rieker said. "As a half-breed, this is probably the most important task I'll be assigned."

Dain swung his head toward Rieker. "Half-breed?"

"Apparently, the members of the Seelie court can tell by looking at me that I have mortal blood as well as faerie blood. The common opinion seems to be that I'm not good enough to wipe the queen's boots."

Dain tilted his head, the feathers surrounding the mask shimmying with the movement. "I see."

Tiki had a hard time looking at the empty, black eyes of the mask. It was as if Dain was some strange, unseeing creature, and she found herself staring at the stone floor to avoid the unnatural quality of his masked face.

"Tell me, what news do you have of the Courts?" Dain asked. Tiki told him of their successful search for the Cup of Plenty, only to find they were too late to save Johnny.

"You actually found the Cup?" Amazement was rich in Dain's voice. "The Tara Stone and the Cup of Plenty? You've found two of the Four Treasures within months of each other—it's almost as if someone wanted you to find them."

"Yes, Larkin mentioned that too," Tiki said. "But what are the Four Treasures? What do they do?"

Dain chuckled. "Imagine, a Seelie queen who doesn't know what the Four Treasures are—now, that's ironic."

"Go on, then," Tiki said with a hint of annoyance. "Enlighten us."

"Certainly, Majesty." Dain started to give a mock bow then stopped as if he were in pain and slowly straightened. "The Four Treasures of Faerie date back to the earliest days of the Otherworld, when only the Seelie Court ruled the land. The Treasures are said to be the most powerful magical objects that exist in our world, though even to this day, their location and ownership have been shrouded in mystery. The stories say the Four Treasures will appear—or be found—when Faerie is in greatest need. Those who wield the treasures will have the power to rule the Otherworld and join the Courts together as one. A rebirth, if you will."

"What could possibly be that powerful?" Rieker asked.

"The first treasure was the *Cloch na Teamhrach*, the Stone of Tara, whose roar would mark a true high queen or king." He held his hand out toward Tiki. "A necessary first step to identify who would lead us to our new world order."

"Don't point at me," Tiki said, giving Rieker an alarmed look. "I'm the least qualified to lead."

"The second was *Corn na bhFuíoll*—the Cup of Plenty—said to offer the four essences of life: healing, wisdom, inspiration and sustenance to those in need."

Tiki frowned. "Sustenance?"

"The third is the Ring of *Ériu*, named after Ireland, herself—a secret-keeper of kings and queens—whose own location is a secret." He motioned at the gold chain that hung around Rieker's neck, the ring at its end balanced against his bare, muscled chest. "I've never heard a description of the ring, but who knows? It could be as simple as the one you wear, though I'd wager to say the ring of *Ériu* hasn't seen the light of day for many a century." Dain shrugged. "For all we know, the ring could already be lost forever."

Tiki and Rieker exchanged a glance.

"And the fourth?" Rieker asked.

"Ah, the mysterious fourth treasure." Dain lifted his palms. "I cannot tell you what it is. The legends are so old they've practically become myth over time. There are a variety of items whispered to be the fourth treasure—swords and spears, to name a few, but I don't think anyone knows for sure, anymore. The paradox of the Treasures is that you must possess the first three to find the fourth."

"What do you mean?" Tiki asked.

Dain paced to the window and stared out past the iron bars. "The secret of the fourth is held within the third—the ring—but you must use the wisdom and inspiration of the second—the cup—to procure the secret from the ring, and only a king or queen, named by the first—the stone—may retrieve the information. And so it remains—only those in possession of the first three Treasures can unlock the mystery surrounding the fourth. Many millenia have passed since the stone last roared, so the promise of the Four Treasures has faded with time."

Dain turned from the barred window where the sky outside had darkened, filling the room with shadows. The blank eyes of his mask stared at Tiki in an unnerving fashion. "Since the Stone has roared for you, Tara, perhaps you are the seeker who shall reunite all of Faerie."

IT WAS ALL but impossible to leave Dain, but both Tiki and Rieker knew they couldn't continue to risk their own safety by staying up in the Tower any longer. Assuring him they would continue to work to release him, as well as to send more food, they descended back down the stairs into darkness.

The swim out was challenging, as night had fallen and there was little light to guide them as they swam. Fragmented pieces of moonlight that danced upon the surface of the water led them to the exit of the cave. Shivering, they climbed onto the rocks, made slippery by the water dripping from their bodies, and carefully worked their way back up to the top of the cliff where Callan waited with their horses.

Tiki could see the guard pacing furiously one way, then the other, clearly distraught at being left behind and unable to protect her. A twinge of guilt twisted her stomach at his evident relief when he heard their approach.

"Majesty," he cried, running up to her and snatching his cloak from his shoulders to wrap around her shivering shoulders. "Please don't ever do that to me again. Every minute was torture, being forced to stay here with the horses like a common stable boy, when my duty is to be with you."

"I..I'm s..sorry, C..Callan," Tiki stuttered. "I..if you would a..agree not to stop me w..whenever I w..want to do something…" the rest of her sentence was lost in a spasm of coughing.

"Sit in front of me, Teek," Rieker insisted, as he helped her on Aeveen. "I can keep you warmer that way on our return."

Rieker wrapped his arms around Tiki, trying to share his own warmth, but he'd been chilled by the cool water, too, and the night air did little to warm either.

THEY RODE HALF the night before Rieker insisted they stop. By that time, Tiki was so chilled she couldn't stop shaking. She'd tried to wrap a blanket from Rieker's bed roll around her shoulders, but it had been impossible to keep it wrapped around her shoulders while they rode, so persistent was the wind at peeling it from her grip.

Rieker quickly made a fire then came to sit by Tiki's side. He wrapped her in the blanket, putting his arm around her shoulders and pulling her to lean against him. Behind them in the darkness, Callan kept watch.

"Maybe you should transport directly to the Palace. I can return with Aeveen tomorrow."

"No." Tiki's tone left no doubt she wasn't going to negotiate. "We stay together."

THEY LEFT AT dawn and continued their journey. The trek seemed to take forever and by the time they arrived at the Palace of Mirrors night was falling once again. They left Aeveen with a guard to brush down and return to the pasture. Rieker held Tiki's hand as they hurried through a side entrance, hoping to avoid being seen. They were almost to Tiki's chambers when a familiar voice stopped them.

"You return empty-handed, *again*, I see."

They both whirled around to face Larkin. She wore a gown of softest green, the color of the first leaves in spring. Her golden hair hung in a loose braid on one side, with curling wisps framing her exquisite face.

Rieker responded first. "And you've returned to the Palace, I see—with the intent to help us, I hope."

Larkin tilted her head, her eyes narrowing in a sly expression. "Yes, well, you do know how it works, William—you help me and I'll help you."

"It's not always about *you*," Tiki snapped. She was cold, wet, sick and worried—the last thing she wanted was to deal with was Larkin's political machinations. "There are others in this kingdom in desperate need. Can't you for *once* think about them?"

The change in Larkin was instantaneous. She was furious and made no effort to hide it. Her words started in a growl. "I have been risking my life, YET AGAIN, on behalf of this kingdom— of which you know so little, yet *think* you are qualified to rule—and I have important news to share. Since I no longer have a study of my own, I am happy to shout it for all to hear in this bloody hallway. THE WAR HAS STARTED. DONEGAL IS ON THE MOVE." She stabbed her finger in Tiki's direction. "YOU ARE HIS TARGET."

Her voice dropped to almost a whisper and a sneer twisted her lips, erasing her beauty. "I've told you before there are other relationships we need to discuss. I think now is the time."

"You're wrong, Larkin." Tiki replied, through clenched teeth. "Now is *not* the time, because I refuse to be intimidated by your schemes any longer. What we *will* do, is call a meeting of the Court in the High Chamber in thirty minutes. You may share what you've learned with all of us at that time and together we'll formulate a plan." Tiki slipped her hand through Rieker's arm and turned away.

"Is that so?" Larkin's voice was deadly. "Even when it involves your precious Clara?"

Tiki jerked around—but Larkin had vanished.

Chapter Forty

"**M**amie." Arthur pushed himself out of the armchair, where he sat reading by the fire, to greet the older woman. "What a pleasant surprise to see you. It's been much too long. Are you well?"

"I'm fine, dear boy, just fine." As a lady-in-waiting to Victoria since she had ascended to the throne at age eighteen, Mamie had known Arthur and Leo all of their lives and the Queen of England for over thirty-five years.

Arthur held his arm out, beckoning the older woman. "Please come in. I'll ring for tea, but I'm afraid Mother has gone to Windsor with Baby."

"I've not come to see Victoria or your sister," Macha Gallagher said. A diminutive woman, with a cloud of white hair wreathing a face soft with wrinkles, her voice was strong and her eyes snapped with intelligence. "It's you and your brother I've come for. Where's Leo?"

"Oh." Arthur stepped back in surprise. "Best to have a seat then, while I round him up. I don't know where he's got off to at the moment, but he can't be far. He's still not himself since the attack."

It was only a few minutes before Arthur returned with his younger brother.

"Mamie?" Leo entered the room, his brow drawn down in a frown. "Is everything all right?"

"Leopold." The elderly woman held her hands out to the prince. "There you are. I need your help, young man."

Leo knelt down next to her chair. "What is it?"

"Your pretty friend? The one with the mark on her wrist? Tara Dunbar?"

"Yes?"

"We need to find and warn her. She is in terrible danger."

Chapter Forty-One

"You play a dangerous game with Larkin," Rieker said quietly as they walked to the High Chamber of Lords and Ladies, half an hour later.

"I'm sick of her manipulations," Tiki retorted, but a wisp of fear burned deep inside her. Why was Larkin bringing up Clara again? The faerie had mentioned she 'knew about Clara' last April, when they'd been at Buckingham Palace and she'd wanted Tiki to go to the Otherworld with her. Another scheme, Tiki tried to tell herself, but the faerie had seemed awfully sure of herself. When it was difficult, if not impossible, for faeries to lie, did Larkin possess the ability to sidestep the truth so convincingly? Or was she speaking some form of the truth?

"Are you sure now is the time you want to introduce me to Court?"

"Yes," Tiki said. "Especially now."

The guards swept the doors open at Tiki's approach and announced her with a stamp of their staffs. Beside her, Rieker inhaled sharply as he viewed the forest-like chamber for the first time. The room was cool as though the breath of Fall hung in the air. Sunlight cast shafts of light through the trees, lighting the gold and amber leaves that carpeted the floor. Birdsong floated in the distance, more sparse today than the previous times she'd been in the room, as if the birds had flown south before an early winter.

"Thank you." Tiki nodded at both guards as she passed through the door. "I'd like another chair brought next to mine for my advisor." She paused to make eye contact with the first guard. *"Now."*

"Yes, Majesty." He bowed and hurried off to do her bidding.

"Majesty." The group murmured, as they climbed to their feet at the sight of Tiki. Larkin was seated at the far end of the table, opposite from where Tiki's chair sat.

"Thank you." Tiki inclined her head. "Please be seated." She stifled a cough and took Rieker's hand to pull him forward until he stood next to her side. "I've brought my most trusted advisor with me today." Her voice was beginning to turn hoarse and she had to strain to be heard. "Allow me to introduce William of London. He will be accompanying me to Court in the future." Tiki stood next to her chair, trying to manage a serene look, but she could no longer hold back the coughing spasm that stormed in her chest and she had to turn away as her shoulders shook with the attack.

Whispers filled the room as the men and women seated along the table discussed the news and covertly glanced at Rieker from the corners of their eyes.

"Pardon Majesty—" Fintan McPhee leaned forward so he could see both Tiki and Rieker— "is he fey?"

"We haven't inducted him into Court," another man harrumphed. "Highly irregular."

A woman's voice could be heard to say, "We don't even know who he is." The buzz in the room grew louder and more discordant.

"How do we know if we can trust him?" Someone else called out. "These are dangerous times. Spies could be anywhere."

"Silence." Larkin's voice rang through the room. She pushed herself to her feet and the talking subsided as abruptly as it had started. All heads swiveled toward her. "I will vouch for William." Her gaze swept those seated at the table. "I attended his birth, here in the Otherworld. I know his brother well. A braver Seelie does not exist."

She motioned at Rieker. "William has much to learn of our ways, but he can be trusted." She shifted her gaze to Tiki and her expression grew cold, as if the ability to trust the queen was in doubt.

Tiki hadn't noticed the Jester when they'd entered the room, but now, the gaudily-dressed man jumped to his feet from where he sat in the corner.

"A consort!" he cried with delight. "Tell us—who might William's brother be?"

A sudden suspicion filled Tiki that the Jester knew perfectly well who Rieker's brother was but was trying to divert the group's attention.

There was a long moment of silence before Larkin turned from her perusal of Tiki and answered the older man. "Dain O'Brien and our William—" she nodded at Rieker— "are twin brothers. Sons of the late Breanna and a mortal lover."

The Jester clapped his hands together in delight. "Ah, another sordid tale of decadence and star-crossed love."

"Lady Breanna of Connacht?" Fintan McPhee asked in surprise.

Beside Tiki, Rieker stiffened at this additional clue to his mother's heritage.

"The same," Larkin replied. "Dain was raised by Kieran McPhee." She raised her eyebrows and gave the man a pointed look. "Your brother, I believe."

"Yes, Mum," the man mumbled, suddenly looking unsure. "I know Dain well—but a brother? It's the first I've heard of this..."

"Shortly after his birth, William was sent to London with his father by the order of Eridanus, ruler of the Seelie Court at the time. In his infinite wisdom, Eridanus could see the advantage of William's dual citizenship, if you will." Larkin looked from one faerie to the next, a challenge in her expression. "I'm sure each of you can appreciate the benefit of having one of our own within the inner circle of Buckingham Palace?"

Gasps of disbelief filled the air. "Buckingham Palace?" Their attention swung back to Rieker, eyeing him with a new level of curiosity. "He knows the Queen of England?"

"Well, William?" Larkin raised her hand to him. "Do you know Queen Victoria?"

Rieker nodded. "I do."

"Would she trust you, do you think—" a smile played at the corners of Larkin's lips— "with the secret of our alliance? Perhaps as a liaison between our worlds?"

Rieker's lips curved in a charming smile, as beguiling as his good looks. "I believe she would."

"Yes." Larkin shifted her focus back to the group seated around the table. "I think so, too. As you know, Dain has been captured by Donegal and at this very moment is being held in the White Tower, in an unknown location, doomed to be the sacrifice of the Wild Hunt on Samhain. I think it is to our advantage to have William work with us to free Dain before that date."

Larkin stared at Rieker for a long moment and her voice softened. "Donegal has murdered the rest of William's family. We can rest assured that he seeks the Winter King's demise as much as we do." With a flourish, she sat back down. "I vote to induct him."

Heads leaned together. Conversation buzzed around the room like a swarm of a thousand bees. After a few moments, Levi MacLia, a tall, handsome faerie with brown wavy locks and aristocratic features, stood. "We agree to put it to a vote."

Tiki tensed. What if they voted no? What would she do then? She needed Rieker by her side. Could she demand that he be present?

The discussion flew back and forth across the table so fast it was hard for Tiki to follow. There was a chorus of 'ayes' and Levi spoke again, this time his tone more formal.

"William of London—"

"*Lord* William," Tiki interjected. A few eyebrows raised around the table before Levi continued.

"Lord William of London, son of the late Lady Breanna of Connacht, we issue you a formal invitation to join Queen Tara MacLochlan's Seelie Court. What say you?"

Rieker gave a short bow. "Thank you very much. I accept."

Levi nodded at Tiki. "Majesty, would you like to preside over his induction?"

Tiki blinked in surprise. She'd missed the induction for Fintan McPhee. She had no idea what the ceremony entailed. "I bow to your greater eloquence, Lord MacLia." Tiki inclined her head. "Please proceed."

The induction was swift and simple. The Jester pulled something from his vest and handed it to Levi. Everyone stood. The faerie slowly unfurled a flag that appeared to be a colorful map of silk with three symbols drawn on different sections. Tiki spied a crown, a harp and what looked like a wing before the faerie attached the flag to a standard and rested the fabric upon Rieker's left shoulder.

"With this flag, we tie you to the five corners of the Otherworld, upon which you pledge to protect and defend to your dying breath, all things Seelie and blessed." He moved the flag to Rieker's right shoulder. "You swear to guard and preserve The Plain of Sunlight and those who inhabit that space, as well as our most blessed queen whether she occupies the Plain of Sunlight, the Palace of Mirrors or any other place."

Rieker stood tall and strong. "I do."

"By your bequeath, we shall mark you as a Lord of the High Chamber and from this day forward, you shall bear the mantel of the Seelie Court."

Someone produced a cape, the same rich burgundy color as those which the other lords and ladies wore, and affixed it around Rieker's neck.

"Henceforth, you shall be known as Lord William of London, Advisor to the Queen." Applause spattered around the room and a few banged their cups against the wooden table. Almost immediately, the guard appeared with the chair Tiki had requested some thirty minutes previously.

Tiki looked around the table. "Thank you," she said. "Welcome Lord William." Clutching her skirt she finally sat. Everyone in the room followed suit.

"Now, let us begin." Tiki tipped her head in acknowledgement to Larkin. Once again the faerie had surprised her, providing critical support when Tiki needed it most, at a time when she had expected it least. "Lady Larkin has news of Donegal and his threats. Please share with Court the knowledge you've gained."

Larkin didn't look at Tiki when she spoke. "Donegal is already marching toward the Palace of Mirrors, impressing solitary fey into his ranks. He has lit a great fire in the Wychwood—to be used as a funeral pyre for our queen." Her voice was flat, unemotional. "It is his plan to murder her and claim the Seelie throne for his own." She shifted her gaze to Tiki. "Toward that end, he's been investigating our new queen and has recently learned where she's been hidden for the last seventeen years."

Tiki stiffened in her chair.

"Is it true you were in London all that time, Majesty?" Lady Beckworth, a plump woman with orange hair and bright blue lips, which matched the blue berries stuck throughout the bird's nest on her head, practically quivered with curiosity. "Hidden and unaware of your true calling?"

"She was in London—" Larkin answered before Tiki could— "waiting for the right time to return. As I was saying, Donegal has targeted the queen and we believe he has UnSeelie fey positioned outside her London residence at this time. The UnSeelies will try to lure those mortals closest to the queen into Faerie, where they will be tortured until Donegal gets what he wants."

Tiki sat forward and gripped the arms of her chair. *"What?"*

Larkin ignored Tiki's outburst. "Because the truce is still intact and being guarded, there is only one who can attack directly: the *liche*. We haven't been able to locate him but we believe Donegal has sent him to London."

"You should have told me." Tiki's chest constricted and she began to cough again, the congestion rattling deep in her lungs.

Larkin feigned innocence. "But you specifically told me to wait, *Majesty.*"

"You know that's not—" Tiki's breath rattled in her throat as she coughed, fighting to answer.

Rieker leaned close and murmured, "Are you all right? Do you need water?"

Tiki waved him off. She needed to concentrate. She needed to stop Donegal. She needed to protect her family. The safest place was probably Buckingham—if Leo and Arthur would have them. At least it would be harder for the UnSeelie fey to reach them there.

"Now," Larkin continued, "Here's what we need to do: we need to make sure...."

The faerie's voice blurred into an indistinguishable drone as Tiki focused on what she had to do: Stop Donegal, hide her family and find a way to free Dain before Donegal's Wild Hunt started.

"Is that clear, Majesty?" Larkin's sharp tone cut through Tiki's musings.

Tiki jerked her head toward Larkin. "What?"

"You must be at the Palace at midnight on Samhain to accept the sacrifice and to transfer the throne to the UnSeelies."

"Accept the sacrifice?"

"Of course. The Seven Year King is sacrificed to the Seelie Queen." Larkin's eyes became slitted. "That's you."

Chapter Forty-Two

Tiki shivered uncontrollably as she rushed back to her chambers. Ice gripped her heart from listening to Larkin speak so callously of Dain's impending death and the threat to her own family. Rieker hurried along beside her, the muscles in his jaw tight with anger. Behind them, Callan trailed at a proper distance, trying to keep Tiki in sight.

"You don't sound good," Rieker said with a worried tone.

"I'll rest when I know my family is safe," she wheezed. But even as she said the words she knew it wasn't true. She couldn't rest until Dain was free, as well. "Given the circumstances, do you think Leo will let them move to the Palace?" Tiki glanced over her shoulder at Callan behind them and grabbed Rieker's hand to pull him around the corner toward her chambers. "Hurry, I want to go before Callan can follow, but I've got to get something. Close the door and wait here." She rushed into another room and returned with the stake of Ash that Dain had given her clutched in one hand. "Ready?" At Rieker's nod, she whispered the words and they shimmered from sight.

THE HOUSE WAS unusually quiet when they returned to Grosvenor Square. Instead of the pitter-patter of feet upon the wood floors running to greet them, there was only an unnatural silence. Chill bumps crawled up Tiki's arms as an eerie sensation of encroaching danger washed over her.

"Something's not right," Tiki said in a low voice, as she scanned the hallway. "Where are the children?"

Rieker paused and peered into the kitchen. The fire was cold and the counters were bare—a sure sign Mrs. Bosworth was not in the house.

"Charles!" he called for the butler. "Are you here?"

Silence greeted his call.

Rieker paused to pull an antique sabre from a wall display before he continued down the hallway, his shoulders squared as though he expected an attack at any time. Tiki was several feet behind, searching for any clue to explain the unsettling quiet, when Rieker made a strangled noise and darted into the drawing room.

"What is it?" Tiki cried and dashed after him. She rounded the corner and stopped abruptly, staring at the shambles before her. A fire burned heartily in the grate, but the furniture in the room was upended and strewn about, as though a terrible fight had occurred. Her heart thrummed wildly in her chest. What evil had entered this room to create such disarray? "What happened in here?"

"I don't know." Rieker flipped a seat cushion from the sofa out of the way with the tip of his sabre. "But I don't like it."

Tiki searched the chaotic contents of the room, trying to sense what had occurred. A patch of white in the corner caught her eye and she hurried over to look closer.

It was a piece of Fiona's fancywork—an embroidered table runner that she'd been working on for months. Most of the fabric had been torn away, leaving just the shred Tiki now held. She clutched the cloth as a sudden surety hit her: the *liche* had been here.

Tiki started to run from the room, but Rieker moved faster and stuck his arm out to block her from exiting the room.

"Stop," he whispered. "We need to be cautious—we don't know where he is right now."

Tiki nodded as she gripped the Ash stake so tight her knuckles turned white. Would she find little Clara lying on the floor covered in blood with her heart sliced from her chest? She tried to shake the horrific images from her mind but a fear filled her, making it difficult to breathe.

"They got away," she whispered, "I know they got away—Shamus would have helped them." But what chance did any of them have against a creature like the *liche*?

They tiptoed down the hall, every footfall sounding like a cannon explosion in the eerie silence. They'd almost reached the entry foyer when a cold, familiar voice spoke.

"I was hoping you might be dear, sweet Fiona, but sadly, I see you're not."

In that instant Tiki died a thousand deaths. She jumped back with a strangled cry, pointing the wooden branch, which now looked small and useless, in his direction. The tall, elegant gentlemen they'd met at the Goblin Market stood before them as if he had every right to be inside the townhome.

"I can smell Fiona's sweet skin everywhere in this house—" he continued in a sultry voice— "but alas, she continues to elude me."

Tiki covered her mouth in horror as she spied Charles lying at the man's feet. The butler's usually-immaculate garments were covered with red and his vest had been neatly sliced down the front, leaving a gaping hole. A puddle of blood circled his dead body.

"What have you done?" Tiki screamed, brandishing the ash branch at him as if she might run him through.

Rieker pushed her away and pointed the sabre at the man's chest. "Get back, Teek. *Now.*"

The *liche* laughed, a low demonic sound, his red eyes glowing as though flames burned inside his body. He flicked his wrist at the dead butler. "His heart was not tender enough to satisfy my wants—" the *liche* licked his lips— "but I've found a better substitute." He nodded at Tiki. "I'm sure the taste of your sweet heart will make me weak with desire."

He feinted at Tiki, the movement making his straight black hair swing forward. At the motion of the black strands, an idea exploded in Tiki's head. She tried to dodge his attack but the *liche* caught the front of her jacket with one clawed hand, ripping it loose and exposing the tender skin of her breasts.

With a scream, Tiki whirled away, holding the ragged remnants of her jacket together. Rieker lunged at the man, nicking his wrist with the tip of the blade and forcing him back.

"You've taken your last heart," Rieker growled.

The *liche* hissed and barred his teeth, growling like a wild beast. Pure evil emanated from his blood red eyes. "You dare to strike me?" His fingernails were suddenly razor-sharp and deadly. "I'll cut your heart from your chest for that and eat it while you watch, you pathetic mortal." In a blinding fast move the *liche* whirled the opposite direction and slashed towards Rieker's neck.

But Rieker was already gone. Faster than Tiki could track he had pulled her away from the madman who threatened them and positioned himself between the two of them. With a backward flick of his wrist he slashed downward with his blade and a ribbon of bright red appeared across the cheekbone of the *liche*.

Rieker didn't take his eyes from his opponent. "Tiki, get out of here."

The creature put his hand to his cheek in surprise then threw himself at Rieker, all claws and teeth, trying to bite, scratch, cut and impale. "You will *both* die for that," he growled.

Rieker dodged away from where Tiki stood, leading the creature away from her, but the *liche* caught his arm and spun him into the wall.

"Don't!" Tiki cried and stabbed at the man's side with the stake of Ash.

The *liche* whirled on her, but Tiki's intervention had given Rieker enough time to recover his balance and he slashed the sabre across the man's arm. Tiki blinked and he suddenly stood three feet away from them.

The *liche* paced to the side, contemplating them. "You're faster than most mortals," he said, his sides heaving with exertion. "Different than the others I've met in London." He smiled, his sharp teeth glistening. "Which makes you that much more attractive. Who doesn't prefer the chase before the kill?" His chuckle was threaded with something dark and evil.

"Except you're the one who is going to die today," Rieker said calmly, his sabre held loosely in his hand as he waited for the man to make a move.

"Where's the bottle Leo gave you?" Tiki whispered. "The one you had at the market?"

"Upstairs, on my dresser."

"What are you whispering about?" The *liche's* lips twitched in a smirk. "Plotting your useless attack before I kill you?" He pointed at Tiki. "I will eat her heart first and make you watch…" his nostrils flared, "or perhaps the other way around." He took a step closer. "I've heard the Seelie queen visits this place—tell me what you know."

Rieker laughed. "You'll burn in hell before I ever tell you anything."

Tiki could barely breathe, so profound was the fear engulfing her. Instinct told her that she and Rieker were no match for the *liche*—but somehow she knew if either of them were to survive, she had no choice but to leave Rieker alone with the creature.

"Keep him at bay," she murmured. "Buy some time—I have an idea." Using every ounce of will power she could summon, Tiki closed her eyes and visualized Rieker's bedchamber. The hallway shimmered out of view and she found herself standing in the very room she'd just been imagining. From the lower levels of the townhome, she could hear the *liche's* shout of outrage as he realized she was not mortal.

Tiki rushed to the dresser and snatched up the little glass jar, the black hairs inside glistening in the lamplight. With the tiny bottle clutched tight in her hand, she closed her eyes and envisioned the drawing room, willing herself to be in that room, next to the fire. In a heartbeat she stood before the fire, the flames crackling and licking the air like hungry tongues. Out in the hallway, the *liche* continued to taunt Rieker.

"Who is your pretty fey friend? She's much too young to be the Seelie queen, but perhaps she's the reason for both mortal and fey guards outside?"

"How did you get in here?" Rieker asked, feinting toward the man, forcing him to dodge the blow.

"Your butler was kind enough to invite me in to wait, once he learned I had important news for you from the Palace." The *liche* grinned. "I didn't mention *which* palace, of course."

"Why did you kill him?"

"He was in my way, just as you are. When I finish with you, I'm going to take your friend away with me. You'll never know what's become of your lover…" his manic laugh echoed down the hallway.

It was all Tiki could do not to run from the room and attack the *liche* herself. How dare something so depraved speak of an emotion like love? He could never understand the depth of feeling that would inspire one to give their own life for another.

She dropped to her knees before the flames and yanked the cork stopper from the bottle. Shaking the strands of hair into her open palm, she shuddered as they touched her skin. With trembling fingers she pinched the black strands and balanced them carefully on the T-shaped portion of the stiletto-like limb.

When she'd seen the movement of the *liche's* hair, she'd finally understood what the dryad had meant: she didn't need to stab the liche with a branch of Ash—she needed to burn him on it. Literally. She held her breath as she slowly moved the limb and strands of hair into the flames.

A wild scream of pain erupted in the hallway.

"Stop!" The *liche* shrieked. "STOP! What are you *doing?*"

Tiki dug her teeth into her lower lip as she watched the flames lick and dance around the branch. "Hurry," she whispered. "Hurry, hurry, hurry."

From the hallway a terrible growl erupted that turned into a roar of terror, horror and excruciating pain. The horrendous noise echoed and grew louder and louder, filling the room until it seemed the windows might blow out with the pressure.

Propping the stick against the grate so it continued to burn within the flames, Tiki pushed off the floor and ran for the door. Her heart leaped with relief as she spotted Rieker still standing in the hallway. She raced toward him and slid to a stop next to his side.

Before him, the *liche* was on his knees writhing in pain. Steam rose from his head where his hair had dissolved into a bubbling mass. His face was melting like candle wax.

"NO!" he cried, "*STOP!*"

As they watched, his clothes caught fire and he imploded into flames. In a macabre echo of Tiki's cry upon seeing Charles' dead body, he screamed, "*You wicked girl—what have you DONE?*"

Chapter Forty-Three

Tiki shuddered as the *liche's* screams seemed to linger in the hallway long after the last of him had turned to ash. Convinced that he was no more, she rushed for the stairs.

"I've got to check for the children," Tiki called over her shoulder as she sprinted away. "Clara! Toots! Shamus! Are you here?"

"Wait for me," Rieker called, as he hurried behind her.

Tiki could barely breathe as she ran from one room to the next, fearful of what she might find, but even more fearful of not looking.

They found the note in Rieker's study. She snatched up the page and opened it with trembling hands.

"What does it say?" Rieker asked, moving to look over her shoulder.

"It's from Leo. He and Arthur came and got the children. Even the Bosworth's, Geoffrey and Juliette went with him," Tiki said, a note of wonder in her voice. "He writes that Charles refused to leave." She looked at Rieker. "How could they have known—"

"Mamie." Rieker said. "She's the only one who could have possibly convinced them. They know enough to believe her, though."

Tiki stared at Rieker, hope and fear reflected in her expression. "They're safe, aren't they?"

"Yes, they're safe." Rieker opened his arms. "And you're safe." He kissed the tender skin of her temple as he pulled her close.

"I was so afraid I might lose you—that he might—" he stopped, unable to finish.

Tiki cupped the side of his face and looked into his eyes. "I'm safe, because you saved me." An overwhelming sense of love flooded her

"I think we saved each other." One side of Rieker's mouth twisted, but not quite enough to erase the fear that still clung to his features. He ran his fingers across her brow, brushing tendrils of dark hair back from her face. "In those moments, when he was here, looking at you, saying you would be his—" he closed his eyes as though in pain— "I couldn't bear the thought that you might not be with me—"

"I'll always be here for you, William." Tiki drew his hand up to kiss his fingers and gasped. "You're bleeding!" She grabbed his wrist and turned his arm so she could assess the injury. "Dear Lord, the *liche* cut you." Panic filled her voice. "We've got to clean the wound—make sure he hasn't poisoned you like he did Leo and Johnny." She dragged him toward the kitchen. "We've got to rinse that cut. How deep is it?"

"I'm fine," Rieker said, only slightly resisting. "I don't think it's deep. Let me take my jacket off and we'll be able to see better." He lifted his arms to pull the garment over his head, revealing his naked chest and torso.

Tiki stared at the lean muscles rippling along his ribs and chest with his movement. He was so beautiful and perfect. She wanted more than anything, to run her fingers along his ribs, to feel the warmth of his skin against hers.

Unaware of her perusal, Rieker dropped his jacket and held up his arm to reveal a three inch cut that stretched between his wrist and elbow. Standing in the kitchen, he put his arm to his mouth and sucked for a moment, then spit a mouthful of blood into the sink.

Tiki choked. "What are you doing?"

"Sucking the venom from the wound, of course." Rieker raised his eyebrows and grinned at her. "Would you like a go?"

Tiki playfully slapped at his shoulder, letting her fingers drift down his arm in an ill-disguised caress. "You're a right disgusting prat, at times, you know that?" But his lack of concern eased her worries, and her panic subsided as she waited while he continued to suck the venom from his arm.

"Let's rinse that now like a civilized person might," Tiki spoke in an overly-prim voice, "and wrap it in a clean bandage, shall we?"

Rieker sighed and leaned against the counter, watching her every move with an intensity he made no effort to conceal. "If you insist. But I think fewer coverings might be a better idea." He brushed the torn front of her jacket, revealing her cleavage and his fingertips lingered against the tender skin, before she moved out of reach.

"William." She shot him an innocent glance from the corners of her eyes. "Whatever do you mean?"

He reached for her waist. "Let me show you."

Laughing, she dodged free of his hands and stepped over to where she'd lined bandages neatly on the counter. "Mind your manners, or I'll put you out with the horses." Rieker stood docilely, but more than once Tiki glanced up to find his eyes not on her face, but on her partially exposed chest. She told herself there wasn't any more skin showing than in some of the dresses she'd worn to parties at Buckingham, but somehow, in this moment, when it was just the two of them, she felt like her very soul was laid bare for his eyes.

Her cheeks began to warm and after a minute her fingers were so fumbly it took twice as long to wrap his arm. Finally, Tiki finished with the bandage and stepped back. "There. As good as new."

"Thank you, Majesty." Rieker bowed and lifted Tiki's left hand to kiss her fingers, reminding her of the first time she'd met the dashing William Richmond at Buckingham Palace. That time when he'd kissed her hand, her birthmark had been revealed and practically caused Leo to have an apoplectic fit. "You have saved me—" Rieker's voice was low and husky— "your humble servant and inconsequential half-breed."

"William." Tiki spoke in a stern voice. "We don't speak ill of the less fortunate." A smile wavered at the corners of her mouth. But instead of relinquishing his grip, he turned her hand over and pressed a kiss into her palm. For a second, she could feel his tongue against her skin and something stirred deep in her belly at the intimate gesture.

"You mean you're not ashamed to be seen—" his lips moved up her arm and kissed the black swirls that twisted around her wrist— "with someone like me?" He slid his other arm around her waist and pulled her close.

Tiki giggled, wrapping her arms around his neck and pressing against his hard chest.

"If you're not ashamed to be seen with a lowly pickpocket."

An expression that was both pleasure and pain crossed his face, before he lowered his lips toward hers.

"Let me prove to you how unashamed I am…" his tongue traced the corners of her mouth, tenderly pulling at her bottom lip before he covered her mouth with his. He kissed her with an urgency that was unfamiliar and primal, as if his patience had worn thin and he couldn't wait any longer.

Tiki was surprised to find the same urgency burning inside her. She pulled him closer, wanting to feel him against every inch of her body. He was hers and she was his and there would be nothing that would ever come between them.

AFTER THEY DRAGGED Charles' body out to the coach house and covered him with a black tarp, Tiki swept up the ashes of the *liche* from where they lay on the floor. They poured the remains through a paper funnel into a plain brown crock she'd retrieved from the kitchen and carefully sealed the lid.

"Where can we put this where it can never be opened?" she asked.

Rieker took the stoneware from her and disappeared into his study. A few minutes later he reappeared.

"Locked up tight." He slid his arms around Tiki and pulled her close, pressing his lips against her hair. "You were brilliant. And brave." He leaned back so he could see her face. "And you've done it. The *liche* is gone forever."

"YOU'VE COME FOR Prince Leo's guests?" The butler asked upon their arrival at Buckingham Palace. "They're in the upstairs library." He stretched his arm out. "By the sounds of it, they're having the time of their life."

Shrieks of laughter could be heard as Tiki and Rieker hurried down the grand hallway. Tension, that had been coiled like knots in her shoulders, began to release as they listened to the sounds of merriment coming through the door.

Another guard stood outside as they approached. "Lord Richmond. Miss." He bowed deeply then pulled the door open.

Tiki and Rieker stepped through the door and paused to take in the scene. Arthur was on his hands and knees while Clara rode on his back as if he were a pony. She was clutching the collar of his shirt and laughing gaily, "giddyup little pony, giddyup!" Nearby, Toots was petting the silky coat of a cocker spaniel, who stared at him with adoring eyes, her tail thumping the carpet. The young boy was holding a stick in one hand and having a heart-to-heart talk with the dog about fetching.

Fiona stood by the fire next to Leo who sat with a grin on his face as he watched his brother's antics. Next to him, Shamus also sat, with eyes as wide as two silver shillings. Tiki smothered a giggle. He looked like he needed a good pinch.

"Teek!" Clara waved happily, as if they all dropped into Buckingham Palace on a regular basis. "Arthur is my pony."

It was all Tiki could do not to burst out laughing at the sheer absurdity of the situation. What would the people of England think if they could see their prince now?

Leo bolted from his chair and hurried toward them. "Wills—Tara." Relief was thick in his voice. "You're all right. Thank God. Mamie convinced us you were in dire straits and we've been worried sick."

"Tiki—" Toots called across the room— "we should get a dog!"

"Mamie was right to be worried," Wills said as he shook the prince's hand. "Thank you for bringing the children back here. But we've brought good news."

"What's that?" Leo looked hopefully from one to the other. "We could use some good news."

"The murderer who has been loose on the streets of London? The one who took poor Charles Bagley's daughter?"

Leo hesitated. "Yes?"

"He's gone. Forever. We won't be bothered by the likes of him again."

Chapter Forty-Four

After visiting for more than an hour, Arthur called a carriage round to take Tiki, Rieker and the others back to Grosvenor Square. Geoffrey drove Rieker's carriage with the Bosworth's and Juliette. Toots and Clara chattered the whole way home about their adventure with the royals.

"An' then Leo said, *'they must come with us'*," Clara pronounced dramatically, imitating the prince, "an' Shamus said we couldn't go without 'im, so off we all rode in the carriage."

"They've more than one dog, too," Toots said eagerly. "The queen has loads of them. And next time Arthur said he'd take me to the mews to see the horses!" He bounced up and down on his seat with excitement.

"What did you think, Shamus?" Tiki asked, nudging the older boy's knee.

Shamus shook his head, even more quiet than usual. He finally spoke. "Me sittin' with the princes of England in Buckin'ham Palace." A slow grin spread across his face. "It was like a bloody faerie tale."

WHEN THEY ARRIVED back at Grosvenor Square, Tiki wrapped her arms around Fi. "How are you?" she whispered in the other girl's ear. "Do we need to go pick a pocket or two to liven you up?"

Fiona gave a half-laugh and hugged Tiki tight. "Do you think that would help?" She clung to Tiki for a long moment, then stepped back and blinked her eyes rapidly. "I'm glad you're home. I've missed you."

"I've missed you, too." She cupped the other girl's face with her hand. "Things are going to be back to normal again soon, you'll see."

Fiona smiled, softening the sharp edges of her thin face. "When has life ever been normal for this lot?"

Shamus approached and held his hand out to Tiki. "Welcome ho—" He shot a guilty look at Rieker— "I mean, welcome back, Teek." Tiki brushed his hand away and stood on her tiptoes to wrap her arms around his thin shoulders.

"How are you, Shamus?"

"Better now that you and Rieker are here." He looked into her face with a serious expression. "Things haven't felt right. It's not the same without you, Tiki. We need you here."

"And I need to be here." She forced a smile, choking back a cough. Her relief at finding everyone safe and knowing the *liche* was no more made her feel lighter than she had in months.

THE NEXT DAY the clock tolled ten p.m. as Tiki and Rieker sat in his study. The others had gone to bed, but only after Fiona had insisted on fixing some tea with lemon and honey for Tiki's cough.

"I don't like the sounds of that, Teek," Fiona had said. "You need some bed rest and somebody taking care of you, for a change, instead of you always bein' the one to take care of others."

"Look who's calling the kettle black," Tiki had grinned, before she'd started coughing.

"Drink this now." Fiona had forced the warm cup into Tiki's hands and stood there with her hands on her hips, like a miniature version of Mrs. B., until Tiki took several sips. The mixture was surprisingly soothing on her throat and Tiki had nodded her thanks.

"Do you think it's safe for the others to stay here now that the *liche* is gone?" Tiki asked Rieker. Her voice was little more than a rasp.

"We have to be realistic—there's no guarantee as long as Donegal wants the Seelie throne. If Larkin is right and he's identified that you live here in London, then there is risk." Rieker moved a bishop in a diagonal across the chess board that sat on a table between them. "But the Macanna are still outside and can keep an eye on things here. Grosvenor Square is probably the safest place for the others to stay at this point." He lifted his head. His eyes were shadowed, the expression on his face intent. "You realize I've got to go back and help Dain. There's got to be some way to free him."

Once again, Tiki fought the sensation of being pulled equally in different directions—she needed to be two places at once. How could she possibly choose? An image of Dain's masked face, with its bottomless eyes staring at her—as if silently begging her to *do something* to save him, hovered in her mind's eye. But even as she thought of Dain, an image of the happy and relieved faces of Clara, Toots, Fiona and Shamus warred with the image. What good was it to be a faerie queen if she didn't have the power to protect all those she loved?

Tiki exhaled slowly, staring at the intricately carved black and white chess figures, frozen in an unfinished game. "I know. We've got to return to the White Tower and try again to find a way to get Dain out. There's only a few days until Samhain." She pushed a pawn forward to block the path of Rieker's bishop, wondering how they were possibly going to free Dain this time when they hadn't been able to figure out a way before. "Maybe you should ask Larkin if she has any ideas on how to release him?"

Rieker's voice was solemn when he spoke. "We may not be able to get him out."

Tiki glanced up. "I've thought the same thing. But if we can't get him out—" she couldn't finish her sentence. They *had* to get him out. "I shouldn't have—"

A sound made Tiki turn. Clara peeked around the corner of the door.

"What are you doing up at this hour, Miss Mouse?" Tiki asked.

"I couldn't sleep." Clara skipped into the room. "Maybe if you read me that story ol' Potts gave us again, my eyes would stay closed." She pulled the *Field of Boliauns* from behind her back. "I've got it right here."

"Well, isn't that convenient," Tiki teased as she held her arms out for the little girl to climb up on her lap.

"I've missed you reading to me at night, Teek," Clara said softly as she snuggled into Tiki's arms. "Toots' misses it, too, even if he doesn't say so."

"And I've missed you and Toots." She tweaked Clara's nose. "Pretty soon you'll be reading books on your own."

"I like it better when you read." Clara smiled up into Tiki's face. "An' when you talk with an accent."

"You mean like a good Irish lass?" Tiki said, affecting a thick Irish brogue.

Clara giggled. "Yes! Exactly like that."

"Let's see what Clever Tom is up to in this story," Tiki said, as she turned the opening pages of the book. Rieker crossed his legs and watched them, a smile tugging at the corners of his lips.

"Yes, let's," Clara said, doing a spot-on imitation of Tiki's accent. "I think he's goin'ta find himself in a wee spot of trouble."

Tiki began to read out loud. "The story begins on one fine day in harvest—it was indeed Lady-day, that everybody knows to be one of the greatest holidays in the year—and clever Tom Fitzpatrick was taking a ramble..."

Clara's eyes grew heavy as Tiki read the story and she fell asleep before the book was finished. Tiki held the little girl in her arms, and gazed down at her perfect face, a sense of pure love warming her heart. She so desperately longed to stay here, safe in this room, but she knew her happiness would never be complete until Dain was safe here with them.

THAT NIGHT, TIKI dreamed of a thousand red garters fluttering in the wind. The landscape of her dream was dark and a terrible fear filled her. She was running, looking for the garter that marked the hidden gold, when the air was filled with the thunder of approaching hooves. Panicked, she looked over her shoulder to see who chased her, but the shadows were too dark. Though they remained unseen, she knew it was Donegal and the Wild Hunt—hunting her.

She turned and ran. The noise got louder and louder until the ground shook with the power of the beasts chasing her. Tiki couldn't keep her footing and began to fall....

Tiki awoke with a jerk, her heart pounding like the horse's hooves of her dream. Through the first light of dawn that crept into the room, she surveyed the familiar corners. Convinced she was alone, she relaxed against her pillows and stared up at the ceiling.

The one thing her dream had made clear was that they had to free Dain before the Wild Hunt. Before Donegal gained control of the Otherworld again. As much as she didn't want to leave London, she and Rieker needed to go back and find a way to release Dain—immediately. Even if it meant asking Larkin for help. Tiki threw back the covers and climbed out of bed, the movement causing a spasm of coughing. She hurriedly donned her clothes shivering in the cool morning air. They didn't have a moment to waste.

"GOOD MORNING, DEARIE," Mrs. Bosworth called out from where she was kneading bread as Tiki entered the kitchen. Flour dusted one side of her middle-aged face as well as her apron and hands. "Another one up early this morning."

"The sun is barely above the horizon," Tiki said as she poured some hot water into a mug for tea, hoping it would help to stop the coughing. "Has Shamus left for the bakery already?"

"Shamus *and* Master William have come and gone already." Mrs. Bosworth wiped a wisp of hair from her forehead with the back of her hand and left another streak of flour. "Master William left a note for you." She nodded toward the other counter.

Tiki froze. "A note?"

The older woman gave Tiki a coy smile. "Over by the pitcher, dear. Couldn't wait until he saw you again, I s'pect. Seems quite taken with you, Miss." She focused on her kneading, humming under her breath. "Quite taken, indeed."

Tiki snatched the small white envelope off the counter. Her name was written in black, block letters on the front. Any other time she would have paused to admire the neat script but she barely noticed as she broke the seal and yanked out a fine piece of embossed stationary, marked with the name Richmond.

Tiki, I'm sorry I left without talking to you, but it's better this way. We're running out of time. I've got to help Dain and you're needed here. Be safe.

Love,

Wills

Chapter Forty-Five

Tiki stared at the page. He'd gone back to the Otherworld without her. He was going to try and release Dain alone. *"Damn him."*

Mrs. Bosworth froze. "Beg pardon, dear?"

Tiki jerked her head up and looked at the housekeeper with a guilty expression. "Nothing, Mrs. B., I..."

"What's wrong?" Fiona's voice came from the doorway.

"Another early bird." Mrs. B. shook her head. "You'd think I live with a bunch of farmers."

Tiki shoved the note into her pocket. "Nothing. Rieker just had to go out of town unexpectedly." She added some honey to her tea and took a sip, trying to suppress the urge to cough. She sank onto a chair next to the small wooden table, her mind racing. She needed to follow Rieker but should she go to the Palace and get a horse, or should she go straight to the White Tower?

Fiona walked across the room to get a mug. "Are you going to join him?"

Tiki hadn't forgotten how angry Fiona had been when she'd left for the Otherworld last time, when Larkin had insisted she claim the throne. Fiona hadn't said she wanted her to stay, but Tiki knew the other girl needed her now, more than ever.

"Only for a few days, Fi, then I'll be home again." A congested cough rumbled in Tiki's chest.

"You sound like you should be in bed," Mrs. B. said. "I don't like the sounds of that cough, one bit."

Fiona was quiet as she poured hot water from the kettle to make tea. She sat down at the table across from Tiki. "Do you need help?"

A twinge went through Tiki's heart. She and Fiona had shared so much in their fight for survival. Now Tiki was fighting for other people to survive and once again, even though her own heart was broken, Fiona was there to help her.

Tiki reached across the table and took Fiona's hand. "It's a dangerous time right now. I won't be gone long."

"What's happening? Is it Larkin?"

"It's more than Larkin," Tiki said in an undertone. "Someone very important has been captured and we have to free them or…" She couldn't bring herself to finish.

"Or what?"

"Or they'll be sacrificed."

THE SOUND OF the front door knocker rang through the house.

"Merciful heavens," Mrs. Bosworth cried, "who could be calling at this hour?"

Mr. Bosworth, filling in as butler until Rieker had time to find a replacement for Charles, appeared in the doorway a few minutes later.

He gave a short bow toward Tiki his wrinkled face alight with astonishment. "Prince Leopold and Lady Macha Gallagher are here to see you, Miss Tara."

TIKI HURRIED TO meet Leo and Mamie in the elegantly appointed drawing room.

"Leo? Is everything all right?" She nodded at the diminutive woman. "Mamie, so nice to see you again."

"Dear Tara." Leo grasped Tiki's hand in both of his. "What a relief to find you safe and sound."

Tiki's brow furrowed as she looked from one to the other. "Why were you worried?"

Leo glanced over at Mamie. "We've had word that caused us some concern for your health. Mamie was at the palace before daybreak, insisting we come first thing this morning."

Tiki fought back a cough. "I thank you for your concern, but as you can see, aside from a small cold, I'm just fine."

Mamie's expression was grave as she stepped forward. She put a hand that shook with age onto Tiki's arm. "Donegal hoped to use your loved ones here in London to lure you into a trap, but last night they chanced upon someone else."

Tiki couldn't breathe. "Who?"

The older woman's grip on Tiki's arm tightened. "William. They've got William. You must be very careful. They will use him to draw you into their deception." She lowered her voice. "William will receive some protection from the truce—but you—given who you are—" she raised her eyebrows—"you're not protected. You must use your wits to save him—and to survive."

Chapter Forty-Six

Tiki stood alone in the Wychwood forest, in the spot where she and Dain had met the Tree Dryads. Mamie had told her they were the best source of information to find where the UnSeelies had taken Rieker. How the old woman had knowledge of what went on in the Otherworld, Tiki didn't know, but she didn't doubt the woman's veracity for a second. From Mamie's description, it sounded like Bearach had been the one to capture him. Tiki couldn't bear the thought of Rieker being tortured at the hands of that brute like Dain had been.

There was no time to be afraid. She'd come here with one purpose: to find Rieker. Together, they would find a way to free Dain. There was no one else she could trust enough to share this responsibility.

"Elder! Can you hear me?" Tiki called out to the trees in a raspy voice as she slowly walked down the path. She was dressed to blend with the wood, her clothing like bark and leaves, shadow and mist. She held a lightweight bow with an arrow notched, similar to that which Sean had carried when they'd traveled through the forest before. "I need your help."

The wind rustled the branches overhead, as if they spoke to each other in a secret language only they could understand.

"The Winter King has taken someone from me." The wind grew sharper. Leaves and twigs began to twirl in small gusts. Tiki raised her voice. *"I want him back."*

She stopped and turned a circle, searching the trunks and shadows for anyone—any*thing*—that might be listening. "Donegal is burning the Wychwood—killing more innocents each day." Tiki forced her voice louder. "We must join forces to stop him. Work together. " She fought a growing irritation at her lack of knowledge as thunder rumbled in the distance. How did one find a Tree Dryad? She felt such an overwhelming urgency to hurry, hurry, *hurry*—there was no time to waste in saving Dain and Rieker. She called out again. "Come now and speak to me."

"Who are you?" The voice was rough, like a piece of bark.

Tiki whirled around. Before her stood the same three women she'd met with Dain when he was disguised as Sean. Their skin was rough and weathered, eyes nothing more than knot-holes. Feathery, moss-like hair hung in long strands over mostly bare chests; their skin brown and bark-like. Had they not spoken, she wouldn't have noticed them among the trees.

Tiki tightened her grip on her bow, but kept the arrow pointed toward the ground. "Which of you is the Elder?"

The tallest in the back waved a long branch-like hand. "I am."

"I need your help," Tiki said. "I'm looking for a young man who rode through here not too long ago…"

"Who are you, that you dare to ask for our help?"

Tiki tried to keep her temper in check. She didn't have time for questions. She needed answers. Thunder rumbled again, closer this time. A shaft of lightning flashed in the distance. The branches of the nearby trees shifted with the wind, their leaves rattling.

"I am Tara MacLochlan, queen of the Seelie Court." The words sounded strange on her tongue. "I am seeking—" Tiki thought fast— "one of my knights. I need to find him as soon as possible. There are many lives at stake. Have you seen him?"

The elder Dryad measured Tiki with her dark eyes. "Is that why you brought the storm?"

Tiki didn't know what she was talking about. "Have you seen him? He's tall with dark hair. Probably riding a white horse."

"You don't look like a queen."

Tiki reacted by sheer instinct. She stabbed at the sky with her right hand and imagined the jagged bolt of lightning. She clutched her fingers around its fiery heat and flung it at the space next to the Elder tree. Lightning charred the ground, so close to the Elder tree that the heat singed her leaves.

Shrieks filled the air as the trees blew to a different spot. Tiki's eyes widened in shock. Had she just done that?

"Don't ask for our help and threaten us at the same time," growled the Elder. "I'll give you the information you seek, o fair queen—for a trade."

Tiki re-positioned her fingers around the shaft of the arrow threaded through her bow. "What trade?"

"We are bound within these trees by the curse of the same Winter King who has taken your lover. For us to leave, someone must stay in our place." The Dryad's woody face focused on Tiki with a powerful intensity. "Help release me and I will help you."

Tiki's mind raced. Just like Larkin, there was always a trade involved when dealing with the fey. The Dryad had made an outrageous and desperate request. There was no one Tiki would or could sacrifice to a life trapped in a living hell. What else could she offer?

"There must be—" Tiki started to negotiate then stopped. There was one person she'd like to imprison forever: Donegal. She adjusted her grip on the bow as an idea took seed in her mind. "How would the transfer be made?"

The Dryad's leaves rustled. "They only need be close enough that I can wrap my branches around their body. As I bring them into the heart of the tree, I will switch places with them and step free." A note of longing rang in the tree's gruff voice. "However, the curse states that it must be someone with magical powers at least equal to my own."

A plan was forming in Tiki's mind. "If I bring you someone, how will I find you?"

"The trees are the heart of the forest. Our roots are connected deep within the earth. Our breath whispers with the wind. Call for the Elder and I will find you."

Tiki inhaled sharply, scarcely believing the bargain she was hoping to make. "Can you travel to the Palace of Mirrors on Wydryn Tor?"

"It's not easy, but there are trees on the Tor. I can go there."

"Then I need you to trust me and be patient," Tiki said. "If you give me the location of where they took my friend, then I will bring you the very man who imprisoned you in the first place: Donegal, the Winter King."

A longing sigh blew through the trees. The woody face contemplated Tiki's small form. "You don't look like much, but I sense your power is great. I will take a chance and trust you once. Bearach has taken your friend to an abandoned village in the Wychwood, very near where—"

"I know where it is." Tiki inclined her head at the Elder Dryad. "Thank you for your help. I will be in touch."

TIKI CLOSED HER eyes and visualized the spot where she and Rieker had met Gestle near the White Tower. She opened her eyes to find herself standing in exactly the space she had remembered. Day was fading and a mist floated just above the surface of the lake, its ethereal fingers beginning to thread their way through the trees. The wind was biting cold and snow threatened—which could only mean one thing: Donegal was close and his power must be growing.

Tiki gazed across the lake to where the three standing stones stood, marking the village. Was Rieker being held in one of those stone buildings? She crept through the underbrush in the direction of the village as silently as she could, coughing into her sleeve when she couldn't suppress the urge any longer. Was it possible they'd taken Rieker to the Tower and imprisoned him with Dain? Was she headed in the wrong direction?

As she approached the village, Tiki stopped. She surveyed the surrounding area, looking for Donegal's troops, Aeveen—anything that might give her a clue to Rieker's presence—but there was nothing. She worked her way through the brush, circling the perimeter of the dark buildings. When she got to the far side, she spotted two horses tethered together, hidden among the trees.

Tiki took a deep breath. Someone was here. She hunkered down to watch and contemplate her next move.

IT WAS LESS than an hour later when two men emerged from one of the buildings. One was clearly a prisoner, his wrists bound in front of him, a rope leash around his neck—the other had shoulders like an ox and flaming red hair. Bearach. Tiki's heart raced as she stared at the tall, slim figure of the prisoner, sure it was Rieker.

As she watched, Bearach jerked hard on the leash, causing his prisoner to stumble and crash to his knees. Across the stillness of the forest Tiki could hear him cough and gag. She jumped to her feet and yanked an arrow from the quiver on her back. She had to do something—could she shoot Donegal's *tánaiste* from here?

"Careful, Majesty. " The scratchy voice spoke from close behind her.

Tiki whirled around. "Gestle." She uttered the man's name with relief.

The impassive face of the hobgoblin leader watched the UnSeelie guard and his prisoner through the trees. "A bit of a risky gamble from this distance, even for me. If you miss, you might kill the wrong person. Then you become the target." He glanced at her. "Don't you have guards of your own?"

Tiki motioned toward the captive. "Is he the prisoner from the Tower?"

"No. They took him away earlier. This is your friend—he's just arrived."

"Dain's gone?" Tiki whispered. "Do you know where they took him?"

"I overheard one of the guards say he was bound for the Palace. Apparently, he's to be the bait in the Wild Hunt." Gestle stroked his long chin. "Never heard of the Winter King hunting a person before. Must think he'll be more of a challenge."

Anger surged inside Tiki and she had to bite her lip not to shout out at the Winter King's cruelty. "And my friend?" She motioned toward the prisoner she now knew was Rieker. "Do you know where they're taking him?"

"Donegal's ordered him sent to the great fire." Gestle pointed a clawed finger in Rieker's direction. "That one'll be dead before the Wild Hunt even starts."

Tiki clutched her bow until her hands shook. Thunder rumbled directly overhead and the Dryad's words echoed in her head: *Is that why you brought the storm?*

In the distance, Bearach jerked sharply on Rieker's leash to force him to his knees, then rammed the hilt of his sword against the side of the young man's head causing Rieker to sag to his side on the ground.

With a low growl of anger, Tiki slung her bow over her shoulder and thrust her arms out in a wide V toward the sky. She let all the fear, frustration and anger that roiled around inside her surge out through her fingers. In an instant, the sky turned black and dark clouds swirled and boiled over their heads like an otherworldly tempest. The wind whipped the branches of the trees in a wild dance and Tiki's skin tingled with power.

With an innate knowledge, she swept her hands toward the ground and rain began to fall in torrents. Gestle stepped back and eyed her with alarm. Bearach shouted as he kicked Rieker in the ribs, trying to force him to get up and onto the horse so they could escape the deluge.

Rage as hot as any flame burned through Tiki to see Rieker treated in such a way. With a flick of her wrist she sent a lightning bolt straight at the red-headed beast. The fiery dagger landed square against the man's chest and sent Bearach flying backwards through the air. He landed on his back ten feet away. Donegal's second-in-command didn't move as a spiral of smoke slowly rose from his great chest.

Gestle let out a low whistle of approval. "Nice shot, Majesty."

Rieker pushed himself off the ground and jerked around to look in their direction. Tiki raced toward him. Recognizing her, he scrambled for the horse, grabbing the reins as he vaulted on. He kicked the horse into a run and held his bound hands out for Tiki. She grabbed hold of his wrists as he flew by and he swung her onto the horse behind him.

"They've taken Dain to the palace," she yelled in his ear. Then she wrapped her arms around his waist and hugged him tight.

Chapter Forty-Seven

When they'd ridden for thirty minutes, Rieker pulled the horse to a stop. The storm had cleared the further they got from the abandoned village.

"Have you got a knife?"

"Yes." Tiki yanked a blade from inside her boot as he twisted and held his hands out for her to saw through the ropes that bound his wrists. As the strands gave way, Rieker ripped off the rope leash.

"Are you injured?" Tiki asked.

He rubbed the red abrasions around his throat, his voice hoarse. "Nothing serious. How do you know they moved Dain?"

"The hobgoblin told me. He said they'd taken him to the Palace." She didn't need to say why.

THE PALACE OF Mirrors was in turmoil when they arrived. Preparations were being laid for a vast feast and workers were scurrying in every direction. Huge pyramids of wood were stacked for bonfires and tables were being set out. In a nearby pasture, scores of horses were pulling at the grass, their breath coming out in frosty clouds.

Tiki stared in amazement. "What is going on?"

The guard who took the horse from Rieker answered. "It's the feast of Samhain. There's always a party when the seasons change."

His eyes glowed with anticipation. "Especially when a Seven Year King is to be sacrificed. It starts tonight."

Rieker stalked away without answering and Tiki hurried to catch up with him. "Do you think Dain is here?"

"There's only one person who would know for sure." He marched on, entering the Great Hall through a side door. Tiki followed Rieker down a long hallway, around a corner and through an arched doorway where he paused abruptly.

"What is it?" Tiki asked, coming to stand beside him.

Before them, the Great Hall was filled with workers. Tall trees of white candles were scattered around the room like a forest of light, casting a shimmering glow. Strewn like ribbons of gold between the tall fluted columns were swaths of glittering fabric. But that wasn't what Rieker was looking at. Perched on the golden Dragon Throne, as if she were queen, sat Larkin.

"The nerve—" Rieker growled.

"That's not what's important right now," Tiki murmured. "We have to find Dain—find out how much time we have."

Rieker strode forward, his shoulders rigid.

"Larkin."

The faerie showed no surprise at their arrival. "William, what a pleasant surprise. I'd heard rumors you were captured by Bearach."

"The *Queen* helped me to escape." He glared at her.

Larkin pushed herself off the throne and brushed her long hair over her shoulder with a flick of her wrist. She looked down her nose at Rieker as she descended the three steps.

"William, I sense antagonism. You understand that what I do is out of concern for the kingdom. I have dedicated my life to protecting this Court and its inhabitants—"

"Why are so many starving, then?" Tiki snapped. "You might think your motives are altruistic but you serve your own purposes, Larkin."

"Then tell me," Larkin's eyes narrowed, "how do *you* plan to protect the Seelie kingdom and battle Donegal? He has amassed an army of UnSeelies, including any solitary fey he can find in the Wychwood into his ranks. "

Tiki clenched her hands into fists. "What does it matter? He's going to be in charge for six months after tonight, anyway. There's nothing to be done until I reclaim the throne in the spring, is there?"

Larkin put her hands on her hips. "What you don't seem to understand is that when the Winter King reclaims control of Faerie tonight he's not going to give it up in the spring."

Rieker stepped closer, his face inches from Larkin's. "What are you saying? That Tiki shouldn't turn the throne over tonight?"

Larkin gave a derisive snort. "We don't have a choice. At this point, Donegal's army far outnumbers ours. In this war there's only one way we can be guaranteed victory."

"What's that?" Rieker asked.

"A few months ago I never would have believed it possible, but now—"

Tiki gritted her teeth. *"What?"*

"The Fourth Treasure, of course."

Tiki groaned as a cough rattled deep in her chest. Not another circular conversation. They didn't have time. "Forget the bloody treasure for now—the first thing we need to do is find Dain and save him before he is hunted like a fox before a pack of rabid dogs."

An expression Tiki couldn't identify flitted across Larkin's exquisite features. "It's too late for Dain. Donegal has him within his inner circle. He is inaccessible. It would be impossible to free him now."

"Then when they set him loose for the hunt—"Rieker sounded desperate— "we'll help him escape."

Larkin gave a short laugh. "Even if you could—which would be nothing short of a miracle—there still has to be a body presented to the Seelie queen at midnight in payment of the tithe." Larkin cocked her head at them. "How do you propose to do that?"

"I don't know—*yet*." Tiki snapped, exhausted and incensed at Larkin's disregard for Dain's life. "But we're not giving up on him. We'll think of something."

"In the meantime—" Larkin surveyed Tiki through slitted lids— "if I were you, I'd find a good place to hide."

Chapter Forty-Eight

Tiki tugged Rieker away from Larkin and led him from the room. They passed the short little man who had told her in Westminster Palace that the Seelies wanted war against Donegal. It seemed he was going to get his wish. He bobbed his head at her as she passed.

"Majesty."

His green pants were held up by suspenders and he wore a well-made pair of shoes with shiny gold buckles that covered his extraordinarily long feet. For the first time, Tiki recognized him as a leprechaun, just like the character in the story she'd read to Clara.

A painful twinge went through Tiki's chest at the thought of the little girl. How she longed for those simple days when she knew nothing of the Otherworld and the battles being waged. When Mr. Potts loaned her books she could read to the children and they would be safe together in whatever spot they were calling home.

Tiki shook her head. But she did know of the Otherworld, and though there were times when it would be easier to pretend none of these responsibilities existed—she couldn't abandon those who needed her.

"Majesty!" Callan raced down the hall toward her, relief evident in his voice. "The Jester said you'd returned."

Tiki hadn't seen the Court Jester, but it didn't surprise her that he knew of their arrival. He seemed to know everything of importance that happened around the palace.

"I have returned and I'm going to rest now, Callan. Please see to it that no one disturbs Lord William or myself, would you?"

TIKI NODDED TO the guard who opened the door for her as she and Rieker entered her chambers. Callan stopped at the door.

"I'll take over out here—give this chap a rest." His voice was bright with enthusiasm. "I'll be right here, Majesy, if you need me."

"Thank you, Callan."

Before the doors had shut another voice spoke up.

"Bless you, Majesty, for what you've done for us this season. We'll wait faithfully for your return next Beltane."

Tiki whirled in surprise. There was no mistaking Ailléna's scratchy voice. Tiki paced back to the entry and found the scarecrow-thin little Redcap on her knees in one corner.

"What are you doing here?" Tiki asked in surprise.

"I've been waitin' for days for your return, Majesty." She threaded her fingers together and bowed her head. "To thank you and wish you the best. I'm not allowed on the Plain of Sunlight on account a' bein' a—" she waved her hand along her body and Tiki wasn't sure if she meant a Redcap or a beggar— "so I won't see you again until Beltane."

Tiki motioned to the small creature. "Ailléna, come into my chambers, please." She led her to an opulently-appointed study where an ornate desk and bookshelf were positioned beneath an expansive diamond-paned window. On a nearby pedestal stood the Cup of Plenty, the blues, golds and browns of the glass goblet glowing softly in the daylight, as if lit from within. Tiki sat down at the desk and Rieker came to stand behind her, his arms clasped behind his back.

Tiki motioned to the cup. "I want you to know, that thanks to your help, we were able to locate the Cup of Plenty and it has been returned to the world of Faerie without the mortal's knowledge. All is, as it should be, again."

The little goblin stared with round eyes at the glass goblet. "Is it true, Majesty?"

"Yes, it's true and you are no longer at fault. The wrong has been made right and you should not waste another moment of your life feeling guilty."

The little Redcap hiccupped then let out a long sniff, trying not to cry. "Thank you, Majesty. It's been a terrible burden to carry all these centuries." Ailléna sniffed again, turning her head to search the room. She wiped the corner of her mouth with one clawed hand. "Pardon my curiosity, Majesty, but what smells so good?"

Tiki drew a deep breath and paused in surprise. There was a delicious aroma wafting through the air that made her mouth water. She glanced at Rieker and she could tell by the puzzled look on his face that he could smell the tantalizing scent, as well.

"It must be the kitchens, preparing for the feast tonight."

"But the Court who is leaving doesn't provide the food," the little goblin said slowly, "the incoming court conjures the food when they take the throne. There won't be any food here until midnight. And, pardon my saying, but UnSeelie food never smells that good."

Tiki pushed herself to her feet and shrugged. "Then I have no answer." She held her hand out to the diminutive creature and Ailléna slipped her fingers into Tiki's. Rieker pulled open the door as Tiki bent down to look into the goblin's eyes.

"Thank you again for taking the time to visit. I'll look forward to seeing you next spring. Take good care of yourself in the meantime and make sure you get enough to eat."

"Yes, Majesty, but there's been no food at the camp for weeks."

"No food?" Tiki shot a questioning look at Rieker who raised his hands and shrugged.

Ailléna gave her a guilty look. "We thought maybe we'd eaten too much in the summer."

"That's ridiculous," Tiki said, but as she spoke, she recalled Gestle telling them that Donegal had burned the hobgoblin's fields. "Of course, you didn't eat too much. I asked that food be set out for the hungry each day, but I'll look into it and make sure there is enough for all."

"It's all right, Majesty. We're used to getting by. We can always beg." Ailléna bowed. "Blessings and good health on you."

AFTER AILLÉNA'S DEPARTURE, Tiki sank into one of the elegant chairs in the sitting area and put her head in hands. She was so tired and there was so much yet to do, beyond freeing Dain. If only she could rest for a few minutes, then maybe she could think more clearly about what to do next. The mouth-watering aroma had dissipated and Tiki wondered if they'd just imagined the delicious smell.

Rieker sat in the chair next to hers, dark circles shadowed the skin under his eyes. The bruises around his throat were more prominent now as if he wore some ghastly purple necklace.

"Teek—I don't know what to do."

The despair in his voice twisted Tiki's heart.

He sighed and leaned his head back against the chair, covering his face with his hands. "I've got to do *something*—but I don't know what. It's just like losing Jimmy and Tommy all over again, except this time I've known it's coming."

Tiki reached over and put her hand on his knee. It was so unlike him to show weakness or indecision—it made her heart break to listen to the anguish in his voice.

"Wills, we've still got time—we'll figure it out. Just promise you won't ever leave me again."

TIKI JERKED UPRIGHT. Rieker stood at the window, talking about the procedure for the Wild Hunt that night. She'd only nodded off for a few moments but in that finite space of time she'd dreamt of red garters tied to boliaun branches again.

Rieker had his hands on his hips, with his shoulders square as if preparing for battle as he stared out toward the blood red sun. "It's only a few more hours now before they set him loose."

Tiki jumped up, hardly able to contain her excitement. "I've got an idea."

THE SUN HAD just slipped below the horizon when Larkin came to find Tiki in the Great Hall where she was surveying the preparations. Larkin had changed to black, her light hair bound in a tight bun behind her head and hidden beneath a dark head drape. Tiki wondered what she was plotting, for the mercurial faerie appeared to be planning to become invisible.

"We need to discuss the procedure tonight. As soon as power has shifted back to the UnSeelies we must return to the Plain of Sunlight and plan our counter-attack. From what I've learned, it sounds like we won't have much time before Donegal pursues us. Luckily, the Macanna are well-trained."

"What exactly is my role?" Tiki asked in a cool voice. She wasn't going to tell Larkin of their plan. She didn't want to take the chance that someone might reveal what they were up to, before it was time.

"The Wild Hunt is launched from the Night Garden. As the moon crests the horizon the UnSeelies will give the prey a thirty minute head start. After that, they follow on foot and horseback. The goal is to bring back the sacrifice—dead or alive."

"Prey? *Sacrifice?* Is that how you refer to Dain now? He told me he'd known you all his life." Tiki curled her lip. "Is it so easy for you to dismiss him as lost?"

Larkin pointed a long finger at Tiki and spoke through gritted teeth. "Don't presume to know what I think or feel. The Seven Year King is a long-held tradition within the Courts, started by Seelie royalty. You seem to want to blame me personally, for a crime *your* heritage began." Her eyes narrowed. "Perhaps if you find these traditions distasteful, it would be best if you gave up the throne for someone more suited for the position?"

"Who?" Tiki snapped. "You?"

The Court Jester danced up to them at that moment. Gold glitter spiraled out from his eyes matching the combination of gold and black stripes, checks and triangles that marked his garments tonight. He raised his hands and revealed nails that had been painted a bright red. Tiki couldn't help but imagine they'd been dipped in blood.

"Majesty—" he bowed low over his knee toward Tiki before straightening to nod at Larkin— "and the Queen's Advisor. I come to bid you adieu for the season." With a flourish, he snapped his fingers and suddenly held a square, razor thin card. The edges of the card were lined with gilt that glittered in the torchlight. He flicked the card into the air and it fluttered toward his cupped hands like a leaf blown by the wind. It landed face down on his fingers with only the black back exposed.

He proffered the card to Tiki, his black eyes locked on hers. "When the clock strikes twelve, Majesty, may the winds of change blow you in your true direction."

Tiki had no idea what he was talking about. "Thank you, Jester." She took the card and tucked it into her pocket without glancing at the image drawn on the other side. "May you be well during the dark season so that you might light our days with your wit and wisdom upon my return in the spring."

The Jester placed his hand over his heart and bowed. "I am your servant, Majesty," he said softly. Then he flung his arm out and whirled away.

"How strange," Larkin murmured, watching the man's departure through slitted eyes. "I've never heard the Fool pledge himself to a sovereign before." She turned to face Tiki. "Have you promised him something?"

"What?" Tiki frowned. "Of course not. Now back to the topic. Where do I have to be at midnight to accept this ghastly offering and transfer the court?"

Larkin waved her arm in an airy gesture. "On the throne, of course."

Chapter Forty-Nine

Tiki stood on the steps of the palace and looked out over the Night Garden. Fluffy snowflakes drifted down from the sky. Already the grounds were coated in a layer of white. As a result of the snow, the world was washed in light at a time when darkness should have made the grounds impenetrable. The branches of the trees that had blossomed so beautifully during the summer months were leafless now and seemed to be retracting into gnarled, grotesque, misshapen creatures.

Rieker stood next to Tiki with his hands on his hips, his lip curled in disgust. "Of all the rotten luck. It's as light as day out here."

"A snow sky," Tiki murmured. In the past, she'd always considered snow a sign of luck, but tonight, it seemed a sign of doom, for it would make the hunt for Dain significantly easier with the world lit by the reflection of white light.

On one side of the Tor, a thick knot of UnSeelies mingled. They were a variety of shapes and sizes, a mix of different creatures from what Tiki could tell, all of them dressed in an array of black garments—some gaudy and decorative, others deadly efficient and designed to hunt, with swords, spears, spiked mallets and knives attached to their apparel. The most disconcerting group, however, stood apart and formed a tight circle in the distance.

Larkin had pointed them out earlier: Donegal's inner circle: Sullivan, Cruinn, and Scáthach—only three with the disappearance of Bearach. The Winter King had not yet been seen.

"If only we could have told Dain of our plan," Rieker said in a low voice. "It would make things infinitely easier."

Tiki clutched his fingers. "You'll have time. Are you ready?"

Rieker nodded. "Callan has Aeveen waiting on the far side of the garden. If you're right—that Dain will take the trail down the side of the Tor—then I'll intercept him at the bottom and we'll ride through the Wychwood to freedom."

Tiki turned and slid her arms around Rieker's neck, uncaring who might see them. "I know you can do this, William," she said softly. "You are brave and kind and clever—if anyone can save your brother—it's you."

"I could never do it without your help." Rieker wrapped his arms around Tiki's waist and pulled her close against his chest. "Teek, if I don't make it out, I need you to know something…"

"Shh," Tiki pressed her fingers against his lips. "Don't talk like that. You've got to make it out because I need you."

"But if I don't—I want you to know I love you, Tiki, more than anything—" he ran his fingers along the contours of her face, as if memorizing her image— "or anyone in my life. You are my life and breath. The reason I'm here. Whichever world we might end up in—I want to be there with you."

"William—"

The blare of trumpets split the night.

"Wait, Teek—" Rieker reached inside his collar and pulled a braided gold chain free. His hand cupped around what dangled from the end and he quickly pulled it over his head. "You need to guard this now. In case I don't make it back—there's more you need to do."

"No—" Tiki tried to stop him, but in one deft movement he slid the chain over her head and slipped the Ring of *Ériu* down the front of her dress. "You should keep it—it might bring you luck—"

"You're all the luck I need," Rieker said in a husky voice. "Kiss me for all time and I'll be protected for just as long."

Panic made Tiki's heart run wild in her chest. He was leaving her—saying goodbye—had he seen an omen that he wouldn't return? A hot pressure burned behind her eyes at the thought of never seeing his handsome face smile at her again.

"No, that's not enough," she whispered. With trembling fingers she snatched a piece of her raven black hair and wove three strands into a tight braid. Plucking the small knife from her belt, she sawed the braid off and kissed the strands before offering them to Rieker. "Take part of me and know you'll never be alone. I'll always be with you, William."

Rieker took the small braid and kissed the strands in the same spot Tiki had. "I'll wear this next to my heart." He slipped his hand inside his vest and tucked the strands into an inner pocket. Then he cupped her face in his hands and kissed her. When Tiki opened her eyes—he was gone.

With a triumphant fanfare, the trumpets stopped and silence echoed across the night air. Tiki crossed her arms over her chest, fighting back tears at the sense of loss that filled her. Everything depended on what happened in the next few hours. She'd never felt so helpless in her life.

Torches, perched on tall posts, stretched in two long rows away from the palace steps. There was movement at the far end and Tiki spied Dain, still trapped behind the chilling mask, standing at the far end of the colonnade.

"Ladies and gentlemen." Larkin's voice boomed across the garden. She stood several steps away from Tiki, no longer dressed in black, but shining instead in a gown of gold. "Samhain is upon us and it is the seventh year—the year in which the UnSeelies must pay a tithe to the Seelie Queen to retain their right to act as a separate Court. At the Winter King's decree, the Wild Hunt will be for the Seven Year King this year. The man or woman who kills or captures the sacrifice will be made an honorary advisor to Donegal's Court. As per our ancient tradition, the sacrifice must be presented before midnight on Samhain. Should the Seven Year King not be presented by that time, another sacrifice must be provided—" her voice rose— "the selection to be at the Seelie Queen's discretion."

"Majesty." A low voice spoke next to Tiki.

She turned to find Callan. "He's safely on his way?"

"Yes. And the other package you requested is wrapped and concealed in your chambers."

"Good. Thank you Callan." Tiki turned back to the row of lighted torches and pressed her hands together in prayer. She pointed them toward Dain and nodded in his direction. To her surprise, Dain put his hand over his heart then held his open palm out to her.

Tears rushed to Tiki's eyes. In response, she crossed both hands over her own heart.

Larkin's voice silenced any conversation. "The sacrifice shall have a thirty minute lead starting NOW." For a split second, everyone froze, as Dain slipped sideways into the crowd. A buzz of conversation set flight above their heads like a flock of birds, before someone called out, "He's gone."

"There!" A deep voice called. "I see him headed for the stables!" The crowd turned to gaze in the direction he pointed.

"No, that's not him—he's over there—by the statue of Danu." The crowd wheeled around to look in another direction.

"Wait! I saw him hide behind that tree…" They shifted yet again as grumbling rose from the UnSeelies waiting to set chase.

Tiki permitted herself a small smile. It had begun. Just like the red garters in the Field of Boliauns, there would be a thousand Seven Year Kings in the Wychwood tonight for the UnSeelies to hunt. The Macanna had donned masks identical to that which Dain wore and they roamed the forest with the sole intent of leading the hunters astray. The difference was, they could remove their masks and blend with the hunters should the UnSeelies get too close.

She spoke in a whisper. "Be clever like a leprechaun, Dain."

Chapter Fifty

Tiki hurried back inside the palace toward the Great Hall, only to exit down the long hallway where she and Dain had snuck out before. She counted down to the thirteenth doorway and paused, glancing up and down the corridor before letting herself out into the side garden.

She was alone among the trees and bushes with the reflected light of the snow making it easy to see across the tor. Tiki closed her eyes and imagined the thunderstorm that had drenched them outside the White Tower the previous day. She pictured the mistreatment that Rieker had suffered at the hands of the UnSeelie guard and let loose the tight clamp she held on her fear.

A familiar tingling began in her skin until power crackled down her arms right through the tips of her fingers. She reached for the heavens and imagined pulling the black clouds toward her, like a blanket, to cover the sky. She flicked her wrist and a bolt of lightning flashed overhead. With a silent roar, Tiki thrust her hands toward the ground and the skies overhead opened up with a barrage of icy hail.

Tiki opened her eyes. The night was dark and stormy, the wind whipping the trees as the torrent of hail made it almost impossible to see more than a few feet. Thunder rumbled overhead like an ominous drum roll. It would be difficult to track anything on a night like this. By the time the Wild Hunt started, there would be no footprints to follow, no easy sighting of their prey.

She slipped back inside the palace.

TIKI STOOD ALONE in her chambers, forcing herself to continue to gather the few possessions she had here in the Otherworld, in anticipation of her return to London. If she didn't keep busy her only other choice was to stare helplessly out the window and wonder what was happening with Rieker and Dain. It was torture not to be with them—to be helping—but she and Rieker had decided he and Dain could travel faster and more inconspicuously without her.

THE HUNT HAD been going on for over two hours, with no sign of victory on the part of the UnSeelies. Each time shouts echoed up from below the palace, drifting in through the window open a crack, Tiki's breath caught in her throat. It was impossible to gauge what was really happening. She glanced again at the 'package' resting on her bed. Wrapped in green fronds, she couldn't bring herself to look at the contents.

She stopped in front of the wooden pedestal that held the Cup of Plenty. The colorful glass shone brightly in the firelight and seemed to wink at her with hidden promises. Tiki thought again of what Dain and Larkin had said of the Four Treasures. Were they real? Was it up to her to find the fourth treasure and reunite Faerie?

Tiki slid her hands into the pockets of her dress where her fingers collided with the card the Jester had given her. She pulled it out, a wave of curiosity washing over her.

The black backside of the card revealed nothing, and she carefully turned it over, not sure what to expect. A drawing, so intricate in its details as to appear to be a stained glass window, teased her eyes and she moved closer to the light to better examine the complex details.

Drawn against a black background was a circle with four sections that looked like the crosshead of a Celtic cross. The perimeter of the circle was an intricately drawn Celtic knot design in green. Across each of the cross bars was a different knot design in gold.

Tiki's heart skipped as she peered closer, for the image in the center was very clearly a queen. With hair that was neither brown nor blond, she appeared to be etched from glass—her image fragile and timeless. The pattern on the inner circle around the image of the queen was eerily similar to an fáinne sí, the birthmark that twisted around her own wrist.

Had the Jester been trying to convey a message to her—or was this just a bit of wit with which to entertain himself during the ever-changing seasons?

Between the spokes of the cross, four pictures had been drawn. Appearing to be cut from tiny pieces of colorful glass, the first looked like a standing stone. In a flash of clarity, Tiki recognized the stone as the Lia Fáil, the coronation stone of the Kings of Tara. It was the stone from which the Cloch na Teamhrach, the Stone of Tara, was said to have originated.

The second image was the Cup of Plenty.

The third image was of a golden ring capped by a fiery red stone that glowed as if lit from within. The Ring of Ériu.

Tiki turned the card like a wheel to peruse the fourth spoke of the circle. Would the card reveal the mysterious fourth treasure? But instead of an object, this section showed a castle made of golden bricks with a tall tower on one end. There was a lake in the forefront, which reflected the image of the castle like a mirror. But there was no object that could possibly be the fourth treasure.

Tiki's brows knit in concentration. What was the message?

"So the Queen is preparing to depart."

Tiki let out a small cry of surprise as she whipped around. She'd asked to be left alone in her chambers tonight. Who dared to intrude upon her privacy?

From the shadows of an adjoining room a dark figure moved toward her. He was dressed in black—silky fabric that rippled like water as he walked. The torchlight glinted off the gold circlet that sat upon his dark hair and a thrill of abject fear shot through Tiki. What was Donegal doing in her chambers? Hadn't he gone on the Wild Hunt?

"I've been waiting for you." His voice was mild, coated in deceit. He took slow, measured steps toward her. "I wanted to be alone with you when I revealed what you've done."

"W..what do you mean, '*what I've done?*'" Tiki stammered. "I've done nothing..."

Donegal raised his voice and spoke over her. "I wanted to be close enough to see the look in your eyes when you see what you've done TO ME." He stepped into the light of the nearby torch and Tiki let out a cry of fright, covering her mouth with her hands.

Before her stood the Winter King, but he didn't look as she remembered him. One side of his head had long, straight black hair as before, along with his normal features. But the other side— Tiki stared in horror—the other side of his face looked like it had melted. The skin was abnormally thin and smooth, stretched down over his eye, nose and half of his mouth. His lip was grotesquely enlarged on that side, forcing his mouth to sag open in a macabre fashion, and where his nose should have been, there was only a blob of melted skin. The hair on that side of his head was mostly gone—looking as if it had been singed off, leaving scarred tissue with ridges of melted skin.

Tiki backed away, trying not to stare at the horrible caricature before her, but afraid to take her gaze from the repulsive vision.

"Do you like what you see, pretty Queen?" He stepped toward her. "Because this—" he jerked a long finger up to point at the damaged side of his face— "is YOUR doing."

"I didn't...I don't...I don't know what you're talking about." Tiki looked around as she took another step back, her mind racing.

What was the best way to flee? Should she scream? Would the guards get to her in time? Should she transport to the Great Hall or...

Donegal flicked his wrist and a thin, green vine-like whip flashed through the air and wrapped around her wrist. "I hope you're not thinking of leaving me." He tugged Tiki closer. "We've so much yet to talk about."

"I demand that you release me." Tiki tried to sound forceful, but panic and her illness made it hard to draw a deep breath. She jerked against the pull of the tether but her movement only seemed to tighten the cord.

An evil chuckle erupted through Donegal's deformed lips and as he came closer Tiki could see his black eyes glittering like the eyes of a deadly snake.

"Without taking my revenge? I think not."

"I didn't do t..that to you," Tiki cried.

"Who else could have been clever enough to kill the *liche?*" A note of anger crept into his voice. "That perfect killing machine was my defeat of that bloody truce—a sure way to control the throne through all the seasons." His voice deepened with emotion. "I had to give up part of my body to raise the *liche* and when you burned him—you burned me."

Tiki struggled against the pull of the vine. How could she get free from this madman? What was he planning to do to her? What could she do to him? She straightened her spine and lifted her chin. "A risk you took when you raised such a creature."

Donegal tilted his head. "Are you not afraid of what I'm going to do to *your* pretty face?"

"No, I'm not," Tiki snapped. "You think by hurting me you'll gain power?" She narrowed her eyes, a familiar surge pulsing through her, giving her strength. "You're mistaken, Donegal—" she spat out his name in distaste. "The fear and intimidation by which you try to rule are going to start a revolution. Those fey out there—" Tiki thrust an arm toward the door— "the ones you're starving, or forcing into servitude, or whose families you've kidnapped and tortured—they're going to stand up to you. Hurting me is only the battle cry they need to fight."

Donegal scoffed at her. "When we present you with the body of the Seven Year King tonight I'll take the Dragon Throne and show you how a truly powerful king rules."

Tiki bit her lip. She wanted to scream that she would never accept the casual brutality of killing someone as a sacrifice for an ancient tradition but she knew it would fall on deaf ears.

"For now, Donegal, you have the right to rule during the dark months of the year, but that doesn't give you the right to threaten and starve those who aren't your subjects. Or anyone, for that matter."

"Kings are above the law." Donegal shouted. "We ARE the law." He glanced over his shoulder toward the door and his voice quieted. "And what do you mean, *for now*?" He raised the one eyebrow on his face, the melted skin on the other side awkwardly pulling at the movement, giving her a look of mock-confusion. "Are you threatening me?" A low chuckle slid from his throat. "You remind me of Larkin. So pretty on the outside, but cold and fearless on the inside— even when you're at my mercy." He reached forward and stroked the side of her face. "Which makes you infinitely more interesting. Perhaps a worthy adversary, after all."

Tiki shrank back, her skin crawling at his touch. The stench of decay emanated from him and she could see blackened teeth through his sagging lip. Revulsion turned her stomach and she clenched her teeth together to stop herself from gagging.

Donegal's hand froze in mid-air at her reaction and an angry hiss escaped from his partially open mouth.

Tiki tried again. "Why are you here? You're not permitted in these chambers until midnight, after the transfer has been made."

She wasn't sure if what she said was true, but she needed to say something—*anything*— to make him leave. "If you don't release me this instant, I will call my guards."

"Your guards are dead. Even that devoted Macanna who followed you around like a puppy is no match for me. The look of surprise is forever frozen on his dead face."

"No!" Tiki cried.

"I'm here to give you a taste of your own justice." The Winter King curved his palm as though he held liquid and blew on his fingers until flames ignited in his cupped hand. "I want you to burn like I have." He reached for her face with his fiery hand.

Fear shot through Tiki like an arrow and she reacted on instinct. In one smooth movement she reached for the ceiling then thrust her free hand toward the ball of flame, imagining a deluge of rain. In that instant, a torrent of water poured from above and extinguished the flames, drenching Donegal in the process.

The Winter King roared in anger. At the same time, Tiki felt the vine wrapped around her wrist relax and she gave a might jerk, snapping the cord. She darted away as Donegal swung around to follow her movement.

"You won't get away from me," he growled as he flung his hand at her. A ball of flame shot across the room in her direction. Tiki dodged the fire and reached for the heavens again, as something heavier than anger filled her. She flexed her fingers and flung her hand in Donegal's direction. A lightning bolt crackled through the room and struck the Winter King in the shoulder, knocking him to his knees.

"Be gone from here, Donegal," Tiki barely recognized her own voice, "or we will both regret what I do next."

"Majesty!" A voice called from the doorway as booted feet pounded toward Tiki's room. "Is everything all right?"

From his knees, Donegal hissed at Tiki, his face twisted in rage. "You and I have only just begun." Then he shimmered from sight.

Toran rushed into the room, a look of alarm on his face, his weapons held at the ready. Two more soldiers raced in behind him, their spears drawn. "The guards are *dead* and we heard shouting and ... and... *thunder*—"

"Thank you, Toran." Tiki sank into a nearby chair, her legs suddenly too weak to hold her upright. "Thank you for being so diligent. I'm fine, now." She put a shaking hand to her brow and rested her head, trying to steady her breathing. "Is Callan...?"

Toran and the Macanna hurriedly searched the room, the other two checking the adjoining chambers. Toran came to stop in front of her. "He died doing his job, Majesty. It's how he would have wanted it."

Tiki covered her face with her hands, fighting back sobs. Of all the times she'd wished the man would leave her alone, it had never occurred to her that he might die—for her. Only now, did she appreciate his sacrifice.

"He was very brave," she sniffed.

"That he was, Majesty." The Macanna guard stared at the floor with a furrowed brow. "Where did all this water come from?"

"What news have you on the Hunt?" Tiki asked, unwilling to discuss what had really just happened in her chambers. She had made a dangerous enemy tonight. Where Donegal had been her foe before—now he held a vendetta against her. The insult had become personal and Tiki knew with an innate surety that he wouldn't rest until she was dead. She wondered at her ability to lure him close enough that she could fulfill her promise to the Elder Dryad.

Toran lifted his head. "There's only an hour left until midnight and they've lit the bonfires. There's been many sightings of the Seven Year King but no sacrifice has been delivered. Usually, it's done in the first hour."

Tiki's spirits lifted with hope. Maybe their plan had worked.

Chapter Fifty-One

"Wills!" Leo stared in amazement at his friend, who stood with his hair plastered to his head, every inch of his tall frame dripping water onto the steps of Buckingham Palace. "I'm so relieved to see you. Mamie has been in a knot over you for some reason." He leaned through the doorway and scanned the area. "But for the love of God, man, what are you doing out on a night like this? It's only suitable for witches and waterfowl out there." Leo motioned him inward. "Come in, come in. Before you float away."

"Leo." There was a note in Rieker's voice that made the young prince pause and turn back around. "I need your help."

Leo frowned. "Of course. What is it?"

"I have a…a friend with me. I need to…" Rieker hesitated, searching for the right words. "Oh hell, I need to hide him until midnight. Can we go to the mews?"

"Hide him?" Leo glanced over his shoulder to check the position of the footman then stepped out onto the porch with Rieker and spoke in a low voice. "Why? What has he done?"

"He has escaped, Leo, that's all. He's done nothing wrong, except to have the courage to risk his life for a court and a queen in whom he believes." Rieker leaned close and spoke in a low voice. "I've got to protect him until midnight, then a bit later, I'm going to ask you for another favor."

Leo eyed Rieker. "And what will that be?"

"I need to leave him with you for a few days. Just long enough for Tara and I to get ourselves organized. He needs to stay hidden—become invisible, if you will. He's gifted with horses—he can help in the stables if you'd like."

Leo was silent for a long moment, searching Rieker's face. "There's more to it, isn't there?"

Rieker nodded. "Much more. Best if you don't know all the details quite yet. You're safer that way. He won't be here long but I don't dare leave him at Grosvenor Square."

"Well bring him in now, then. Why wait until midnight? If he's in the same shape as you, he'll catch his death of cold by then."

Rieker hesitated. "Thank you for your hospitality, Leo, but he can't be seen until after midnight." At Leo's questioning glance, he shook his head. "It's complicated."

Leo waved his hand. "Fine. You know your way to the mews as well as I do. Do you want an escort?"

"No, better that we go on our own. We'll stay out of sight." Rieker grabbed Leo's hand and gave it a hearty shake. "Thank you, Leo."

"I'll wait up for you. Perhaps you can tell me more after the bell has tolled the midnight hour. Come to the side entrance by the kitchens at two a.m. I can sneak you in easier there." A smile creased Leo's thin face. "I do love adventure."

Chapter Fifty-Two

Tiki changed to a gown of shimmering gold. What the future held for her, or the world of Faerie, was unclear, but she was going to leave the Seelie Court with a powerful image to hold onto during these dark months. Where Donegal was dark—she would be light. She would replace the fear he inspired in the fey with hope for better days.

After Donegal's departure she had found the card the Jester had given her on the floor, wet, but not ruined. She had dried the waxy surface and stared again at the images drawn there seeking answers—but there were none. She'd put the card inside the Cup of Plenty and taken those, along with a few other mementos back to Grosvenor Square.

She'd arrived in the darkness of the coach house, the familiar scent of horse hair, leather and hay a comforting welcome. How she longed to know if Dain and Rieker had truly escaped the Wild Hunt. She hurried through the quiet house, silently checking on the others who were tucked safely into bed.

Tiki imagined how Rieker must have felt, returning to Grosvenor Square after the death of his parents and two younger brothers and having to live here, alone. What had once been a place of love and security must have seemed like a prison to him. His tortured words came back to her now: *'Everywhere I looked, there were memories of my family. Especially my younger brothers. They were everywhere around me, yet I was alone. So unbearably alone.'*

A tear ran down Tiki's cheek at the thought of losing her loved ones again. Losing her mother and father had been almost more than she could bear—if she lost Clara or Toots, Fiona or Shamus, Dain or Rieker—her mind wouldn't go any further.

She'd hurried back downstairs toward Rieker's study. She set the Cup of Plenty on one of the bookshelves, her fingers lingering on the colorful glass.

"You'll be safe here," she whispered, as she glamoured the cup to look like an ordinary green glass vase— "until I come back for you."

THE LONG TRAIN of Tiki's golden dress flowed behind her as she walked down the corridor in the Palace of Mirrors, the jewels and sequins embedded on the gown glittering in the torchlight. Nested upon her head was a small circlet of gold, thickly encrusted with jewels that glowed with a remarkable luminescence.

Toran and several other palace guards were in front of and behind her, escorting her to the Great Hall where she would accept the sacrifice. Her heart pounded like the roll of a kettle drum and Tiki clutched at her skirt as she walked.

"Dain and Rieker are safe," she whispered to herself, a cough rumbling in her chest. "The Macanna are clever and cunning. They have escaped the UnSeelies tonight. All will be as we've planned. Dain and Rieker are safe..." she said the words over and over, as if by repeating the words she could somehow make them true.

They entered the Great Hall and Tiki came to a stop. For a second, she thought she was looking at her reflection in one of the enchanted mirrors, but then she realized it was Larkin, dressed in a gown very similar to hers.

The faerie came to stand before Tiki. They were like a mirror image of each other, except Larkin's hair was the color of wild wheat and Tiki's was raven-feather black.

"We've ten minutes until midnight," Larkin said. "There has been no sacrifice provided as of yet." She raised her eyebrows. "You do know you'll have to pick a new Seven Year King if Donegal doesn't provide the body."

"Yes." The same sense of betrayal that Tiki had felt previously at Larkin's lack of action over Dain's plight filled her mouth now with a bitter taste. She was anxious to be gone from the faerie. Perhaps now that the courts were in balance again for the moment, she would have a reprieve from Larkin's incessant need to meddle in her life. "I've made provisions."

A look of surprise flickered across Larkin's exquisite face. "I see."

Tiki kept her voice cold. "Is there some procedure I need to follow when they present the sacrifice or do I just accept the body?" She missed Rieker desperately. She was used to having him by her side to offer support and advice. More than once, she'd whispered a prayer that they would never be separated again.

"Once you accept the sacrifice you can speak if you'd like. After that, you must descend the throne and the UnSeelie King takes the seat." Larkin gave an eloquent shrug. "In the past, the Seelies would return to the Plain of Sunlight until Beltane. This year, however, things will be different."

"How's that?"

"We will be at war, this year." Larkin's jaw was set. "One way or the other."

Tiki thought of the threat Donegal had uttered from his knees in her chamber and knew Larkin spoke the truth.

"The Seelie fey will need a strong hand to guide them, to lift them up when they sink in defeat," Larkin continued, "for there will be substantial losses at first. Donegal has amassed too great of an army to be easily overcome."

The blare of trumpets sounded from outside and Tiki put her hands over her stomach, fearful she was going to be sick.

"That's your cue." Larkin held out an arm. "You're needed on the throne."

Without a word, Tiki clutched her skirt and marched toward the golden chair. The Great Hall was rapidly filling with an astounding array of fey. Members of both Courts jostled for the best position to see the offering. They were a mixture of beauty and beast, grace and awkwardness, magical and common—dressed in an assortment of finery and rags. Even the homeless faeries had ventured from their camp on the Tor to see the changing of the seasons.

Tiki's steps faltered as she spied the golden table that had been positioned in front of the Dragon Throne. Clearly, it was an offering table—the place where the body would be presented. She took a deep, calming breath and continued toward the seat.

As she walked up the three steps to the throne, everyone in the Great Hall got down on bended knee. The deep voices of the Macanna started the chant.

"Tarr-uh! Tarr-uh! TARR-UH!"

Tiki reached the throne and turned, gazing out over the sea of bowed heads. A confusing mix of emotions swept through her—surprise, still, that they bowed to her and called her name; responsibility to provide a better life for these people who would die for her; fear, that she couldn't be who they wanted and needed her to be, along with something else—was it gratitude—or love? In the face of death, starvation and war, these people still had the fortitude to rise up and celebrate, to share their love of life with one another and believe that a better day was coming.

Tiki lifted her arms. "Please rise. Let the ceremony begin." She sat down on the throne and straightened her skirt, fighting the need to fidget. How she longed for Rieker to be here with her.

Toran and the other Macanna positioned themselves on the four corners of her throne, their weapons drawn, eyes scanning the crowd for any threat.

She searched for Donegal, contemplating the moment he would take the throne from her. Would he try to hurt her again? Would there be an opportunity for her to lure him outside so that the Elder Dryad might wrap her arms around him?

Larkin stood off to one side, not far from the throne, looking as regal as any queen. Sullivan stood speaking to her and Tiki wondered what thoughts were going through her head at this moment. She'd fought for so long to reclaim the Seelie throne, to regain the power that had been lost with Eridanus' murder—planning to be queen herself, Tiki was sure. Now war loomed on the horizon, another queen had taken the throne and the power of the Courts was passing back to the UnSeelie's. What was she plotting now?

As if sensing her perusal, Larkin turned and stared at Tiki, her face as unreadable as the mask that had covered Dain's face these last months. The faerie nodded to Sullivan and walked toward the throne. A flare of hope ignited inside Tiki.

Larkin climbed the steps to the throne and leaned close. "Donegal's representative has informed me that the Seven Year King has escaped. You will have to choose your own sacrifice." Larkin turned and stretched an arm out to encompass the room. "You may take your pick."

The crowd went silent as if in sudden understanding of this unexpected turn of events. The expressions of anticipation on those who had gathered turned to looks of trepidation and fear. For one evil moment Tiki wanted to ask Larkin if she was included in the pool of potential victims, but she bit her tongue.

"Thank you, Larkin. I'll need a moment of consideration."

Larkin nodded and stepped down from the throne.

"Toran."

The young Macanna jumped to face Tiki. "Yes, Majesty."

Tiki spoke softly. "Please unwrap the package in my chambers and bring it to the offering table." She put a hand on the guard's arm to stop him. "Be gentle."

"Of course, Majesty." The young guard hurried out of the Great Hall to do her bidding, while Tiki surveyed the crowd. She worked to keep her face impassive. Whispers buzzed through the hall, but they were muted, as if the speakers were afraid to draw attention to themselves.

It was difficult to pretend she might be considering sacrificing one of them, but Tiki understood there was a pretense that went along with being queen—the pretense of strength, and perhaps a bit of intimidation.

After a few long moments had passed Toran returned carrying a dead body.

Tiki hurriedly looked away as he approached. "I have made my selection," she said as loud as she could, her voice rough and scratchy. "A sacrifice has been made to the Seelie Court." An audible sigh of relief went up in the room, as people craned their necks to see what was happening.

Toran carefully laid the body on the golden table, gently crossing the victim's arms over his chest. Tiki took a deep breath and pushed herself out of the throne. She still had not looked at the body. She slowly walked down the steps, her back straight and head held high. She stopped before the golden table. Sullivan had come to face her on the other side.

Tiki nodded at him. "I accept this sacrifice on behalf of the UnSeelie Court. Consider your tithe paid for another seven years. Samhain has arrived and I relinquish the Dragon Throne to the

Winter King until Beltane." Trumpets blared at the back of the room and cheers went up

"On King Donegal's behalf, I accept the throne for the UnSeelie Court." Sullivan shouted and raised his fist in the air. Music began playing and the crowd began to dance. Bottles appeared and wine flowed freely.

It was only then that Tiki allowed herself to look at the sacrifice. Her breath caught in her throat as she gazed upon the young face. If she didn't know better, she would say Johnny was asleep.

Chapter Fifty-Three

Tiki didn't wait to see what Larkin, Sullivan or any of them were going to do. Her time here was done for now. She slid her arms underneath Johnny's thin body and picked him up, hugging him close.

"Majesty—can I help?" Sympathy was etched across Toran's face.

"Yes, thank you." Tiki looked directly into the Macanna's face. "Please don't follow me." She saw his jaw sag as he realized what she'd done before she shimmered out of view, with Johnny clutched in her arms.

TIKI ARRIVED INSIDE one of the vacant bedrooms on the fourth floor in Grosvenor Square. She carefully tucked Johnny into bed and smoothed his brown hair back from his pale forehead.

He was so thin she could see the bones of his face protruding, as if his skin was just a sheer fabric draped over his skull.

"Oh Johnny," Tiki whispered, tears slipping down her cheeks. "Why couldn't we save you?" She perched on the bed next to him and took his fingers in her hand. But he was as cold as the winter wind that blew outside and it wasn't long before Tiki became chilled and withdrew her fingers. "At least we can bury you at home, and watch over your grave, in a place that Fi and the rest of us can visit."

Tiki pulled the covers up and stared at his face a moment longer. When she'd inquired about his condition in the resting spot where they'd taken him, the faerie nurse who'd help to tend him had told her that he wouldn't have changed much from when he had died. If anything, he looked more at peace.

THIRTY MINUTES LATER Tiki was dressed like a boy. Her garments were worn and comfortable—like putting on a familiar skin. She'd become invisible. It was a change she welcomed.

She'd hadn't bothered to wake the others to let them know of her return. She'd checked on them again and they all slept peacefully. There was time for reunions another day. Hopefully, with everyone present.

AN HOUR LATER she stood in the shadows across the street from the royal mews, just as she and Rieker had planned. If he and Dain escaped, they would meet her at the end of the mews closest to St. James Park. She was prepared to wait for as long as it took.

Tiki looked both directions before she left the shadows of the building and headed across the street. The long brick wall of the mews stretched along the road, blocking the interior of the royal stables from view. She stopped at the far end, close to the door to the kitchens where she'd snuck into the palace the night she'd stolen the Queen's ring. Had it only been a year ago?

"Not here to pick a pocket, are you?"

Though soft, it was a voice she'd recognize anywhere. She whirled around to face Rieker. Next to him, like a blurry shadow, stood Dain—the mask gone, his handsome face returning her smile.

Tiki gave a cry of joy and looked from one to the other, not sure who to hug first.

Rieker solved the dilemma and swept her into his arms, twirling her in a circle. "We did it," he said, his voice filled with uncharacteristic emotion. Tiki wrapped her arms around his neck and held him tight, laughing and crying at the same time.

He set her feet on the ground and released her. She wrapped her arms around Dain, who twirled her in another circle, their laughter filling the night air. "You both did it," he said, hugging her tight.

"With a little help from Larkin," Rieker added.

Dain slowed and set Tiki down, holding onto her hands. He looked into her eyes as he spoke. "Thank you for saving me, my queen."

He released her and Tiki swayed on her feet as she tried to regain her balance. "Rieker, what did you say?"

Rieker tilted his head. "Didn't she tell you? Shortly after the Hunt started Larkin found us in the Wychwood. Apparently, she knew which path Dain would take, as well. Rather than riding out, which would have taken us more than two days, she transported us to London. We've been hiding here for hours, waiting for midnight to pass."

Tiki searched his face for the truth. Had Larkin helped, even when she'd seemed indifferent to the treacherous position that Dain had been in?

"I'm not surprised she didn't let you know, Tiki," Dain said, as if sensing her need for an explanation of the faerie's motives. "She's lived a double life for so many years, it's probably hard for her to trust anyone now. Even you. Maybe especially you. I suspect you're the only one who might be powerful enough to best her."

"WE HAVE TO see Leo, Teek. He'd send the royal guard after me if we didn't let him in on some of the fun," Rieker said.

"*Fun?*" Tiki stared from one to the other as Rieker and Dain looked at each other and laughed.

TIKI HELD BACK giggles as Leo snuck them into the palace. The prince tiptoed and used hand gestures to make sure they remained unheard. She was tempted to remind him that he could certainly bring whomever he wanted into the palace, but she bit her lip instead. It was obvious Leo was having too much fun pretending he was pulling off some clever caper.

When they reached the drawing room the prince got his first good look at Dain. His face twisted into a frown of confusion. "You look familiar."

"A distant cousin of mine I've just learned about," Rieker said in a breezy sort of way as he went to stand before the fire.

Leo propped his hands on his hips and surveyed the newcomer. "And from whom did you just escape?"

Dain's eyes widened and he looked to Rieker for an explanation.

"Oh right," Rieker said, "I did mention that, didn't I?"

"There was also mention of your *cousin*," Leo said the word lightly, "risking his life for his court and queen. Who might that be?"

Dain didn't flinch this time. Instead, he bowed toward Tiki and extended his hand. "Queen Tara, of course."

Leo raised his eyebrows. "Tara? A...*queen*?"

Dain winked at Leo. "Perhaps even you have been tempted by her magic?"

Leo glanced uncertainly from Rieker to Dain to Tiki and back again. Finally, he laughed and threw up his hands. "Who isn't enraptured by Tara?"

Dain smiled as he nodded. "Exactly my point."

THEY TOLD LEO what they could of the war in the Otherworld before returning to Grosvenor's Square. Rieker gave no further details of Tiki as queen, nor did he ever admit that Dain was from that world. Thankfully, Leo didn't ask.

IT WASN'T LONG after daybreak that Clara, Toots and Fiona arrived downstairs for breakfast to find Tiki, Rieker and

Dain seated at the table. Behind them, Mrs. Bosworth puttered at the stove, humming happily.

"Tiki!" Clara cried, running around the table to throw her arms around Dain. "You've saved Dain. I knew you would!" She laughed gaily, the sound like wind chimes, as she hurried over to Tiki and smothered her face with kisses until Tiki laughingly cried for help. "Was he tricky like that ol' lep'reecon in the story about Clever Tom?"

"Yes, exactly like that," Tiki laughed.

"I knew he would be!" Clara held up her ragged stuffed animal. "Doggie told me so."

Toots gave Tiki a quick hug then hurried over to shake Rieker's hand and then Dain's, anxious to ask about the horses.

"We've brought Aeveen with us," Dain said with a big smile. "I was hoping you could help me exercise her."

Toots eyes were as round and shiny as two quid as he jerked his head up and down. "Yes sir!"

Fiona came and gave Tiki a tight hug. "I'm so glad you're home safely." She leaned back so she could look into her face. "Will you be staying now for a while?"

"Yes, Fi," Tiki nodded. "For a long while, I hope."

They tucked into platters of eggs and sausage with biscuits that were so fluffy they seemed to melt in Tiki's mouth. Clara chattered happily the whole time. Tiki couldn't help but wonder what Ailléna would think about some of these mortal dishes, but before she could finish the thought another thought intruded: would Donegal provide any food for Ailléna and the others?

IT WAS AFTER breakfast when Tiki told Fiona that she'd brought Johnny's body home. Fiona's eyes instantly welled up with tears, but she clutched Tiki's hands and thanked her.

"Maybe I can sleep now, knowing he's home and we can watch over him," she said softly. "Where is he?"

AFTER A BRIEF discussion, it was decided that Toots and Clara would remain downstairs with Mrs. B. and Tiki, Fiona, Rieker and Dain would go upstairs to view Johnny's body before Rieker would start the process for his burial in London.

It was a solemn group who climbed the stairs up to the fourth floor. The house was quite cool on this level, with no fires lit to heat the unused rooms. The gray light of the day did little to reach into the corners of the house and illuminate the shadows.

Fiona held Tiki's hand as they walked down the hallway, her grip tightening with each step they took closer to the bedroom where Johnny was lying. Tiki paused in the doorway.

"Are you sure you're going to be all right?"

"Yes." Fiona nodded but her face looked uncertain.

"Here we go. I'll be right here for you, Fi," Tiki said softly as she led the other girl up next to the bed. Fiona sniffed then released Tiki's hand. Rieker and Dain stood silently behind them.

"Oh Johnny," Fiona cried, sitting down on the bed next to the still body and running her hands gently over his frozen features. "Why did that horrible creature have to hurt you?" Her tears dropped onto Johnny's cheeks and rolled down the side of his motionless face until it looked like he was crying, too.

"I love you, Johnny," Fiona whispered brokenly, "I'll never forget you."

Before Tiki could stop her, Fiona leaned forward and pressed her lips tightly against Johnny's. After a long moment, Fiona sat back, her shoulders shaking with anguish.

There was a long, audible gasp, as if someone was sucking in air after holding their breath for too long.

"What was that?" Tiki glanced around.

There was another one, less painful this time.

"It's J..Johnny," Fiona stammered, a look of fright on her face. "I think he's breathing."

"He can't be," Rieker said, as he stepped forward to investigate.

Johnny's thin chest shuddered with the effort but it was clear to all that his bony ribcage had risen and fallen on its own.

"Johnny." Fiona cried in a mixture of hope and disbelief as she shook his arm. "Wake up. It's Fi. Wake up and talk to me."

Tiki stared at the young boy in amazement. Was he truly breathing on his own? How was it possible? Behind her, Rieker and Dain were speaking in low tones.

On impulse, Fiona leaned forward and kissed him on the lips again. This time, he took a deep breath, then opened his eyes. There was a moment of stunned silence, then Fiona cupped Johnny's face in her hands and kissed first one cheek and then the other.

"You're alive," she said, laughing and crying at the same time. "You've come back to me."

Tiki moved closer to Rieker and Dain. "How is that possible?" she asked quietly.

Dain slid his hands into his pockets. "True Love's Kiss." He nodded at Rieker. "William said you've fed the boy from the Cup of Plenty. Legend has it that the cup will cure all ills, but they also say that should a *mortal* drink from the cup it will cast them into a deep sleep, only to be awakened by True Love's Kiss." He shrugged. "I think they've written a few stories about it in the mortal world and you can be sure they didn't just make it up."

"But Larkin said he was—" Tiki stopped as her mind raced, trying to recall what it was exactly Larkin had told them. Tiki glanced over at Dain. "She knew to drink from the cup would put him to sleep, didn't she?"

Dain nodded. "Of course she did."

Chapter Fifty-Four

Other than being weak and painfully thin, Johnny seemed normal. He stretched his thin arms over his head and grimaced. "Good lord, Fi, I feel like I've been run over by a horse and buggy. How long have I been asleep?"

"Quite a while," Fiona answered, shooting a conspiratorial glance at Tiki. They had decided not to tell Johnny that he'd ever left London. "What's the last thing you remember?"

Johnny had insisted on getting out of bed and getting dressed. He was sitting in a chair by the fire in the drawing room and he leaned back, his brow furrowing as he stared at the ceiling in concentration.

"Let's see now, I think I remember meeting Rieker, but he was really Lord Richmond..." his voice faded as he tried to recall. "It's all a bit fuzzy now..."

Fiona and Tiki both started laughing. "Lord William Richmond a pickpocket?!" Fiona cried. "You better be careful what you dream, Johnny Michael Francis O'Keefe, or you might find yourself thrown in Newgate for speaking ill of your betters."

His lips curved in a sheepish grin. He shook his head, his mop of brown hair shifting with the movement. "Don't know where that hare-brained idea came from."

LATER, TIKI AND Dain sat with Rieker in his study. Though also much thinner, Dain was his usual charming, mocking self, though the coolness with which he had regarded Rieker in the past had evaporated. Instead, he seemed anxious to know his brother better.

Tiki had told them of her encounter with Donegal in the Queen's chambers at the Palace of Mirrors, leaving out his threat to burn her as he had been burnt.

"He doesn't intend to relinquish the throne next May 1st," Tiki said. "If Larkin is correct, he's going to attack the Seelies soon, in an attempt to decimate the court well in advance of Beltane. From what I've seen, I think she's right."

"We've got to make a plan to leave Grosvenor Square for now," Rieker said. "The last thing we want Donegal to know is that we were involved in Dain's escape or that you've recovered three of the Four Treasures. I don't know what meaning or power the Treasures might offer—if any—but it's to our advantage to keep our cards close to our vest and lie low for a while."

"Where will we go?" Tiki asked.

"A better question might be, where would Donegal expect us to go?"

"Ireland," Dain answered. "It's Tiki's heritage, it's our spiritual home. Ireland is the place we should go to gather strength and insight into what our destinies might hold."

Tiki crossed her arms and looked from Rieker to Dain. "Excellent point, Dain. That's why we'll be going to Scotland."

Chapter Fifty-Five

It was easy to prepare to leave. Rieker informed the staff that they were going to Paris for a month or more.

"I should talk to Shamus and see if he wants to come," Tiki said.

"Maybe it's better if he doesn't know the whole truth," Fiona replied. "You can't give away what you don't know. Besides, I think he'd rather stay here."

Tiki turned from where she was folding clothes to take with them and looked at Fiona over her shoulder. "Why do you say that?"

Fiona gave her a bright smile, the dimples showing in both her cheeks. Tiki couldn't help but notice what a change had come over Fiona since Johnny had awoken and was glad for how happy the girl was now.

"I think Shamus fancies Juliette."

Tiki's hands dropped to her lap. "What?" With all the excitement they'd had over the last few months, she'd barely paid any attention to Rieker's housemaid. The poor girl was usually being ordered around by Mrs. Bosworth or one of the other staff and rarely spent any time around Tiki and Rieker.

"Yes, in fact, I'm quite sure of it." Fiona sang a little melody under her breath, grinning happily.

"I'm sure of it, too." Clara piped up from where she was pretending Doggie could fly. "I saw him bring her a rose one day when Juliette was dusting the hallway. His face was all red an' he acted all fumbly and strange. I thought maybe he was sick, or something." Clara threw Doggie up in the air and jumped up to catch her. "See? Doggie can jump like Dain's horse. Hmm...I wonder if I should put some red ribbons in her hair...."

"And what does Juliette think, do you s'pose?"

"Seems like she thinks it's a fine idea," Fiona said, "because she giggles a lot when Shamus is around."

"Well, imagine that," Tiki murmured, turning back to her folding. A happy smile creased her lips.

THE NIGHT BEFORE they were to leave Tiki stood at the window in her room and stared out toward the square. Their trunks had been packed, arrangements made for travel and they were to set out in the morning.

She gazed around the now familiar room. Grosvenor Square had come to be home, not only for Rieker, but for her and her family, as well. What did the future hold? Would they return to these grand hallways and rooms as a true family one day? Or would there be heartbreak and catastrophe in their future? Tiki was almost happy she didn't know.

"Let each day bring what it may," she whispered. "We will celebrate our successes, learn from our mistakes, and be grateful for each day we have together."

"IT APPEARS YOU'RE leaving."

The voice woke Tiki. There were so many things on her mind it had been difficult to sleep lately and when she did drift off, even the most minute sounds woke her. At first, she thought Larkin's voice was part of her dream, but then the faerie spoke again.

"Before you go there are matters to be discussed."

Tiki jerked up right, suddenly aware that she wasn't dreaming. "Larkin, what are you doing here? It's the middle of the night."

"Exactly," the faerie said. "That's why I've come now. I knew we could be alone. It's time we talked about Clara."

Tiki's stomach clenched as she leaned over and lit a bedside candle. "What about Clara?"

"You need to know the truth." Larkin's eyes glittered in the half-light of the wavering flame. "Clara is my daughter. Surely, you've noticed the resemblance?"

Tiki froze. She couldn't have heard the faerie correctly.

Larkin laughed, the sound like wind chimes, and a slow smirk twisted her lips. "I would have thought you'd have figured it out by now. I'm quite sure William has known for the longest time."

Tiki fought to breathe. Was this a nightmare? Was Larkin telling the truth? Could it be possible that Rieker knew of this? But even as questions raced through her mind—the answers were undeniable. There were too many things—the blond hair, the blue eyes, the laugh, the uncanny ability to know of things beyond a normal child's grasp, not to mention Clara's ability to see visitors from the Otherworld when others couldn't.

"I don't believe you," Tiki cried.

"Yes, you do." Larkin scoffed at her. "When have I ever lied to you? Do you think it was coincidence that Clara was directly in your path on Craven Street that day? Have you never wondered why *you* were the one who found her—among the masses who inhabit London?" She stabbed her thumb into her chest. "It's because I wanted you to find her. I, alone, knew who you were—the destiny that was waiting—and I knew she would be safe with you, filthy little pickpocket that you were."

Though her hands were shaking, a surge of anger made Tiki's voice strong. "I don't care if she's your daughter or not—you gave her up and she belongs with me now."

Larkin gave a derisive laugh, her gaze suddenly as cold and deadly as a well-honed dagger. "I *loaned* her to you, but that is beside the point. I dare you to try and take her from me." The faerie's voice changed to a conversational tone. "However, as with most things in life, guttersnipe, you do have a choice. If you relinquish the Seelie throne to me, I promise I will never bother the two of you again. You can go off with your mortal family and never have another worry about those in the Seelie Court."

She gave a delicate shrug. "It's quite simple, really. But if you don't, then it's time for Clara to return to Faerie with me." Larkin lifted her palms. "It's up to you. Which do you choose: a child or a kingdom?"

Though THE SEVEN YEAR KING is a work of fiction, you might find it interesting to know that **The Luck of Edenhall** is real and on display in the Victoria & Albert Museum in Kensington to this day.

An actual drinking vessel dating back to at least the 14th century, the Luck was owned by the Musgrave family of Edenhall for centuries, its association with faeries known even then. In 1791, Sir William Musgrave wrote in the Gentleman's Magazine, *'a party of Fairies were drinking and making merry round a well near the Hall, called St Cuthbert's well; but being interrupted by the intrusion of some curious people, they were frightened, and made a hasty retreat, and left the cup in question: one of the last screaming out,*

"If this cup should break or fall
Farewell the Luck of Edenhall!"

In 1926 the luck was given to the V&A Museum, which to this day, references the Luck's historical link to faeries. For more information, check the online listing at the VAM here: http://www.vam.ac.uk/content/articles/t/the-luck-of-edenhall-history-and-myths/.

Additionally, **the Isle of Man** is well known for its association with faeries and otherworldly creatures. There is not one, but two faerie bridges acknowledged on the island in present times.

Prince Arthur was indeed born on May 1st, which is Beltane, an important holiday in the faerie world.

Across Europe and especially in Britain, **the Wild Hunt** is an ancient folk myth that has been reported and recorded by mortals for many centuries.

The **Rollright Stones** are a complex of three Neolithic and Bronze Age megalithic monuments located near to the village of Long Compton on the borders of Oxfordshire and Warwickshire in the English Midlands. Of the legends associated with the stones is one that says they were a king and his knights frozen in time by a vengeful witch.

Thank you for reading THE SEVEN YEAR KING. Tiki's story continues in book four, THE FAERIE QUEEN, available from Fair Wind Books in 2014.

Kiki Hamilton
March 1st, 2013

Acknowledgements

Thanks to Carly Hamilton, for her sharp eye and innate knowledge of story structure. Her comments were invaluable and I look forward to the day when her own books will be on the shelf. Also thanks to early readers Amy Fellner Dominy, Jean Martin and Paula McLaughlin for their insightful comments and continued support.

Thanks to the many, many fantastic bloggers, librarians, booksellers and readers who have offered their support in promoting this book and THE FAERIE RING series as a whole. I couldn't do this thing I love so much without you guys! Thank you!

Finally, to the many wonderful readers who have written such sweet and heartfelt notes — your kindness means more to me than words can describe. Thank you!

About the Author

Kiki Hamilton is the author of THE FAERIE RING fantasy series and the YA contemporary novel, THE LAST DANCE. She believes in magic and the idea of hidden worlds co-existing with our own. Kiki lives near Seattle, though she dreams of living in London one day.

Visit Kiki's website and blog at www.kikihamilton.com. For more information about Tiki and the faerie ring, visit www.thefaeriering.com.

Hamilton, Kiki
The Seven Year King #3
33500011799178 lcn

Made in the USA
Charleston, SC
23 January 2014